The Christmas Wish Quilt

a novel by
Ann Hazelwood

 American Quilter's Society
www.AmericanQuilter.com

Located in Paducah, Kentucky, the American Quilter's Society (AQS) is dedicated to promoting the accomplishments of today's quilters. Through its publications and events, AQS strives to honor today's quiltmakers and their work and to inspire future creativity and innovation in quiltmaking.

EXECUTIVE BOOK EDITOR: ELAINE BRELSFORD
COPY EDITOR: ANN HAMMEL
PROOFING: HANNAH ALTON
GRAPHIC DESIGN: LYNDA SMITH
COVER DESIGN: MICHAEL BUCKINGHAM

 American Quilter's Society

PO Box 3290
Paducah, KY 42002-3290
americanquilter.com

Additional copies of this book may be ordered from the American Quilter's Society, PO Box 3290, Paducah, KY 42002-3290, or online at shopAQS.com

Library of Congress Control Number: 2019946204

Dedication

I would like to dedicate this book to "sisterhood." As we celebrate Christmas once again, I couldn't help but think of my sisters Shirley, Betty, and Marilyn. Their memories will always remain in my heart.

I have also been fortunate to have enjoyed the sisterhood of two sisters-in-law, Shirley Meyer and Mary Hazelwood.

A sisterhood can also be enjoyed with good friends who "get" who you are and share your joys and sorrows. In my life, you know who you are. Thank you all for being my sisters!

My stories of laughter, love, and support gave me the excitement to write about fictional sisters Loretta, Laurie, Lynn, and Lily Rosenthal. I have become quite fond of them as well.

Sisterhood is a blessing I wish for all of you.

LeMoyne Star Block

Chapter 1

"What do you mean, we have another sister?" Lynn asked. "Have you been hitting the wine bottle?"

I snickered to myself.

She continued, "The last time I counted, there were just four of us."

"I'm serious, Lynn," I assured her. I began by telling her that I'd had an unexpected visit from our Aunt Mary's daughter, Ellen. That surprise alone shocked Lynn, since we hadn't seen or communicated with Ellen until I'd recently called her just to make contact.

"Did she know about our dad and her mother having an affair?" Lynn asked.

"Yes, she did, but she felt we girls needed to know more, so she wanted to visit me in person."

"Like we need to know more about what, for heaven's sake?"

"Guess."

"No, please don't tell me that's what you meant by saying that we have another sister."

"I'm afraid so. The way she explained it, she'd suspected the deception for years. After our father died, she confronted her mother."

"How awful!"

"I suppose Aunt Mary thought her secret was safe at that point, but Ellen persisted until she admitted it."

"Good gracious! Have you told Laurie and Loretta?"

"No. I had to adjust to the news myself before calling you. It's a shock, but can you imagine how Ellen must feel? She'd been denied knowing her real father just to protect her mother."

"Did you ask if our mother suspected?"

"Ellen said no, but who knows the truth at this point? She did say that Aunt Mary's husband treated her as his own, so that's good, I suppose."

"Our own father had to know, and that makes me furious. I will never forgive him."

I hung up feeling sick to my stomach. I wished now that Ellen had kept this to herself, but the truth always prevails somehow. No wonder Ellen and Aunt Mary had been estranged over the years. I wondered if Lynn, in anger, would now call Loretta and Laurie. Would she also call Aunt Mary and give her a piece of her mind?

I poured a glass of wine. In time, I'd have to share Ellen's news with those close to me like Marc, my sweet significant other, and my best friends, Holly and Alex. Alex would relish the drama and also probably give me advice.

I stared out the back porch window and enjoyed a beautiful sunset. Early fall leaves were sprinkled over the green acreage behind my house. The summer had flown by too fast, and fall events in wine country would soon begin.

Lily Girl's Quilts and Antiques was now an integral part of Augusta's business community. I not only had to participate, but also felt a responsibility to make this community successful.

Chapter 2

I loved fall, but I loved spring even more. The thought of another hard winter ahead was not comforting. The Augusta Harvest Festival was this weekend, and it was always a big deal. I remembered little from last year since I had been busy opening my shop. I did know that there would be a 5K run, which had to be very challenging with hills going in every direction. The parade was at ten but would not be coming by my shop. There would be artists everywhere, plus a corn husking competition and pony rides for the children.

Gracie, who had just opened a quilt shop in town, asked if I would go to the Fruit of the Harvest dinner with her. It advertised eight courses under the stars and a variety of wines. What was not to like?

There seemed to be so much to do this time of year. I had promised Marc that we would go the National Baseball Hall of Fame and Museum in Cooperstown, New York. We shared a love of baseball, but we had never traveled together, so the trip could be risky. I had convinced Marc to wait until fall, so I couldn't think of backing out now.

Alex and I had been determined to hike Klondike Park ever since I'd moved out here. We had planned to go on a Monday since my shop is closed that day.

To my surprise, Alex was becoming a closer friend to me than Holly, who seemed to be tied down with drama at home most of the time. Alex and I shared a long history of working together at Dexter Publishing. He had left before I did to pursue freelance writing. Last Christmas, he introduced me to the owner of *Spirit* magazine, who graciously offered me my own column called "Living with Lily Girl." Without the extra income, I may have had to throw in the towel on retail, which wasn't very lucrative. So far, I'd never struggled for ideas to write about. My readers seemed to love quilts and the fact that I live in a charming little town in wine country. It was always surreal when some reader would stop by the shop to take a photo or request an autograph.

It was late afternoon when three women entered the shop. They looked exhausted and said they had been shopping all day.

"I told Stella that I just had to visit the yellow shop before we could go home," one of the ladies said.

"Well, you're all welcome," I responded. "Let me know if I can help you or answer any questions."

"Pardon my boldness, but what would make you paint this charming old house such a bright yellow?"

I smiled. "It was this color when I purchased it from a friend," I explained. "It's become a local landmark in that regard. I actually love it and don't plan to change it at this time."

She nodded in assent, but her expression was one of disbelief.

"Well, it brought us here, right?" one of her friends pointed out. "I see you have a whole room full of quilts!"

"Yes, I've collected quilts for a long time. I happen to be attracted to red-and-white quilts, which is why you see more of them."

"I see," another woman responded. "I can't believe people pay these prices, especially for an old, used quilt."

"I can see it for a new quilt," Stella said. "Remember the prices we saw at that quilt shop for just the yardage alone? It takes a lot of time. I sure wouldn't think of making one."

"I do like linens," her friend said as she handled some of them. "This big crocheted tablecloth is way too cheap for all of that work."

"Well, try giving them away, my friend," Stella remarked, using a sarcastic tone. "No one in the family wants mine."

I left the room to let them discuss my inventory. It was hard to keep defending everything. Because they were older women, I could see why none of them would want more stuff to get rid of. They finally made their way to the front room.

"Well, I'm going to buy this tablecloth," one woman announced. "It needs a home where it will be appreciated."

"That's nice to hear," I said, taking the tablecloth to wrap up as the other two ladies gave her a look of disapproval.

I thanked them for coming by and got only a slight nod in return. I doubted that I would see them again.

Chapter 3

Before I opened my shop the next day, I decided to pay a visit to Centennial Farms, which was across the street from the library. They carried seasonal fall produce and other items like mums and pumpkins. I walked away with fresh bread sticks, two pumpkins, fresh honey, a jar of apple butter, and a yellow mum that was as bright as my house. When I looked across the street, I saw Susan, my quilting instructor, get out of her car to go into the library.

"Susan!" I called.

"Good morning!" she returned, giving me a friendly wave.

I put my things in the car and went over to talk to her.

"You are certainly out early this morning," Susan joked.

"Well, I think it's going to be a beautiful fall day, and I wanted to see what the farm was all about. The foliage is about at its peak, don't you think?"

"Yes, there are some spectacular spots right now. Will you be at quilt class on Monday?"

"I'm sorry, but I promised a friend that we would go hiking at Klondike Park. Alex has been hearing me talk about it, and the foliage will still be gorgeous."

"Alex? Is he a boyfriend that I don't know about?"

"No, just a friend from where I used to work."

"I was hoping you'd bring your Christmas quilt with you. I'm going to talk about how to choose quilting designs."

"Oh, that would have been helpful. I'm sorry to miss the class."

"Edna and Marilyn cancelled also, so I may just have to cancel the class. I have some great ideas for the Christmas season."

"It will be here before we know it. I guess I'd better get back and open the shop."

"Enjoy your hike tomorrow."

"Thanks!" I got on my way, and when I returned to my place, Snowshoes was dropping off my mail.

"Here you go," he said as he handed it to me. "Looks like your place is going to be covered in leaves soon."

"I know. I hope I can find someone to help me out since I won't have Kip and Tom around."

"I'll keep my ears out for someone. Before you know it, I'll have to get out my snowshoes!"

I laughed and started bringing in all my purchases as Snowshoes went on his way. As soon as I got inside, my cell phone started to ring. It was Marc.

"Hey, Lily, I wanted you to know that I have our plane tickets. You can't back out on me now!"

"Wonderful!"

"We'll fly into Albany and take a car into Cooperstown, which is supposed to be a gorgeous drive."

"Alex and I are hoping for some gorgeous scenery tomorrow when we hike at Klondike Park."

"Someday, I might decide to be jealous of him, but it wouldn't do much good, right?"

I laughed. "You're right!"

"I've got to be on my way. I'm heading to Chicago for just a couple of days but wanted to catch you up on our trip."

"Thanks, and I'll talk to you later."

Marc was an easy boyfriend to have. We both liked our freedom, and each of us had no desire for our relationship to include marriage. As I put Rosie's rocker on the porch to start my day, Carrie Mae pulled up.

"Good morning," she called as she got out of her car.

"What did I do to deserve this visit so early in the morning?"

"Several things, I suppose. Betty said that Ted, her grandson, is looking for odd jobs around town. He's trying to buy a vehicle now that he is sixteen, so I told Betty you may have more for him to do than I do right now."

"Fabulous. The timing is good. Right now, leaves are piling up everywhere, and I want the trim painted on Doc's house before it gets too cold."

"It's best to go through Betty to get him there. I think he's at her house most of the time."

"Okay, thanks!"

Chapter 4

Carrie Mae continued, "The other matter to discuss is that Butler is talking about coming out next week to have lunch. He wondered if you would be free."

"Most likely, but I hate closing the shop with these fall tourists coming to town."

"Okay, we'll make it a quick lunch."

"I've been thinking about Doc's house," I said, placing my hands on my hips.

"Oh? Are the Dinner Detectives involved?"

I laughed and shook my head. "I think I'm going to fix up Doc's office and use it during the Christmas season. I can see a Santa Claus sitting in there."

"Are you sure? That sounds a bit risky to me. If Santa knows how spooky it is, I doubt that you'll get him or anyone to sit in there."

"When there's no Santa, I'll use it for a Christmas display. Last year, I put a wreath on the door, and it was so inviting. It will get people's attention, especially if there's a light going on and off like there is sometimes." I smiled. "It might discourage some of the rumors. I'll use white lights and greenery. I can see it now!"

"Lily Girl, I admire your spirit. It will be the talk of the town."

"I think I'm already the talk of the town."

We laughed as she went on her way.

I didn't know what I'd do without Carrie Mae. I thought back to our long history and how I used to visit her to buy quilts when I still lived on The Hill in St. Louis. When I purchased the inventory from Rosie's antique shop after Rosie's murder, Carrie Mae offered me the yellow house to store things in while I made up my mind about what I really wanted to do with them.

When I saw the apartment upstairs, I realized that I could live upstairs and have a shop downstairs. With that idea in mind, Carrie Mae offered me a reasonable price to buy the house, so I jumped at it. When I restored the upstairs and downstairs porches, it became home. I left alone some of the original things—like the untouched 1940s floral wallpaper in the bedroom—just because of the charm.

The interesting thing about the move was that Rosie's spirit came with me. In her inventory was an elaborate rocking chair with a "not for sale" sign on it. I wanted to keep it as well, as a remembrance of her, so I placed it on the front porch each day and displayed a quilt on it. Occasionally, Rosie would remind me of her presence and rock the chair.

The traffic was quiet on these chilly fall mornings. Things usually picked up around noon when folks ventured out for lunch. I decided that while I had time, I would check my sister group email. I was so grateful that we'd started this frequent communication because it served as a wonderful way to keep us in touch with one another.

I was pleased to see that there was an email from Laurie, who lived in Fish Creek, Wisconsin. She had recently finished radiation treatments for breast cancer and was doing well. She reported that many shops were already closing before Christmas because of the colder weather. Laurie always kept her shop, Trinkets, open until Christmas Eve. It was nice to read that her spirits were up.

Lynn reported that she was behind in her work on commissioned paintings. She reminded us that we'd all agreed to come to her place for Christmas this year. Last Christmas, we were with my sister Loretta and her family in Green Bay, Wisconsin.

Loretta said she would do everything she could to get Sarah and Lucy, her daughter and granddaughter, to come with her at Christmas. Lucy was born one year ago, and it would be fun to celebrate her birthday on Christmas Day. Loretta also informed us that Laurie would join her on Thanksgiving Day.

My contribution to the conversation was telling my sisters that Marc and I were planning a trip to Cooperstown.

Loretta immediately responded by saying that the relationship sounded serious and asked if there was any talk of wedding bells.

I wrote back asking when big sisters quit picking on their little sisters.

Loretta then asked if I'd heard from Aunt Mary since her visit. I wanted to respond that I'd had an unexpected visit from Ellen, but I didn't want the revelation of having a new sister told to Loretta in an email. I noticed that Lynn, who knew about the new addition to our sisterhood, also stayed silent about our discovery in the email exchanges.

I said goodbye to them when I saw a customer pull up in front of the shop. I was surprised to see that it was Lisa, a former quilt collector who lived in Marthasville. Carrie Mae and I had visited her marvelous estate to have tea with her one day and to see her quilts. She'd ended up selling me several of her antique quilts at fantastic prices because she'd wanted to thin out the number of quilts that she owned.

Chapter 5

"Hey, Lisa!"

"How have you been?"

"Really well. I can happily say that I've sold some of the quilts that I purchased from you."

"That's great! I can probably find more for you. I just stopped by to tell you and Carrie Mae that we've put our place up for sale."

"No way! You live in total paradise out there!"

"It's no longer paradise when there's no love in the home."

"Lisa, I hate to hear that."

"Divorce is hard. I'll continue living there until it sells."

"Where will you go?"

"I've been looking online, but I'm not sure yet. I'm hoping to take my dog, but I'll miss the horses and other creatures that visit us every day."

"Surely your dog can go!"

"He was my husband's dog before we married, but I'm fighting for him."

"Oh, how sad."

She nodded. "Please pass on the word about the place being for sale. If you're serious about buying more quilts, I'll bring them by, or you can drive out to see them."

"Great. I appreciate it."

"Your shop looks fabulous, and so does Augusta with all the fall colors. Well, I'm sorry we had to see each other when I am delivering sad news. I need to be on my way."

"Sure. Please take care of yourself. I wish you the best as you make this transition." As I watched her leave, I felt so sad. It is easy to be envious of those who look like they have it all. Now her life had taken a totally different turn.

I was suddenly distracted by a mother coming toward the shop with two little children who looked to be under five years old. The mother looked somewhat desperate.

"Randy has to use the bathroom. May we use yours?"

"I suppose so, but there is a public restroom up the street," I offered.

"That won't work," she said abruptly. "Here. You take Elizabeth while I take him. Where is it?"

"In the next room to the right," I said reluctantly. The next thing I knew, Elizabeth was in my arms. She looked to be about a year old.

The mother yanked little Randy by the arm and headed toward the restroom.

"Hello, Elizabeth," I said in a gentle voice. She leaned back to get a clearer look at me, and her face puckered up. The next thing I knew, she was shrieking for her mother. I couldn't put her down since I didn't know if she could walk. I headed toward the restroom. Considering the amount of time that had passed, I thought the mother had made good use of it as well. As soon as they came out, she took Elizabeth from me.

"Let's hurry, Randy," she said, grabbing his hand. "Daddy is going to be looking for us."

There was not a glance my way or a word of thanks as she headed to the door. It was quite odd, and I was afraid to open the restroom door. Would I ever get used to dealing with the public?

Judy walked in the door as I headed back to the counter.

"How are you, Lily? Are you having a good day?"

I laughed out loud. "Not really! A friend came by to announce her divorce, and then a child came in to use the restroom. Those are the highlights."

She giggled and shook her head.

"You are just the person I wanted to see," I said.

"Well, I'm glad to hear that." She smiled.

I told her about wanting to go to Cooperstown with Marc. Judy had filled in for me at the shop when I went to Green Bay last Christmas. She had a part-time job at Kate's Coffee, but she was usually available. She nodded her head as I described when I would be gone and for how long. She made a point to write down the dates and said she would check her schedule and get back with me.

"You know I'd love it. I like dusting things and seeing things up close. It was fun when I did it last time. It will likely work out."

Chapter 6

Judy continued, "I was sorry to hear that our quilt class was cancelled, but there would have been just a few attending."

"Well, I seldom take off, and I decided that a little fun once in a while can't hurt anything."

"You most definitely deserve to go. By the way, I thought I'd tell you that I met a friend of yours who seems to be quite fond of you."

I smiled, curious. "Who might that be?"

"His name was Anthony, and I've forgotten his last name, but it's very Italian. You know him, right?"

My heart stopped. "Was he in the coffee shop?"

She nodded. "Randal had some sort of meeting and Anthony arrived early, so we chatted."

"How did I enter into the conversation?"

"He asked if I knew you. When I told him about our friendship, it didn't take him long to start singing your praises."

"Well, that's odd, as I barely know who he is."

"Don't you like him?"

"I have no particular feelings about him. Buzz and Karen introduced me to him at their dinner party a while back."

"He'd be a good catch, Lily. He is so handsome, and that accent is delightful and sexy."

I chuckled and shook my head. "I have a nice man that I'm seeing, remember?"

"Okay, I get it. Say, do you still have that ceramic creamer and sugar set that had grapes on it?"

"I do. It's Royal Doulton, and rare, from what the tag says. It's not cheap."

"My aunt collects sugar and creamer sets. She would love it. How much is it?"

When I told her, her face dropped in disappointment. "I'm sorry, but the previous owner had it priced at that amount," I explained.

"Oh, I totally understand. I will think of something else. I just can't afford to spend that much on her."

"Can you afford to spend half of that on her?"

She looked at me oddly. "Yes, but you can't sell things at half price."

"Yes, I can, because I'm the owner. You do so many nice things for me. I would be happy to know the set will be going to a real collector."

She smiled, made the purchase, and went on her way.

That was how the rest of the day went. It had its low points and high points. I brought in the rocker at about four thirty. I was ready for a glass of wine. I went to my wine rack in the first-floor kitchen and opened a new bottle of Vintage Rose merlot. It made me think of Anthony because he'd introduced it to me when I'd first met him at the Ashley

Rose restaurant. It seemed most folks knew Anthony here in Augusta since he was in the wine industry. He was great about keeping our friendship confidential since I was seeing Marc. Augusta is a small town, and it wouldn't take much to connect me with him. That is why I chose to not even tell Alex and Holly about meeting him. My sisters would kill me if they thought I was seeing another man besides Marc. As innocent as my friendship with Anthony was, it still made me feel guilty that I admired him so.

I went upstairs to relax on the porch. When I looked outdoors, I saw lights flashing once again in Doc's office. I shook my head, not understanding how that could possibly happen without any electricity in that building! The activity no longer scared me, but it gave credence to the rumor that the place was haunted. I was learning something nearly every day about the strange life of the doctor who once practiced medicine on this property. Tom and Kip, the young men who used to help me out with jobs around the house, had found a tin box containing Doc's books and a patient journal when they were tearing down the barn. According to the journal, it appeared that his patients were all women, listed by their first names. Carrie Mae and Betty were helping me discover more information. We called ourselves the Dinner Detectives since we always had dinner as we performed our research.

Chapter 7

The Harvest Festival seemed to be in the air throughout the town. Locals were excited and were expected to participate. I could hear the start of the parade in the distance. I decided to close the shop for a bit and walk up the hill to Walnut Street to catch some of the excitement.

I was surprised to see there were as many costumed pets as there were parade participants! Schoolchildren placed on wagons were waving and yelling their little hearts out. There were small decorated floats and tractors followed by numerous Boy and Girl Scout groups. Every now and then, a lone musician would walk by, playing some familiar tune to get the bystanders involved. Marge, Randal's wife, came my way to say hello. She told me she was one of the judges for the pie contest this year. Her civic pride was beaming all over her face.

"A pie contest? You would be the perfect judge! What a tasty job."

She laughed and nodded. "You should enter! They have a cream and fruit category."

I laughed. "Right! I've never made a pie in my life, Marge. Isn't that terrible?"

"You don't mean it! Well, Lily Girl, I'll have to teach you sometime."

I smiled politely, knowing it would never happen.

There is nothing quite like a small-town parade. It is the perfect opportunity for every hopeful politician to connect with the community. It is certainly entertaining, and the Harvest Festival gave me a sense of community pride, even though I was still new to the area.

I decided that while I was out and about, I would walk over to Carrie Mae's shop. She and Betty were standing side by side, watching the parade and waving to everyone they knew. They each had a warm cup of coffee in their hands, which was a grand idea.

"Betty, I'm told that your grandson is looking for some work," I said.

"Yes, he's doing odd jobs for folks who will let him. Do you need some things done?"

"I sure do. Would you have him stop by sometime?"

"Absolutely!" she said with excitement. "He's trying to buy some kind of pickup truck since he just turned sixteen."

"That would be great. I guess I'd better get back to work in case any of these folks come down the hill." By now, the chill was penetrating, so when I got to the house, I went straight to the coffeepot that was still on from the morning. My cell phone rang. It was Alex.

"Do you have hiking shoes?" he asked humorously.

"Do you?" I shot back, laughing.

"Be sure to bundle up, Lily Girl. I'll bet the wind will be quite chilly in the hills. I'll bring some sandwiches from the deli if you bring a bottle of wine."

"You may need the wine to warm up, but I'll bring my coffee thermos, thank you."

"Whatever, but I should be there at about eleven."

"Sounds good." After I hung up, I decided that the hike would be a good time to tell him about my newly discovered sister, Ellen.

After the parade was over, a few people trickled into the shop. Some of them were families, which didn't usually result in any sales. I thought I had made a sale to a customer who fell in love with a blue-and-yellow Irish Chain quilt that seemed to be perfect for her décor. At the very last minute, she folded it up and put it back on the shelf! We were both disappointed, but my hope was that she would come back again to purchase it. After the shop was closed, I went upstairs to get my things together for the next day. I checked the weather and learned it was supposed to be forty degrees and very windy.

As I prepared for bed, I turned on the TV to catch the last of the Cardinals game. They were ahead, but likely wouldn't make the playoffs. I had almost drifted off to sleep when my phone rang. It was Lynn. "Are you okay?" I asked. "It's late for you to be calling."

"I'm sorry, were you asleep?"

"No, I had just crawled into bed. What's going on?"

"It's the Ellen thing. You have got to tell Laurie and Loretta. I hate knowing it and them not. Please do it soon."

"Okay, okay. I will. Don't worry about it so."

"How can you take this so lightly?"

I detected anger and frustration in her voice and remained quiet, hoping to hear her real concerns.

"We all have to decide what this means. Do we invite her for Christmas?" Lynn questioned.

"Frankly, a lot depends on her. She chose to keep this to herself for so long. If you ask me, yes, we should include her on our Christmas list. Leave it up to her as to whether or not she wants to join us."

After I hung up, I started feeling guilty that I hadn't said anything to Laurie and Loretta. I would do it first thing in the morning. I tried to envision another sister in the family. Her name didn't start with an L, but if you said the name Ellen, it sounded like it started with an L.

Chapter 8

I woke up excited about having a day off. I stayed in my robe and wandered downstairs to get my coffee. When I looked out the back window, I remembered that it was the day I would call the sisters about Ellen. I knew that Loretta was always up early, so I called her first. "Are you sitting down?"

"I am. What's up? Did you get engaged?"

"Get that out of your head right now!"

She laughed.

"Our cousin, Ellen, paid me a visit recently, and our conversation was very enlightening."

"Oh? What was the occasion for her visit? Was it the affair that she wanted to talk about?"

"Yes, you might say that, but she took it a step further. She said that we share the same father."

There was silence.

"Why am I not totally surprised? Good heavens, why weren't we told sooner? I'm not sure whether to laugh or cry."

"I think it meant a lot to Ellen when I called her after

Aunt Mary's visit. I think she felt it was time to tell us. I personally don't have a problem with it."

"I can't remember what she even looks like. Does she look like our father?"

"I can't tell. I did call Lynn right away, but I haven't said anything to Laurie. She has been through so much."

As we finished our conversation, I was pleased that Loretta didn't overreact. I then got the courage to call Laurie. "Did I wake you, sweetie?" I asked softly when I heard her groggy voice.

"Not really. I just can't seem to get going. What's up?"

"Our cousin Ellen came to see me."

"Good God! I haven't seen her in ages!"

"We had an interesting conversation, and she had a reason for her visit."

"Like what?"

"She claims that we have the same father. She's known for a long time, and it's been the big problem between Ellen and her mother." There was the same silence that Loretta had given me. "Laurie, do you understand what this means?"

"That is crazy. Do you believe her?"

"I'm sure she has proof, and Aunt Mary doesn't deny it."

"I don't want to hear any more of this. What does she want? I guess she's after an inheritance."

"I can't answer for her, but she is reaching out to us. How much we reach out to her is the question. Christmas is coming, and she's been without much family all these years."

"That's too bad. Whose fault is that? You all do what you want. I can't digest this right now. I need to go, Lily."

"I didn't mean to upset you, Laurie."

"I'll be fine. I'll talk to you later."

I hung up feeling sick to my stomach. There had been no question that each of us would process this news differently. As I had guessed, it was more emotional for Laurie after what she had gone through with breast cancer. It had been a trying year for her.

I went up to shower and dress. I prayed to God that we would all be able to deal with this and that it wouldn't come between us as sisters. We all needed some time. I checked my group email to see if there had been any reactions, but there was nothing. I shook my head, wondering where all of this would lead.

Chapter 9

Alex arrived all chipper and dressed like he was going to appear on some outdoor TV show.

"Would you like a cup of coffee before we go?" I asked as I filled my thermos.

"Not now, but we'll need it the way that wind is blowing."

"Do we have a blanket or something to sit on when we get to the top of the hill?"

"I've got one. Let's go, Lily Girl!"

"Okay, okay."

Off we went in Alex's classy Jeep. It truly made me feel like we were on a great adventure. As we drove through the winding hills, I held on tightly. Alex loved flying around the sharp corners.

Klondike Park was located on the outskirts of Defiance. It was once a huge, active quarry that offered the most incredible views. When I first moved to wine country, I went alone to check it out.

"We can park by the Conference Center, which is at the bottom of the big trail. This was originally built as a residence and was a bed and breakfast years ago. It was called the Quarry House."

"It's amazing out here. Why would anyone go to Colorado?"

I laughed.

"Look at the color over there!" Alex marveled.

"Wait until you see it from the top of that hill."

We went inside to use the restrooms before we started on the trail. We were glad we had brought sock caps, as the wind was picking up. It didn't take long for me to begin huffing and puffing. Was I that out of shape? Alex made fun of me, but I could tell he was challenged at times as well. Finally, we got to the top, and Alex pulled me up the last few steps. He spotted a flat rock, and that's where we spread our blanket and took a drink of our bottled water.

"I'm ready for lunch!" Alex said, rubbing his stomach.

"We decided to wait until we get back to the car, remember? The trail is hard enough without dragging more things. Just relax and take it all in."

"Binoculars would have been cool to have right now, but it is amazing. I'll have to tell my buddies about this place."

As we got more relaxed, I ended up telling him about having a new sister.

"That's pretty cool, Lily. Look at it as a gift. I'm sure it's one for her."

"A gift?"

"Yeah. She's part of your flesh and blood, for heaven's sake. You do believe her, right?"

I nodded. "I told my sisters, but I'm concerned about Laurie's response. She didn't want to believe it."

"Give her time. Life is too short to ignore it, if you ask

me."

"Good advice. Now tell me what is going on with Mindy from Minnesota."

He chuckled. "Not a thing. She has moved on… hopefully."

"That's great if it's mutual, I suppose."

"So, you are about to have your first out-of-town trip with Mr. Marc. How do you see that working out?"

"Well, I'm really just a traveling companion for him so he can see the Baseball Hall of Fame. He is totally concentrating on that alone. I'm surprised he even mentioned it to me."

Alex burst into laughter and shot me a look like he didn't believe me. "I think it says a lot. If this goes well, don't be surprised if he starts talking about marital bliss."

"Stop that kind of talk right now. Marc and I understand each other."

He shook his head, still laughing. "Hey, look over there. That's a bald eagle, I think." Alex pointed to the east, where a tree had grown out of the hillside.

I immediately jumped up to see the discovery and stepped too quickly off the rock I had been sitting on. "Ouch!" I said, falling to the ground in pain. I wanted to cry, but not in front of Alex.

"Hey, hey! I don't know how you did it, but you've turned your ankle. Sit for a bit before you put your weight on it."

"This is just what I need!"

"Relax. We need to get you back down the hill and attend to it before it starts swelling too much. Here, grab ahold and let's see if you can stand up."

As I stood up, the pain increased. It was hard to put weight on it, but I had to grin and bear it. It was necessary to get back down the hill.

"Well, old lady, hang onto this guy. We'll take it slow and sit down every now and then."

"I'm so sorry, Alex."

"Hey, you always were a pain in the you-know-what, so let me be in charge for once."

So, with a lot of sarcastic remarks and giggles, we slowly made it back down the hill. Alex opened his Jeep door so I could sit down while he went inside the building to get some ice.

Chapter 10

Once the ice arrived, it helped the pain enormously.

"Do you want to head on back?" Alex asked as he fussed over me.

"No, I want that picnic we talked about. I'm hungry. Let's hobble over to that picnic table by the tree. I'll be fine."

Alex reluctantly agreed. He quickly spread the tablecloth and set the food on the table. There was something about food tasting better outdoors. The leaves were falling like a rain shower. It was a perfect fall setting—except for the invalid sitting on the picnic bench!

"If you ever needed a glass of wine, it's now, Lily Girl," Alex said as he popped the cork. "You will feel no pain very shortly."

We both burst into laughter. Alex was so darn sweet and funny.

"Here's to my clumsy Lily Girl!" Alex said, making a toast. "May this wine keep you from whining all the way home!"

"That was cruel, my friend, but I'll make a toast to my strong and able companion who practically carried me down the hill. Thank you!"

He shook his head, not expecting such a compliment.

"I'll have a little of that wine," I said, holding up my glass. "Let's talk about something else. Do you think Richard is still pleased with my articles for the magazine?"

He nodded. "Trust me, if he wasn't, you'd be hearing about it. The way you're hearing from your readers, I think you're on the right track."

"The only complaint I ever get is that some have asked to read more about quilts."

"Well, don't you belong to a quilt class? I'll bet there are always a lot of things you learn other than how to make a quilt."

"That's for sure. I guess everyone thinks what happens at quilt class stays at quilt class."

Alex chuckled and said, "Hey, I don't mean to whine, but it's starting to sprinkle. Maybe we should think about packing up and getting home."

"Oh, it probably won't last. Have some more wine. It's sure helping me."

"Remember one of the Dexter Christmas parties when I had to take you home because you'd had so much to drink?" he asked.

"I don't remember such a thing, my dear. You were likely in the same shape."

"I remember because you also took a bottle home with you and I covered for you."

"Whatever. I guess you were a good friend. I'm so glad we both made it out of that black hole."

Suddenly, a big clap of thunder surprised us. Alex quickly grabbed our picnic basket and tablecloth, and I grabbed the bottle of wine. Things happened so rapidly that I didn't think of my pain as we scurried back into the Jeep. We giggled and chatted nonstop all the way back to Augusta. Traffic was slow. It seemed as if the rain had changed many plans for the tourists on the road.

When the rain let up, Alex helped me into the house. He thought I should have someone look at my ankle, but I just wanted to get in the shower, dry off, and rest. Alex went on his way once I was safely inside.

After my shower, I put on a fluffy robe and stretched across the bed. Despite the throbbing of my ankle, it had been a wonderful day. I got a text. It was Alex.

Made it home. How is the ankle?

I'll be fine. Thanks for lunch.

The wine came in handy, too. ☺

Relaxing on the bed, I recalled the conversation Alex and I had had about my column. I knew I had to write something about sharing the beautiful fall season with a good friend and enjoying delicious wine. I decided to make it about the changing seasons. "Fall Back and Look Forward" was my title. I could describe the beautiful wine country in the fall while sharing the joy of the season.

Chapter 11

The next morning, I called Judy to remind her of the hours she needed to cover for me while I was gone. I wanted her to know that if the weather got bad, she should close and go home.

"I will, Lily, but please forget about Augusta and have a wonderful time. I've always thought that Cooperstown would be a great trip."

"Thanks so much, Judy. Call me if you have any concerns."

I started my day by looking forward to The Fruit of the Harvest Dinner. It would be a new experience for me. I ignored the pain I was still feeling in my ankle. I saw a mailman coming toward my place and noticed that he was someone other than Snowshoes.

"Good morning!" I said as I took my mail from him. "Is Snowshoes on vacation?"

"No, his wife, Pauline, took sick, so he has to be with her for a while."

"Oh, I'm sorry to hear that. My name is Lily."

"I thought it might be. Folks call me Barney. It's short for Barnard Davis."

"It's nice to meet you, Barney. Please give Snowshoes my best if you see him."

"I will. You have a lovely day."

I knew nothing about the personal life of Snowshoes, yet I felt like I knew him. I hadn't known him to miss a day of work since I'd moved here. I received a text, and it was Gracie. I sat down to get the weight off my foot.

> Sorry, Lily. I am backing out of tonight's dinner. I have an offer I can't refuse. I know you'll understand.

My heart sank in disappointment. I guessed that her better offer was with the man she was having an affair with. When she'd told me in confidence that it was her sister Glenda's husband, I could hardly believe it. I surely wasn't interested in going to the dinner alone, so I chose to look at it as a free evening to get ready for Cooperstown.

Tomorrow, there was quilt class, and then the trip. There was no homework for the class, and Susan would likely have the same program planned since class was cancelled last week. I put out Rosie's rocker and chose an attractive brown-and-orange quilt to display on it, which looked like fall. It was a beautiful day as I observed from my porch. I looked over at Doc's office and began to consider how I wanted to decorate it for Christmas. I wanted to check again about what was left inside, so I went to get the key.

Once I had the key, I hobbled over to unlock the door

and pushed it open. Spiderwebs greeted me, and I pushed them aside. This should have been a haunted house for Halloween instead of a Santa house! Pressing forward, I looked at the shelves. They would be perfect for displays. There was plenty of room to include a chair for Santa. I decided a whitewash would clean it up nicely, if I could get Ted to do it for me.

I could easily run a cord from the house to hang Christmas lights all over the place. I knew folks would be most curious and would come this way. With greenery and some red bows, the tiny structure would be irresistible. As I closed the door, I saw two women arrive.

"Good morning!" I greeted.

"Good morning!" an elderly woman responded. "Are you Lily?"

I nodded and smiled. "How can I help you?" I asked as I headed inside the shop.

"I told you, Clara," the blonde with the old woman scolded.

"We came to see your quilts," Clara stated with a smile.

"Well, I'm happy to show them to you," I assured them while walking them toward the quilt room.

"I read your column," Clara said.

"Oh, thanks so much!" I replied, although I noticed that she didn't exactly give me a compliment.

"Oh!" the blonde woman exclaimed. "How come they seem so old?"

"I've always loved and collected antique quilts," I explained. "They fit right in at this antique shop."

The woman gave me an odd look.

36

"How can these used quilts bring so much money?" Clara asked, shaking her head.

"Well, they all have their attributes and shortcomings," I said with a chuckle.

Chapter 12

"I am looking for a new baby quilt for my great grandchild, but I don't think I'm going to find it here," Clara said as she looked around.

"There's a quilt shop in town, but I don't think she has quilts for sale," I informed her.

"We tried there first," Clara explained. "I was shocked to see the prices of the fabric!"

"Yes, it isn't inexpensive to make a quilt these days," I agreed.

"I thought by the way you wrote that you were quite an authority on quilts," Clara stated. "I thought you would have a variety for quilts for sale."

I wasn't sure how to respond. "I never claimed to be an authority," I said slowly, taking time to gather my thoughts. "I love quilts and care about how people use them. I also love history and the quilts people have made through the years. That said, I have lots to learn—just like everyone else."

They looked at me like I was referring to them, so it worked!

"Well, I'm ready to go, Clara, if you are."

"I'm sorry I couldn't provide you with a baby quilt, but please come back." I said politely.

"Well, could we at least get a photo of you and me?" Clara requested.

"Why, sure!" I responded as her friend prepared to take the picture.

"No, we must go out by your sign or folks won't believe it's you," Clara insisted.

"We can do that," I said, following them out the door. After a couple of attempts at the photo, they got in their car and were on their way. I walked inside the shop feeling totally confused. I just couldn't please everyone, and as a retailer, that was difficult to accept. In dismay, I elevated my ankle and turned on my laptop to check my group email, hoping to get my mind off those ladies.

Loretta was the only one who had emailed. "Sarah got fired from her part-time job. Don't tell her I told you, but she may have deserved it. She probably called in too many times using Lucy as an excuse. I also doubt that she is making progress on her online degree."

I felt I had to defend Sarah. "Don't be too hard on her. She is young and wants some independence. I'll send her what I can to help out."

I closed the laptop when I saw that Judy had arrived.

"You're a day early," I joked.

"I was in the area, and I just thought I'd check in on you to see if there is anything you wanted to show me."

"You did well last time, so don't worry about anything. I think I'll close early today. Do you want to go have a drink somewhere?"

"No, I'd better not. I need to go to my aunt's house from here. How is your ankle doing?"

"Much better. It talks to me every now and then. I'm going to make a phone call to my niece and then get some dinner."

"Sounds good. Thanks for the invitation."

After Judy left, I locked the shop and went upstairs to call Sarah. "I guess it didn't take long for Mom to tell you that I lost my job," Sarah said sarcastically. "She even suggested that I move back home."

"She just cares about you, that's all."

"I'm not going back."

"I'll send you a little money until you can find some work."

"Thanks, Aunt Lily. I really want to come to Missouri for Christmas with the others."

"I hope you can."

Sarah then proceeded to ask questions about Marc and Alex. She sounded homesick when she asked about Carrie Mae and the other folks in Augusta. I gave her a pep talk and hung up with mixed feelings about her situation. I changed clothes and decided to go to Ashley Rose for a glass of wine and some comfort food. It wasn't Thursday, so I wasn't concerned about running into Anthony. As I stepped outdoors, I noticed that the temperature was cooler, so I decided to drive. My foot didn't need to be walking up that hill! I walked into the restaurant and couldn't believe my eyes. The first thing I saw was Esther and Chuck having dinner with Anthony.

Chapter 13

"Well, look who's here!" Chuck happily greeted me.

I smiled at each of them.

"Are you here for dinner?" Esther inquired. "If so, please join us. You've met Anthony before."

"Oh, sure. Hello!" I responded awkwardly. "Thanks, but I just wanted to pick up something to go."

"Well, sit a bit," Anthony said, getting up to pull out a chair. "Go place your order and have a glass of wine with us."

His eyes were so penetrating that I almost couldn't respond.

"Good idea!" Esther encouraged.

"Okay, just for a little while," I conceded. "I didn't mean to interrupt your dinner."

I went to the counter, where Sally was ready to take my order. Without thinking, I ordered the special just to keep things simple. Right behind me was Anthony, which startled me for a moment.

"Put her dinner and drink on my tab, Sally," he instructed.

"Sure enough," she responded with a wink.

"Don't panic, Ms. Rosenthal," Anthony whispered. "I won't blow your cover."

I looked up at him and took a deep breath. "Thanks," I said as I walked back to their table. "So, no B&B guests tonight?" I asked Esther and Chuck.

"We have one late arrival, and dear Anthony will be spending the night with us," Esther explained.

"I have an early appointment in Washington, so I decided to check into my room here."

"Your room?"

They chuckled.

"I've stayed there a few times because it's such a marvelous place," he explained. "I even took advantage of the pool last summer."

"How nice," I said as Sally placed a glass of wine in front of me.

"Are you having Vintage Rose, by chance?" Esther asked.

I nodded. "I love it."

"Well, here's to a happy fall, y'all!" Chuck said, raising his glass.

As Anthony tapped his glass to mine, he flashed me a flirtatious smile. I hoped that no one noticed.

"Have you been to Lily's shop?" Esther asked Anthony. "It's the cute yellow house down the hill."

"I would love to see it sometime," Anthony responded. "I love quilts and antiques."

"Well, you know what they say—the highest form of flattery is a purchase," I quipped.

We laughed, and I prayed that my order would come soon. Instead, Randal and Marge arrived. I felt even more uncomfortable now.

"Here you go, Lily," Sally said as she delivered my order.

"Oh, thanks!" I said as I nearly jumped out of my chair.

After I said my goodbyes, I went to say hello to Randal and Marge so they would know I was not with the dinner party. When I neared the exit, Anthony approached me to see if I needed any help going home. As I had many times, I reminded him that I knew my way.

I was glad to get home. I took the food upstairs to the porch and turned on the fireplace to knock off the chill. As I sat and watched the flames, I wondered if I'd appeared foolish around Chuck and Esther. I didn't know what it was about Anthony that seemed to raise my blood pressure. I'd certainly never felt that way around Marc, and I was in love with him—or was I?

I forced myself to think about the Cooperstown plans. As I thought about what to take, I realized I didn't have any fancy, sexy sleepwear. Would it matter? Would Marc have arranged for separate bedrooms, or should I assume that he wouldn't? Should I expect him to pay for everything? Should I care about any of that? I wasn't a teenager anymore. Was I thinking about this whole visit too much? I was tired of thinking, so I settled into bed and pulled the covers over my head.

Chapter 14

The next morning, when I entered the library for quilt class, it appeared that I was late, and it felt as if everyone was staring at me. Susan had made hot cider for the chilly morning and Heidi had brought some donuts. It hit the spot, and everyone became talkative.

"It's so good to see everyone here," Susan spoke above our chirpy voices. "We have some things to discuss before I show you how to mark a quilt."

"Oh, Susan, I'm so glad I didn't miss this class," Judy exclaimed.

Susan nodded and smiled. "Let me begin by asking if you know what a secret sister is," she said.

"Like a secret Santa, right?" Marilyn asked.

Susan nodded in agreement. "Good! I thought we would all draw names for Christmas. You can acknowledge that person in any way you decide. It can be quite fun, because it's a secret! After the holidays, we will reveal the name we have drawn today. That means you should all pay attention to your secret sister for ideas. Please do not spend a lot of money. Think of simple things."

"How fun!" Heidi exclaimed.

"I have names already printed out, and I have taken the liberty to include myself. I hope that's okay. After you draw your sister's name, do not look at her, or it will give it away."

We laughed.

"Please pick a name as you leave today. Now on to the next matter of business," Susan continued as she pounded on the table. "Most of you know that I am very active with the Christmas Walk committee."

Everyone got quiet.

"We have an unusual problem this year. We have lost the Santa that we have had for many, many years," Susan stated.

"How can you lose Santa?" Marilyn asked.

"Unfortunately, he has a terminal illness and cannot do it this year."

"How sad," Edna said quietly. "He was quite good."

"Yes, he was," Susan sighed. "I am on a search now to replace him, but as you can imagine, most Santas are booked by now."

"Can't anyone around town fill in?" Judy wondered aloud.

"Not likely," Susan said, shaking her head. "We would like a full-bellied fella with a real beard, not to mention a happy personality."

"I see," I said slowly, thinking about my idea for Doc's office. "I need him to be at my place as well. I have the perfect little house for him."

"Do you mean Doc's office?" Judy asked.

I nodded as everyone got quiet. "It will be adorable when I finish decorating it," I assured them.

"It's a wonderful idea, Lily, but you'd better have plan B

in mind if I don't find one. So, if any of you hear of someone, please let me know."

Susan then moved on to showing us how she marked her quilts. She showed us various ways of marking and cautioned us not to leave much blank space on the quilting designs. She said the quilting lines should connect in some fashion. It was interesting to watch her demonstrate and to hear what she had to say.

As our class ended, we all exited and picked a name out of Susan's hat. I didn't unfold my name until I got to my car. I was hoping to get Judy's name, but I got Susan's. That would be a challenge for me. I liked Susan a lot, but I also assumed she had everything a quilter would need. I would have to start paying attention!

Chapter 15

Before I left for the trip, I kissed nearly every one of my quilts goodbye. I told Rosie to keep an eye on things and to wish me well! When I got in my car, Doc's lights were flashing in his building. I took it as a wave goodbye. I stopped at the coffee shop to get a cup of coffee to go. Randal said that I was his first customer of the day. He seemed a bit envious when I told him I was off to Cooperstown. He lifted my spirits as I left my little town.

I was surprised at how much traffic there was at this early hour. When I got to the highway, I pulled over to send a text to Marc to tell him that I was on my way. It had been a while since I'd seen Marc, so I was excited.

Marc was waiting for me in his parking garage by the freight elevator. "Good morning, sweetheart." He greeted me with a hug. "Are you excited?"

"Not as much as you are, I'll bet," I quipped.

"My things are in the car, so as soon as we add yours, we can take off."

"Great!" I could tell that Marc was in seventh heaven. He

was Mr. Baseball! We got to the airport in plenty of time to have our second cup of coffee. The traveling crowd was very light. I hadn't flown since I'd made a trip to Green Bay to see Loretta. I'd hated the hassle then, and I hated it now.

Once we were boarded, Marc began to describe the Cooperstown Inn B&B where we would be staying. He explained that they had transportation available, but he thought we should have our own car in case we wanted to do other things. The flight became quite bumpy at times, so Marc continued to hold my hand.

When we arrived in Albany, we headed to a luggage carousel and then to the car rental place. It involved a lot of walking, which aggravated my ankle, but I didn't say anything. I loved to people watch, and it kept me entertained for most of the travel experience.

When we got in the rental car, Marc explained that our B&B was established in the 1800s and had an old-world décor that he thought I would enjoy. It had to be quite large since they advertised fifteen rooms on their website.

Our arrival was most interesting. Marc had booked one of the B&B's large suites instead of separate rooms. Somehow, that didn't surprise me. The sweet girl who showed us to our suite told us we would love our view and that it was very close to the Hall of Fame. Marc gave her a generous tip, and he followed up by giving me a slight hug that indicated to me how happy he was.

I felt like a princess as we got settled. Although I never lacked opinions of my own, I liked the way Marc took charge of things. The trip was about him, so I was just pleased to tag along.

"We'll have dinner at that cute little café we passed next

door, if that's okay."

"Of course. Let's keep it simple tonight. I'm rather exhausted."

We stayed in our travel clothes, and I felt right at home in the small Italian place that reminded me of The Hill. As we ate our pasta, Marc told me about some of the other attractions around town, like the Cooperstown Bat Company. He said they had tours showing how they made all kinds of bats. The excitement in his eyes didn't quite match mine after the long day. Our first night was sweet and not as awkward as I thought it might be. We were both tired, yet we were comfortable with each other. Tomorrow would be full and much more exciting.

Chapter 16

The next morning, we were moving slowly and barely made it to the last serving of breakfast. Neither one of us was used to such a full and fancy breakfast, so it was a real treat. We visited with other couples who were also experiencing Cooperstown for the first time. Marc had a wonderful way with new acquaintances, which likely came from having a law practice. When we left the inn, I wanted to see the entire picturesque town, but Marc was chomping at the bit to get to the Hall of Fame. As we approached the building, I was surprised that it was smaller than I had envisioned. Greeters were waiting for us when we walked inside.

The guide told us there were 40,000 artifacts on display. Especially impressive was the big hall, where 323 Hall of Fame members were honored with gorgeous gold plaques. Of course, Marc knew most of them, but my knowledge was limited to names like Babe Ruth and Jackie Robinson. As I watched the slow pace of Marc as he read every word, I suggested that we split up and go around at our leisure. A gentleman in a red jacket advised us to visit Doubleday Field, where the annual Hall of Fame game had been played until 2008. He said it was just two blocks away.

I took my time checking things out so that later I could discuss some of the information with Marc. It didn't take me long to find the gift shop. I started shopping and found a Cardinals nightshirt for Holly, who was a big fan of the team. Alex did not care much for sports, but he wore baseball caps. A cap for Alex was perfect. Just as I was thinking of some things for myself, I received a text from Alex.

Having fun yet?

I laughed to myself.

Yes, I'm having a blast! Do you wish you were here?

Cute! Behave yourself!

I continued shopping and found a snow globe of the museum that was fascinating. Perhaps I could save that for Marc as part of his Christmas gift. I also chose a long-sleeved T-shirt in red and white that I could see myself wearing. Half an hour later, I left the shop and saw Marc standing down a hallway. We continued together until we heard the announcement that the place was closing. I was ready. Marc, not so much.

When we left the building, a light rain was coming

down. So much for a late-night walk. I was ready to rest. We decided the night would be best spent in front of a fireplace. We ordered pizza and broke open a complimentary bottle of wine. I changed into a sweatshirt and jeans. Marc quickly did the same.

"Hey, Lily! We could have gone to the 'bloopers' theater tonight!"

"The what?"

"I guess it's a place where you can see baseball bloopers replayed, including the Cardinals'. Would you have been up for that?"

I chuckled. I went over to the high-back chair where Marc was sitting and boldly sat on his lap. "I think I like exactly where I am right now, Mr. Baseball Man."

He drew me close for a passionate kiss as he let me know that he was exactly where he wanted to be as well.

The next morning at the breakfast table, a sweet couple described their visit to the Heroes of Baseball Wax Museum. I was intrigued as they described the realistic figures. It was nearly noon when we got back to the Hall of Fame. We both wanted to take more photos, and I wanted to cherish every minute before heading home in the morning. I took the time to call Judy now that I knew the shop would be open.

"Hey, you're not supposed to call and check on me," Judy scolded. "Marge actually showed up to buy something this morning and to see if I was doing okay."

"Well, that was sweet of her."

"She spotted that blue-and-white ceramic muffin tray and fell in love with it."

"Wonderful, and she'll likely use it, too."

"She will! Now, forget about Augusta and enjoy the rest of your trip!"

"Thanks, Judy!" I drew in a breath of relief.

Chapter 17

It was always satisfying to get a good report when away from home. It gave me the freedom to enjoy my last day away. At the recommendation of some of the guests at the inn, we chose the Cooperstown Back Alley Grille for dinner. There didn't seem to be a lot of choices for fine dining in the area. We speculated that it might be because tourists, mostly families, desired more casual dining options.

"Are you glad you made the trip?" Marc asked after we'd ordered a drink.

"Absolutely! I feel very privileged to have shared this with you. I hope I didn't hold you back on your adventure."

He looked at me strangely. "You were a bonus, Lily. The beauty of having a wonderful experience is sharing it with someone. I'm glad I didn't have to describe all of this to you when I got back!"

I smiled. "I agree. It's like trying to explain a beautiful sunset or a special kiss."

"Like this?" he said, leaning forward slowly and giving

me a soft kiss on the lips.

"Exactly!" I blushed and looked around to see who may be watching. "I'm ready to experience some food and spirits! I'm starving!"

"I'm in!"

The rest of the evening was nearly perfect. Leaving for the airport at an early hour would come soon.

We were quiet the next morning as we went through the rituals of getting to the airport and returning the car. Our flight home was running late, which tested the patience of my lawyer friend. He was making phone calls and already getting back to the grindstone of work. The trip for two began to separate into our independent lives filled with our own responsibilities. Our goodbye back at Marc's place was quick. In no time, I was traveling on the winding roads of wine country, making lists in my head for when I returned. When I pulled in front of my shop, I saw a young man walk toward my door. I got out of the car to see what he wanted. He didn't look like the typical customer.

"Can I help you?" I asked as I stopped him.

"Thanks, but I'm looking for Ms. Rosenthal, who owns this shop," he said.

I'm Lily Rosenthal. I'm just getting back from being out of town. I'll bet your name is Ted."

He smiled and nodded. "Yes. How did you know?"

"Well, I told your grandmother that I needed some help, and she offered your services."

"That's right. I am looking for some work."

"Can you start as early as tomorrow?"

He agreed and grinned from ear to ear.

Before I went in the house, I explained to Ted my plans for Doc's house, just to make sure he was up to the mission. My first priority was for him to rake all the leaves and dump them in the large sinkhole further down on Carrie Mae's lot behind me. He kept nodding and even offered to bring his own rake.

"My grandma may bring me. I don't have transportation, but I'm saving to get a truck of my own."

"It's nice to have an incentive. Come early tomorrow, then."

He smiled and was content to leave with the promise of returning in the morning.

When I went inside the shop, I heard Christmas music playing.

"Merry Christmas, girlfriend!" I teased.

Judy laughed. "I hope it's okay, but the music seemed to put the customers in a good mood."

"I couldn't agree more. I'll be doing some early decorating before Thanksgiving. Hearing these Christmas songs makes me want to get started."

"Oh, Lily, you will never guess what I sold while you were away."

"What?"

"That very strange papier-mâché Santa you had standing over there."

I knew just the one she meant. "That's good news! He certainly scared some of the children who have been in the shop. His eyes seemed to follow them everywhere."

"An elderly woman who stopped by said that her family used to have a similar one when she was growing up. She didn't bat an eye at the hefty price you had on it."

We chatted a bit more before a couple entered the shop. I asked Judy if she could stay the rest of the day since I had things to do. She was more than happy to, which worked out very well for me.

Chapter 18

I changed clothes, unpacked, and then checked my laptop to see if there were any group emails. Lynn reported that she was going to Carl's parents' for Thanksgiving this year. She said I was more than welcome to join them.

Loretta was cooking, and this year they were including an elderly couple who lived next door to them. They were anxious to see Lucy, of course. Laurie had also agreed to join them, so I was glad she would not be alone on the holiday.

When it was time for me to respond, I thanked Lynn for the invitation but said that I was perfectly happy to spend Thanksgiving here in Augusta. I asked if anyone had asked Aunt Mary or Ellen to join them. There was no response from Laurie, but Loretta said when she told Sarah about Ellen being one of us, Sarah was thrilled to have another aunt. I'd have bet Ellen would feel the same way if she got reacquainted with Sarah and met little Lucy.

I went through the mail, and there was another issue of *Spirit* with my column in it. It reminded me that I needed to be thinking of another topic. The green-and-red Feathered Star quilt that Butler had given me last year popped into my head. I couldn't wait to bring it out this season. The quilt was a great gift that kept on giving. It had started in his family, traveled to dealers, and ended up back at Butler's for some reason. Butler knew I had fallen in love with it, but he knew I would never be able to afford such a quilt. To my surprise, he felt the right owner should have it. I could use such an example in my next column since it was getting close to Christmas. I could call it "The Gift That Keeps On Giving."

I went downstairs when I knew Judy would be leaving. "I can't thank you enough," I said as I handed her a check and a scarf from the Baseball Hall of Fame.

"Thanks so much! I really enjoyed it. I guess I'll see you at quilt class, right?"

"Yes, I'll be there."

When she left, I poured myself a glass of wine and put a frozen pot pie in the oven. I was interrupted by a phone call from Carrie Mae.

"How was Cooperstown?"

I smiled. "It was great! What's going on here?"

"Butler wants to have lunch tomorrow. Don't you have quilt class?"

"Yes, but I can leave early if I have to. What's the occasion?"

"Oh, I weakened and sold him the little Lincoln painting I've had for many years. It's time that I move some of these things on, and he's the perfect one to own it."

"Well, it will be good to see him. I'll pick you up at

eleven thirty. Where are we going?"

"Wine Country Gardens. I can't wait to hear more about your trip."

"Oh, by the way, Ted is coming tomorrow to rake leaves, but I don't have to be here. The next day, I want him to start scraping the trim on Doc's house."

"It's a good thing that we have a new helper. Ted stacked some firewood for me last week. He's quite a nice young man."

I ate my dinner and decided to get to bed early. I received a text as I was getting out of the shower.

How is my baseball buddy?

She is about to drop into bed after a great trip!

You were a trooper!

Anything to keep my baseball man happy.

Love my baseball lady.

Well, that was a pleasant message to hear before bedtime. Perhaps I loved Marc more than I was willing to admit. I opened my laptop when I crawled into bed. There were no additional emails from my sisters. I was sure that was my fault for suggesting that Aunt Mary and Ellen be invited to someone's Thanksgiving festivities. Would Ellen ever qualify to be in this private sister email group?

Chapter 19

When I went downstairs to get coffee the next morning, I was shocked to see Ted already raking leaves. I quickly ate a bite and then had to get ready for my quilt class, so I decided not to engage him in conversation right then. What could I wear to class that would also be suitable for lunch with Butler? There was no choice but to wear black.

As I left the house, I complimented Ted on his work. I handed him cash and told him to come back tomorrow to begin work on Doc's house. I asked him not to come until nine since I had to set him up with the right tools and paint.

"My grandma has brushes," he offered.

"I have all of that, but it may take longer than you think to scrape all the wood."

"Yes, ma'am," he replied. "Grandma said this is going to be a Santa house of some kind."

"That's right, but it first has to be cleaned out before it can be decorated."

"No problem. I've done almost everything for Grandma before."

"You're quite fond of her, aren't you?"

"I don't know what I'd do without her."

I knew there was a sad story there, but that's all I needed to hear for now. "I can keep you pretty busy. You'll probably want that truck before Christmas, right?"

His face lit up. "That would be awesome, but I don't think it'll be possible."

"Anything is possible if you wish it so, Ted."

He grinned. "Well, thanks for the money. It's more than necessary."

"You finish up here. I need to get going." I looked at my watch and saw that I was running late.

It appeared that everyone was there when I walked into the quilting class. Susan was about to start. "Okay, ladies. I have a few announcements before we talk about today's lesson."

Everyone got quiet.

"Last week, I reported that we had lost our Santa Claus for Augusta, but I am pleased to tell you today that I have located one that is too good to be true."

"Really?" Heidi questioned.

"I found him online, but since he lives in the city, I decided to call and tell him about our situation. He actually lives near The Hill, I think."

"Great!" I responded.

"For starters, he is quite chubby from the looks of the photo, and he has a real beard. He sounded quite jolly as I talked to him. I liked him right away."

"Expensive?" asked Edna.

"That's the kicker!" Susan said. "He said he would take whatever we could afford. He said he doesn't do it for the money."

"No way!" Heidi exclaimed.

"How long can we have him?" I asked, thinking of my own needs.

"He said we could use him as many days as we like," Susan reported.

The whole thing sounded fishy to me, but I was thrilled at the same time.

"Here, let me pull up his photo," Susan offered as she opened her laptop.

He did indeed look perfect, just as Susan had described. He had a quilt on his lap, which I thought was odd, so I mentioned it to the others.

"He has to be a good guy if he likes quilts," Marilyn laughed. "Sign him up!"

"Don't forget, Randal wants an appearance, and he'll have to be at the tourist station," Judy said.

"I'll take him when no one else needs him," I stated. "It would be nice to have one of the nights during the walk."

"Where on earth would you put him, Lily?" Edna asked.

"I'm turning Doc's office into a Santa house," I reminded her. "I can even light it up for him. Oh, Susan, I hope he's for real. Why hasn't anyone else booked him?"

"I hear your concerns, but after talking with him, I think he's for real."

"What will you do about those lights that keep going on and off?" Judy wondered aloud.

Everyone got quiet.

"That's a good question," I responded. "It will just draw more attention, I guess."

They all nodded without smiling.

"Lily is certainly adding a new attraction to the Christmas season," Susan bragged. "I can't wait to see how it turns out."

"Well, I'll tell Randal right away," Judy said with excitement in her voice. "This will be such fun!"

Chapter 20

Susan finally got around to what she had planned for class. The topic was labels. She showed us some of her quilts that had labels on them, and then she demonstrated several types of markers that could be used when creating a label. She informed us that most people look on the lower backside corner for a label, but assured us that they can be placed anywhere. Everyone in the group needed to label last year's Christmas quilt that we'd made, and Susan shared many great ideas for what we could do. I wanted to put a label on the Christmas quilt that Butler had given me last year, but I wanted him to sign and date it so it would be clear to others that it was a gift and not a quilt I had made. It would be a good idea for me to take a piece of muslin with me today for him to sign when we met for lunch. By the time class was over, I was more than excited.

Carrie Mae was ready for me and decked out for the occasion. She wore a suit accessorized with plenty of antique jewelry. She would only do that for Butler. She blushed as I gushed over her.

"I think the world of him, as you know," Carrie Mae admitted.

"You must, or you would have never let go of that Lincoln painting."

She smiled, confirming that my observation was correct.

Butler graciously greeted us as soon as he saw us. He was such a dapper man in every respect. "You ladies look magnificent!" he said kindly. "I know this is a busy tourist time for you, so thanks for taking time to meet with me."

"We were anxious to catch up with you," I assured him. "You look great as well!"

Butler ordered a bottle of wine, but Carrie Mae and I decided to have iced tea.

"I remembered to bring Lincoln," Carrie Mae said as she handed him a wrapped package.

"Ahhh, grand!" Butler responded. "I have your check, and I added in a little extra for you because we both know it is worth a lot more than you asked."

Carrie Mae shook her head stubbornly.

"Well, I want to know about you," I said, trying to change the subject.

"You are referring to the suicide foundation in James's memory, aren't you?"

I nodded.

"It is doing extremely well, and I find it very rewarding to help others who have lost loved ones—sometimes when the family was not even aware that there was a problem," he explained.

"Have you been traveling?" Carrie Mae asked as she touched his arm affectionately.

"No, not as much," he answered. "I've had a few health

issues that have kept me close to home, plus nearly everything I do businesswise is conducted online."

"That's the new way now," complained Carrie Mae. "I hope your condition isn't serious."

"No, so please don't worry yourselves about it. I'm getting old, too, remember?"

We chuckled.

"Now, Ms. Lily here seems to be looking younger and younger. How is the Christmas quilt doing?"

"I'm glad you brought it up. I brought a fabric label with me. I want to sew it on the back of the quilt so that in the future, people will know where it came from. Would you mind signing it for me?"

"Good idea!" Carrie Mae exclaimed.

"I'd be happy to," Butler agreed. He paused in thought after I handed him my indelible marking pen, then he wrote: "This family quilt belonging to Butler Hayes of St. Louis, Missouri was given to Lily Rosenthal as a Christmas present. Enjoy!"

"Lovely. Now sign and date it, please."

"Your handwriting is wonderful," Carrie Mae noted.

"Thanks so much, Butler," I said as I looked it over. "I'm going to do some embroidery around the edge, I think."

"You truly love it, don't you?" he asked quietly.

"I do! I would never be able to purchase anything that nice."

"You must wish it so," he said, his tone now more serious. "Don't hold yourself back," he advised as he pulled his gaze from me and turned to Carrie Mae. "She is truly in the right business, isn't she, Carrie Mae?"

"She is indeed!" Carrie Mae beamed.

Then, in an unexpected moment, Butler said, "Tell me more about what's going on in your personal life, Lily."

He'd caught me off guard. My breath caught as I tried to think of a response.

Butler took advantage of the pause and added, "You are such a pretty gem hidden in such a little town."

I could feel color rising from my neck to my cheeks.

"Oh, you would be surprised how the men seem to find her," Carrie Mae joked.

"That is good to hear," he replied. "If any of them give you any trouble, contact me."

"Oh, most definitely," I returned, hoping my composure would return quickly.

Our lunch lasted a full two hours. I loved hearing about his world. It seemed so different than mine. When it came to what I wanted for my own life, maybe I should wish it so, just as I'd advised Ted.

Chapter 21

The next morning, I was happy to see sunshine, which meant Ted could keep working on Doc's office. He was right on time and got to work.

"What's inside here?" Ted asked innocently.

"Just junk and dirt. A lot of things have already been hauled away. Just think, a doctor once saw patients in this tiny place."

"That's hard to believe. Grandma said not to be alarmed if lights start going on and off."

I laughed. "It's harmless activity, Ted. The brushes and paint are on the back porch. I'll order sandwiches from the coffee shop when you are ready for lunch. I always did that for Kip and Tom, the young men who used to do some work for me."

"Yeah, I've heard about them."

I left him to work and went to get Rosie's rocker to put on the porch. It was a chilly fall day, but I had hopes of tourists coming in. I was doing paperwork when a man came into the shop.

"Good morning," he greeted me pleasantly. "Are you Lily?"

I nodded.

"I'm a friend of Marc's. He told me to stop by when I was out this way. My name is Will."

"How nice to meet you. Are you interested in quilts or antiques?"

"Neither, really. However, I've inherited three quilts from my mother and grandmother, and I want to sell them. They haven't been appraised, but I thought I would find a reputable dealer, and we could just agree on a price and be done with it. Marc sang your praises regarding being fair, so I thought I'd stop in to see you."

"That was kind of Marc. I'll do what I can to help. When can I see them?"

"Do you make house calls? I'd be happy to pay you, of course."

I smiled and shook my head. "I tend to be very tied down here, Will."

"Well, how about I invite you and Marc over to the house and you can take a look?"

"That may be possible, but arrange it with him. I lived near The Hill before moving here. I understand you are familiar with that area. I really miss the restaurants and bakeries."

"Yes. The restaurants and bakeries are like no other. You have a very nice shop. I am pleased to meet you."

"Thanks, Will. Hopefully we'll see each other again."

That was an interesting situation. That done, I called Kate's Coffee and ordered some sandwiches and lemonade for lunch. Every time I looked out the window, Ted seemed to be working hard. Then, Susan surprised me with a visit.

71

"Hey, what's going on?" I asked.

"I'm on a mission to get the scheduling arranged for Santa. I can't believe all the requests I'm getting! You know, they call him the 'Make-a-Wish Santa.' What do you make of that?"

"It makes sense to me. We all make wishes, especially at Christmastime. I can't tell you how many wishes we marked in the Sears catalogs when I was growing up."

Susan nodded and laughed. "It was the J. C. Penney catalog at our house. Would you look at the schedule I have so far and tell me if it works for you?"

I examined the schedule Susan offered me while I began to think about this special Santa. I suggested, "You should use his title in the advertisement. I can also write something about it in my column that comes out around Christmas. I'd need to do it soon, though."

"Great idea!"

"What would you wish for from Santa, Susan?" I was thinking about her being my secret sister.

"Of course, there's good health, but I'm a sucker for more fabric, chocolate, and of course, wine."

"You love your wine and know so much about it. I wish I knew more."

"What can I say? I see you already have someone getting Santa's house ready."

"Yes, just in time."

"I've got to run. Does this schedule look okay to you?"

"Sure. I won't be picky!"

Chapter 22

Ted and I sat on the front steps and ate lunch. I was learning that he was quite a pleasant young man.

"I can start painting the trim on Doc's house tomorrow, if you like."

"Good. When that's done, we'll clean out the inside to get it painted. I don't want Santa sitting in a dirty room."

"You really will have him sitting in that little place?"

I chuckled. "Yes. He'll be here at various times, but I get one of the nights during the Christmas Walk. He's called the Make-a-Wish Santa, and I can just picture him there."

"Boy, I wish I could ask him for a truck for Christmas. I guess I'm a little too big to expect that, huh?"

We laughed, but then I wanted to know more. "Wishes do come true! Are you getting anywhere close to having enough money?"

"Afraid not," he said, fixing his eyes on the ground.

Some customers were about to enter the shop, so Ted went back to work and I returned indoors. When I saw that Ted was close to finishing for the day, I decided to close and bring in Rosie's rocker. I needed to go by Johann's to get groceries because my cupboard was bare. I also knew I had to get some strings of lights while he still had them.

Johann always seemed happy to see me. He directed me to a big box of lights that had just come in. "You are the third person requesting lights today. 'Tis the season, and now folks decorate before Thanksgiving."

He was right about that!

"How's the world treating you, Lily?" he asked as he rang up my purchases.

"Not bad," I assured him. "This will be my first Thanksgiving in Augusta, and I want to make it special."

"Well, if you don't want to cook, one of the churches will have some mighty nice food."

"Oh, that's good to know."

Johann helped me carry my things to the car. "You have a nice Thanksgiving. I can't wait to see what you do with all those lights!"

I chuckled and waved him on. I was about to park in front of Ashley Rose to get dinner when I saw Anthony's car. I had to think about what day of the week it was. I thought it best to drive on, so I did. As I unloaded my car when I got home, I thought about how silly it was that I just couldn't acknowledge his friendship. That meant tonight was going to be a frozen pizza or a salad. My phone rang just as I had put away the last bit of groceries.

"Lily, this is Ellen."

Ellen. We hadn't spoken since she had shared the news that she was my half-sister. "Hi, how are you?"

"Just fine."

"How's your mom?"

74

"She's fine. I'm not interrupting anything, am I?"

"Not at all. I just got back from the grocery store."

"I decided to be brave and ask if you have any holiday plans for Thanksgiving or Christmas."

"Actually, I am going to stay here in Augusta for Thanksgiving because Lynn and Carl are going to his parents' house. At Christmas, it's Lynn's turn to have everyone. Last year we were in Green Bay at Loretta's. Why don't you join us if you don't have plans?" There was no response. "Ellen?"

"I'm here. Are you sure the rest of the family wouldn't mind?"

"Of course not. I'm sure Lynn has plans to ask you. The family has its way of doing things, like going to church on Christmas Eve together, and then on Christmas morning, we open presents. Last year on Christmas Day, we were all preparing dinner when Sarah decided to go into labor as she was making mashed potatoes!"

I could her hear her giggle quietly. "It sounds so nice. I think I would like to be with you all if there are no hard feelings."

"As far as I'm concerned, you are our Christmas gift this year. It's not every day that you get a new sister!"

"Okay, then. If you could email me the details, I'd appreciate it. It's been ages since I've seen everyone."

"What about your mother?"

"I won't be seeing her this Christmas, but she'll be pleased to know that I'll be joining you all."

"I'm glad you called, Ellen. Lynn also has a large house if you want to stay over."

"Oh, I need to think about all of that. Gee, I haven't gone to church on Christmas in a very long time."

"Well, I think it's time," I said encouragingly.

With that, we hung up. I didn't know whether to be happy or to worry about what had just occurred. I should have checked with the others about the invitation. It was Laurie I was most worried about. I would need to talk to her about that.

Chapter 23

As I sipped on a glass of wine with my pizza, I wondered how best to break the news of inviting Ellen for Christmas to the rest of my family. Should I casually mention it in an email? Would Laurie back out of coming to Missouri if she found out that Ellen would be there? I felt I'd better get some advice from Lynn before doing anything, since she was the hostess.

The ringing of my phone startled me. It was Alex.

"I did a very brave and presumptuous thing," I confessed before either of us had a chance to say hello.

He snickered. "Let me guess," he responded sarcastically. "You asked Robert for a raise."

"Oh, heavens, no."

"You accepted a date from a man, hoping Marc would understand."

"You are so mean, Alex."

"So, tell me!"

"I invited Ellen—our newly found sister—to have Christmas with us at Lynn's."

"That's it?"

"Yeah, but I didn't check with anyone else."

"I can't imagine you not inviting her after all these years."

"That was my feeling, exactly, but it's Laurie that I'm worried about."

"Well, think of it this way: look at the damage and hurt you would have caused by not inviting her. You are all grown women. It's not like you're someone asking to play in the sandbox with the new kid in the neighborhood."

"You're right. I'm making too much of it."

"Speaking of Lynn, did she mention anything about having an open house at her gallery this year?"

"No, but I don't know why she wouldn't. You would be there, right?"

"Sure. I was your date last year, remember? Now you'll be with Marc, I presume."

"I guess. Why don't you ask Mindy?"

"Nah, I can do better than that."

"Oh, really! Aren't you picky-wicky? I'll bet you have quite an inventory of numbers in that phone of yours."

"Funny you should bring that up. There's an app now that's called Little Black Book."

"Did you ever have one of those?"

"Sorry, I'm not that old. Lily, you're still single, so you could download the app as well."

"I don't think so."

"So, you're saying you don't have any other men in your life besides Marc? What about that guy Butler that you've mentioned? Should I go on?"

"I'm hanging up now. I don't like this conversation."

"Okay. I guess I hit a hot button. Tell me how the others

react to Ellen coming for Christmas."

"I will. Thanks for all the great advice!"

He laughed. "Hey, before you hang up, what are you doing for Thanksgiving?"

"I plan to spend it in Augusta for the first time. Lynn and Carl will be out of town. Do you want to come out here for dinner?"

"You can't be serious. Now if you want to come here, I can whip up something in the kitchen for us."

"You know, I think I just want to be here for a change. I might just bake a small turkey breast."

"Whatever, Lily Girl, but my invitation stands, okay?"

"Got it." When I hung up, I wondered if it was too late to call Lynn, but I had Ellen on my mind. I took another sip of wine and made the call.

"Aren't you usually in bed at this hour?" Lynn asked when she realized it was me.

"I'm having a late dinner and had something on my mind."

"Oh, no. Now what? Is it bad?"

"No, I actually think it's quite good."

"Spill it."

"Ellen called, and we chatted about Christmas coming up."

"And?"

"I asked her to join us without checking with you or the others."

"Well, for heaven's sake, it's fine! There will be so much commotion that it shouldn't be that awkward. I'll bet she was pleased!"

"Yes, she was, but what about Loretta and Laurie?"

"Loretta's been used to family dysfunction for some time. All she'll be thinking about is Sarah and Lucy."

"But Laurie has not taken well to this news. I'm afraid she won't come if we tell her that Ellen will be there."

"Well then, we won't tell her. Who knows? Ellen may change her mind and not show up. Trust me, Christmas has a way of working its magic."

"Thanks, Sis. I feel better."

"That's what sisters are for. You confess your thoughts, tell what's on your heart, and then go on with life, right?"

Her estimation of things made me pause for a bit. In the end, I thought that her words rang pretty true!

Chapter 24

The next morning, I was delighted to see Ted at work. He took it upon himself to find the brushes and paint on the back porch. I threw on my bathrobe and went out to say hello. "Aren't you ambitious today!"

"Hope you don't mind that I get an early start. I promised Grandma that I would help her with something this afternoon."

"That's no problem. Please come back tomorrow if you can."

"Don't worry, I will," he said with a big grin.

"I am going to make some vegetable soup today, so if you get hungry, come on in the house."

"Wow, thanks so much!"

I went inside to get some coffee. When I walked upstairs, I turned on the gas fireplace to take off the morning chill. As I sat there, I tried to picture what Thanksgiving might feel like out here by myself. The day was about being thankful, and I certainly had a lot to be thankful for. All of the shops would be closed, so maybe I should be different and be open.

Maybe I could have an open house since shop owners might be available to come. It was time that I gave back to this community. I could invite anyone and everyone as a thank you, but what could be the draw to get them to come?

I welcomed the opportunity to think of something creative. Thanksgiving was all about turkey and pie. Why not have a pie party? I'd never been invited to a pie party where there would be lots of different pies. I did make a pie crust once, but if I remembered correctly, the pie was awful, so that was the end of that. Maybe Alex could help or give me some advice. Who wouldn't stop by for a free piece of pie, despite having it at their Thanksgiving dinner table? Perhaps there were others like me who would find themselves alone on Thanksgiving Day and would welcome a rather unique way to celebrate the day.

I called Alex before I lost my train of thought.

"And why do I deserve this early morning call?" he asked in a groggy voice.

"Oh, I'm sorry if I woke you. I just had an idea."

"That's dangerous. Is it about your column?"

"No. I want to offer some sort of thanks to Augusta and the community, so I've decided to have a pie party on Thanksgiving Day."

"Okay, so like an open house? Hold on. I need to get some coffee. I take it that you're serious."

"Remember the time you showed me how to make a pie crust? I could have all kinds of pies for people to choose from."

"I think I did the work and you watched. Am I remembering that correctly?"

I laughed, recalling that he was completely right. "Well,

yes, but I can do this. I will need your help, though, since you have no plans. I'll need help with fruit pies. Please, please say you'll help me bake some ahead of time."

"What if no one comes and you're stuck with all those pies? Thanksgiving is a family day."

"I've thought of that. I'll just deliver a pie to certain friends as a thank you afterward. Who wouldn't love that?"

"Lily Girl, this takes the cake! You sure make it hard to say no. I have to admit that I've never been to a pie party before."

"Is that a yes?"

"Sure. Tell me what kind and how many."

"Oh, Alex, thank you, thank you! I owe you!"

"Yeah, you always say that."

"Forget about the turkey and dressing this year. It's going to be all about pie!" I was pretty sure that he hung up wondering if he'd had a dream. He was the greatest!

Chapter 25

My veggie soup was a big hit with Ted, but he especially liked the corn bread I served with it. I was amazed at how big a growing young man's appetite could be! As we ate, I shared how I envisioned Doc's house would look when it was decorated. His expression changed a bit when I reminded him that it needed to be cleaned inside before being painted, but the accumulating hours made him feel better.

"Well, I'd better be on my way," Ted said, getting out of his chair. "You are really nice to have lunch for me. Thank you very much."

"You are very welcome. Tell Betty hello, and I'll see you tomorrow."

He nodded as he left, and I paused for a moment to be thankful for Ted entering my life at this time when I needed some additional help, then cleared the table and set back to work myself.

I was getting a fair amount of traffic as the afternoon went along. In between conversations, I designed a flyer for my pie party. Alex's help gave me the confidence I needed to go through with the idea. I also made a note to find my pie cookbook so I could get more ideas. I had cookbooks galore—it would almost convince someone that I actually cooked!

"Hey, Lily," Randal said as he came in the door.

"Hi, Randal. What's going on?"

"I just came from our Christmas Walk committee meeting, where I was put in charge of carolers. Would you mind if some of them hung out here during part of that day? They are mostly around churches at night."

"Of course. Santa will be inside Doc's house, so anywhere on the lawn will be fine."

"Great," Randal replied, clearly relieved that a portion of his responsibilities had been so easily checked off his list.

While he was there, I explained my idea about the pie party. He listened intently, and I knew he had some questions about my plans.

"Everyone will be closed that day, so I thought I'd give people a reason to get out and enjoy a piece of pie. I hope you and Marge can come over for a bit, if you're not tied down. If you were open, I would never want to compete, of course."

He grinned. "We'll be here. So... you like to bake pies?"

I knew that surprised him most. "Well, I'm getting some help from a friend who is a great baker, and I've got a great pie cookbook. I want every pie to be homemade."

"Well, if Marge gets wind of this, I know she'll want to help."

"I'll probably politely turn her down, because it's my turn to give back to folks like you who have been so helpful to me."

"You are a kind soul, Lily. I'd better get going. Thanks for helping us out."

Getting Randal's approval for my silly pie party was huge. They made and sold wonderful pies at his coffee shop. Within minutes of his departure, two girls came dancing into the shop, spilling over with giggles as they entered.

"How much is that bar quilt on the front porch?" one asked.

I had to think about what she meant. Then it came to me. "Oh, that's called a Log Cabin quilt."

"It's called a log cabin?" she asked, smiling and wrinkling her nose as she tried to discern if we were indeed talking about the same thing.

"Yes, I'll bring it in for you to look at."

"I noticed that all the center squares are red, which is kind of neat," her friend added as I retuned inside and spread the quilt out so they could see more of it.

"The bars, as you call them, are the logs of the cabin, and the red centers represent the fire in the fireplace," I explained. "It's a very traditional pattern that goes back to the 1800s. It has some wonderful madder prints that help determine the age."

"Madder prints?" the first girl asked.

I smiled, realizing that it probably sounded like I was speaking a foreign language. "They are prints that get their colors from the madder plant, like this rusty red," I pointed out. "They can be beautiful reds or nice shades of brown. Most of the quilts I have are not this old," I confessed. "Why don't you look at the quilts in the next room? I have a newer Log Cabin quilt from the 1930s that's in pastel colors."

Intrigued, they headed to the quilt room while I greeted a family of four that was entering. None of them seemed to be thrilled to be there, so they quickly scattered throughout the shop, which made me nervous. In no time, the two girls came back to the counter.

"I need to own this Log Cabin quilt," one said. "Someday, I want to live in a log cabin. I could put this on the wall."

"Wonderful," I said as I folded it up. "It's a bit fragile, so make sure you have support across the quilt when you hang it."

"Sure, but that won't be until years from now," she assured me.

I wrapped it in tissue paper and put it in a shopping bag as she watched with excitement. As they left, I wondered why everyone couldn't be as pleasant as those two. The family of four finally followed each other out the door, which was honestly a bit of relief to me. I wanted the day to end on the happy note of serving the two who were delighted to learn something new and embrace something beautiful.

Chapter 26

    I was pleased to see the pleasant weather the next day because it meant Ted could begin cleaning out Doc's office. Betty came in to say hello when she dropped Ted off. "I brought you some banana bread I just made," she said cheerfully as she handed it to me. "I want to thank you again for being so good to Ted. He loves working for you."

    "I'm the one who is thankful. He does an excellent job."

    "I have to tell you that he's a little concerned about working in Doc's office today," she nearly whispered. "He's heard the rumors about that building being haunted, I'm afraid."

    "I intend to help him, so I hope that will ease his concerns."

    "Okay, sweetie. I need to be on my way so I can deliver some bread to Carrie Mae."

    "Sure. Would you do me a favor and have her call me when she can?"

    She nodded.

    "Thanks for the bread. I think I'll have some with my

coffee here shortly."

Ted retrieved the key, and I told him I would join him as soon as I got a broom, some rags, and a big trash bag. When we turned the key and opened Doc's door, lights started flashing.

"Oh, maybe we'd better not disturb anything," Ted said nervously.

"The lights are harmless, Ted. We'll be able to see much better with them." As I looked around inside the building, it was still impossible to see where the lights were coming from. "Hold this bag open for me while I throw some of this junk inside," I instructed. Broken furniture legs, whiskey bottles, an old rug, and empty cans filled the bag.

"You're going to get pretty dirty," Ted warned me.

"That's okay. Take this broom and go after those cobwebs. We'll have this cleaned out in no time." When Ted saw that I was serious, his energy increased, and he was ready to tackle the job.

"Hey, Lily!" Barney called as he came into the yard with the mail. "What on earth are you doing?"

"Cleaning house for Santa Claus," I responded as I wiped a cobweb from my face.

"Where in the world is that light coming from?" he asked, leaning inside.

"I'm not sure, Barney, but it's helping out our cause right now," I replied.

"You two are working too hard!" he said as he scratched his head. "I'll see you folks tomorrow!"

For once, I was pleased that I had no early customers, for we were making substantial progress.

"Look at this," Ted called out as he held up a worn

magazine. "It's got a date of 1910. I'll bet it's worth something."

"It looks like it got wet a few times. If it were in good condition, it might be worth a few dollars. Put it aside, and I'll look at it later."

He nodded and placed it on the front porch. When it got close to noon, the building was empty, and the next step was to sweep it and wipe it down.

"Let's take a break for lunch," I suggested.

"Sounds good to me. I'll wash up on the back porch."

"Would you like some grilled cheese sandwiches and tomato soup?"

"That's one of my favorites, so it sounds great!"

While I was grilling the sandwiches, Carrie Mae came inside the shop. "Just in time for lunch, Carrie Mae," I told her.

"It smells good, but Betty said you wanted to talk to me. When she said you were working on Doc's house, curiosity got the best of me."

I laughed. "Well, have a seat. I wanted to share my idea about something I have planned for Thanksgiving Day."

Chapter 27

Ted came in the kitchen just as I was beginning to tell Carrie Mae about my pie party.

"A pie party?" Ted inquired.

"Yes! I decided I wanted to thank the community for everything they have done for me. Shops will be closed, and nothing says love like pie from the oven!"

They laughed at my silliness.

"You know how to be poetic, but do you know how to make pie?" Carrie Mae questioned.

"I'll bet she does, Carrie Mae," Ted chimed in. "We always have Grandma's pumpkin pie that day, but I can eat pie more than once. My favorite is banana cream, by the way."

I laughed aloud at his enthusiasm, and Carrie Mae just shook her head.

"We'll have many kinds to choose from," I explained. "If I have any pies left, I plan to deliver them to folks who have been good to me."

"Girl, the things you think of!" Carrie Mae declared. "Again, have you ever made a pie before?"

Ted looked at me for an answer.

"Of course," I quickly assured them as I looked the other way. "Alex has agreed to make fruit pies for me. I'll make the cream pies. Isn't that a great idea?"

"I'm in!" Ted cheered. "I'll help that day if you need me. It'll have to be after Grandma's dinner, of course."

"I haven't made pie in years, but if you need me to contribute, I will," Carrie Mae said as she shook her head in disbelief.

"Absolutely not!" I replied with certainty. "You and Betty are some of the people I owe a big thank you to."

"Well, it's crazy, but who wouldn't stop by for a piece of pie?" Carrie Mae admitted.

"I have to rearrange a bit so guests can sit at various places," I thought aloud. "Of course, with clear weather, I could seat some people outdoors, except that I don't have any tables."

"I have some long folding tables in the basement if you want them," Carrie Mae offered. "Ted, you'll have to figure out how to get them here, I suppose." The thought of tables outdoors was exciting. I could visualize them being covered in old quilt tops. How fitting for my shop!

"Well, that's next week, so I'd better get baking," I joked. "Right now, we have other things to tend to, don't we, Ted?"

"Yes, we do," Ted agreed. "I'll get back to work."

Carrie Mae left, and Ted and I resumed dusting the interior. I then hooked an extension cord to my vacuum cleaner so the vacuum could reach Doc's house.

"Who is moving into Doc's house?" a voice asked nearby. It was Buzz, Karen's husband.

"Oh, hi, Buzz." I turned off the vacuum. "We're getting

this ready for Santa Claus. He will visit during the Christmas Walk," I explained.

"I think I did hear something about that, but what's up with the flashing lights?" he asked.

"I think it's Doc's way of helping us out," I joked. "It's pretty dark in here without them."

"Doc's still around?" he asked with a grin. "Is that what you're saying?"

"Who else could it be?" I said, shrugging.

"Wait until I tell Karen. I told her that we had a spirit of some kind in our shop, but she doesn't believe me. Things are always getting misplaced, and she blames me! Well, I need to be on my way. I just couldn't resist stopping to see what was going on."

"We need to get together soon," I suggested. "I owe you two a dinner."

"We would like that," he said as he got on his way.

Around four, Ted returned the vacuum to the shop, and I joined him. "I think we're ready to paint, Ted," I announced. "Let's do that tomorrow, if you're free."

"Sure! I'm going to meet Grandma at Carrie Mae's, so I'd better be on my way. By the way, I sure like your pie party idea."

Chapter 28

After I took a shower, I was completely exhausted as I fell into bed. I pulled the laptop from my bedside table with plans to see if there were any emails from my siblings. I was pleased to see that Loretta had sent of a picture of herself holding Lucy. Lucy was growing up before my very eyes, and what a cutie she was! I often wondered if she looked like her father. Loretta said she was babysitting while Sarah was at a job interview. Loretta also mentioned how much she was looking forward to getting away. They'd already had snow, which I knew was not pleasant for her. She and I both had a dislike for winter. Lynn said she was focused on her commissioned paintings for Christmas. Laurie responded that the snow was helping customers get in the Christmas-buying mood.

My addition to the conversation was how much I missed them all. I briefly explained my pie party for Thanksgiving Day, telling them they no longer had to worry about me being alone. That certainly got their attention, and their remarks were comical for the most part. I then remembered to tell them that Alex was going to help me out. I could see them shaking their heads, wondering what their baby sister would do next. I fell asleep with the laptop resting at my side. I had a dream that turned into quite a nightmare when tons of guests showed up for pie and all I had were burnt pies to offer. I sat up in bed in horror, knocking my laptop to the floor.

Finding it hard to get back to sleep, I got up to write my column for Richard. I had thoughts about Christmas wishes and how diverse everyone's wishes were. I started my first line by asking the readers, "If Santa gave you one wish for Christmas, what would it be?"

I then went on to say that Santa not only brings things to children, but to adults as well. I thought of the contrast between Ted wishing for his first truck and someone who just desired good health. After a few pages, I closed by saying that I hoped everyone would get their wish for a Merry Christmas and a Happy New Year. I crawled back into bed and fell sound asleep until nine, when my phone rang. It was Holly. I hadn't heard from her in a while. "Good morning, Holly."

"I called to tell you that I had to call an ambulance for Maurice this morning. I'm in the waiting room at the hospital now."

"Oh, my goodness! What happened? I am so sorry."

"They're doing tests now. He passed out in the foyer this morning. I couldn't get him up. You know I have a bad back, so I called the ambulance. He wasn't too happy about that."

"You certainly did the right thing. He should be in good hands now."

"I feel so guilty."

"About what, for heaven's sake?"

"That I really want him to…" She stopped before she said the word she really wanted to say.

"Everyone understands, Holly. It's too bad you have to go through all of this with no love for him."

"It's my duty, Lily," she said as she started to weep.

"Listen, use these quiet moments to take care of yourself, and call me if there's any change. I will pray for both of you."

"Thanks, Lily. I love you."

"I love you, too."

As I went down to get coffee, I pictured her sitting alone.

Chapter 29

Ted came to the door, so I let him in.

"Good morning!" he said cheerfully. "If you have Doc's key, I'll get started painting."

"Do you think you can do it without me? I'm not exactly dressed to paint."

"I'll be fine. I hope Doc turns the lights on so I can see better."

We laughed.

I watched Ted as I carried Rosie's rocker onto the front porch and stretched a red-and-blue quilt across the back. I wished I had cut greenery to make it look more festive. I went back inside to eat a bite of breakfast and kept thinking of Holly sitting there completely alone in the hospital. Perhaps her friend Mary Beth would keep her company. Did God have a plan for all of this? Could a serious health situation give Maurice a change of heart? If God decided to take him, would it give Holly a happy life at last? Was it bad to think of their situation in that way?

"Good morning," Barney said, coming in the door with

my mail. "I see you are making progress out there."

"Yes, we are! Say, any word on how Pauline is doing?"

"She's still in bad shape and Snowshoes won't leave her side."

"Please tell him they are in my prayers."

"I sure will. The whole town is praying for them."

I followed him outdoors and walked over to check on Ted. Sure enough, the lights were flashing. "We need to hang greenery from this ceiling," I suggested, looking up. "It would make it smell good in here, too."

"You don't want me to paint up there?"

I shook my head. "I like the bare beams. What you've painted so far is making quite a difference, Ted."

He grinned. "Well, one coat is doing great since this has never been painted before."

"This is a silly question, Ted, but do you feel any presence in here?"

He smiled and paused before he said, "I don't know if I really am, or if I'm pretending I am."

I smiled and nodded, understanding what he was saying.

"It's a good feeling, just so you know. Funny, my Grandma asked me the same question."

"That's good. I'm glad that's your perception."

I went back inside to decide how I was going to decorate for the holidays. I wanted it done before the pie party. I also thought about how I could make more room for guests if they wanted to sit down. I didn't want them eating in the quilt room, so I might have to make a little sign telling them not to take food into it.

"Hey, Gracie," I said as she walked in the shop. "How are you?"

"Really good! I just had to stop and see what you're up to out there."

I chuckled. "You mean the progress on my Santa house?"

She nodded. "I peeked inside. The paint is doing wonders!"

"It will be so cute. Just wait and see."

"It certainly will if you have anything to do with it."

"I'm sorry I haven't been to your shop lately, but I've been so busy."

"Same here. My dad is putting a big tree in the shop today. It's pretty exciting to celebrate my first Christmas here."

"Believe me, I know how you feel. I remember how excited I was last year."

"I apologize again about cancelling our dinner plans. Did you go anyway?"

"No, I didn't. When I get a cancellation, I look at it as a gift of free time."

"That's a terrific way to look at it. So far, business is good, and that quilt class you attend has been a blessing."

"I'm sure it has been. I wish you could join us. You would be such an asset."

"Maybe someday."

"We drew names for secret sisters, and I have Susan's name. If you know of anything she really likes, please let me know."

"Funny you should ask. She went nuts over a line of fabric we just got in. It's called Holiday Fun. We have some precuts of that if you'd like me to hold some back."

"Perfect! Please do!"

Chapter 30

I was happy with the results of Gracie's visit, so I checked on Ted. He was drawing attention, and folks were stopping to see what he was up to before they came into the shop. Deciding not to interrupt his progress, I went back inside, and as I did, I heard my cell phone ring. It was Marc. I happily told him how Doc's office was coming along.

"I called to tell you that I'm flying out to Meg's for Thanksgiving. I know you were probably wondering why I hadn't asked you about your plans."

"That's great, because I actually have plans of my own."

"Oh, have you, now?"

I began explaining my thoughts about giving back to Augusta, and how I thought serving pie on Thanksgiving was a charming way to do it. I couldn't tell what he thought of the idea, but I was pretty certain that I heard a snicker every now and then. He did react when I told him Alex had agreed to help me make some pies.

"You're lucky that guy is always there for you."

I wondered if there was an underlying meaning to

his comment. I replied by saying, "He offered to cook Thanksgiving dinner since he knew Lynn had other plans, but I told him I was determined to spend the holiday in Augusta."

"Good for you!"

"You know, if this is successful, I hope to make it an annual event. Please give Meg my best, and we'll get together when you get back."

"I hope you save me a piece of pie!"

"Of course! What kind is your favorite?"

"Cherry crumb."

"Cherry crumb it is!"

A group of ladies came into the shop, so I wished Marc a happy Thanksgiving and welcomed the customers. They were very chatty and seemed to be having a lot of fun.

"We all work together, and we hired a small bus to take us to the wineries and shops," one of the ladies explained.

"That's great! How in the world did all of you manage to take off at this time of year?"

"We planned ahead," she replied. "There are just eight of us. Some are browsing in other shops."

"I'm Lily, and if you love quilts and antiques, you've found the right place," I assured them.

"I love quilts!" the shortest of them exclaimed.

I showed her the quilt room, and she was delighted.

"Oh my goodness, you do have a lot," she said.

"Do you have any preference of color or pattern?" I asked her.

"I love soft buttery yellows," she said.

"I do too, but you'll see it used with other colors most of the time," I replied.

She picked up a Dresden Plate with a butter-yellow sashing and border.

"Oh, that is lovely," one of her friends remarked.

I helped her open it up all the way, and her eyes lit up. She had no interest in checking the price tag.

"I'll take this one," she said, folding it up.

I gladly took it from her as the others looked around. Each of them picked up small things to purchase, so I was a happy camper.

Ted came in the front door with a big grin on his face. "I think I'm done, so do you want to have a look?" he asked eagerly. "Tomorrow, we should be able to hang the lights."

"Yes, let me see," I said as I followed the ladies out the door. "Would you look at this?" I cheered. "You did an excellent job. What a difference a coat of paint makes!"

"Do you have a small rug or something we can put on the floor? It'll be cold out here."

"I do." I nodded. "I have just the chair picked out for Santa, too, but I won't put that out here just yet."

We both were quite happy with the outcome. Ted's face lit up when I brought him more cash for his truck fund. Ted walked home and I locked up the office. As soon as I did, the flashing lights stopped. I smiled.

Chapter 31

"You can count on cherry, apple, and blackberry pies," Alex said as we planned the party over the phone.

"Could you make one of the pies a cherry crumb for Marc, please? It's his favorite, and I told him I would save him a piece for when he got back from New York."

"Aren't you a sweetie pie?" he teased.

I supposed I was.

"I'll bring them out the night before, so you'll have them first thing. That means I'll spend the night. You're going to need more help than you realize, sweetie pie."

"You would do that?"

"Look, I've never been one to miss a party, much less a pie party!"

I laughed. "Well, Judy and Ted will be available to help as well. Ted is stringing lights on Doc's house first thing this morning."

"When are you doing your baking?"

"I'll start today and finish up tomorrow."

"Okey-dokey! If you think of anything else you need, give

ANN HAZELWOOD

me a holler."

"I will! Thanks so very, very much! I don't know what I'd do without you!" We chatted for a few more minutes and then hung up.

"Lily, Lily, are you here?" Barney called from the front door.

"Barney, I'm sorry. I was on the phone. Good morning!"

"I just wanted to tell you in person that Pauline died yesterday," he reported.

"Oh, no! Poor Snowshoes."

"The word is just getting out. I'm sure arrangements will be announced in time. Randal said he'd post them."

"Oh, good. Please give the family my sympathy."

"I sure will. I'm afraid you may not see him come back to work."

"He certainly is old enough to retire, isn't he?"

"He is, but he loved his job more than anything," Barney said as he went on his way.

As I watched him leave, I felt so sad. Losing someone during the holidays makes it so much harder for everyone. In between customers, I managed to do some baking, which made the shop smell heavenly. So far, nothing seemed too difficult. The first person to interrupt me was Betty.

"Lands, girl," she said in surprise when she saw me baking. "What are you of all people doing in the kitchen?"

I laughed. "I'm making pies! Didn't Ted tell you about the pie party?"

"He said something about pies, but he's always talking, and I don't pay much attention. I just stopped by to look at his handiwork and to tell you how much I appreciate all the hours you're giving him. Doc's office looks nice, and so will

104

all those lights you're stringing out there."

"I'm very pleased so far."

"Do you have another apron? I can help you roll out some dough while I'm here. I think you have some customers walking this way."

"You would do that?"

"Lily, this isn't my first rodeo! I make a pretty good pie crust, and rolling it out is one of the tricks."

"Thanks, Betty," I said, handing her my apron.

"What are you going to fill these with?"

"We'll have banana cream, lemon meringue, pumpkin, and chocolate. My friend Alex is making the fruit pies. I have no idea if I'll have enough. When they're gone, they're gone."

"You'll be fine until someone wants to help themselves to a second piece."

I smiled, thinking that would be a good thing. "Well, I'll be happy to oblige!"

Chapter 32

"Is anyone here?" a voice from the front room inquired.

"I'm here!" I responded when I saw a mother with a young daughter of about eight years old.

"My, what smells so good?" the mother asked.

"I'm making Thanksgiving pies," I explained.

"Well, you are on the ball!" she said, smiling. "I'm looking for a quilt for Claire's bed. I understand that you have quilts for sale."

"Yes, I do," I responded. "This must be Claire. Come on into the quilt room. These are antique quilts, so their smaller sizes may be just perfect for you."

"Oh, Mommy, look at this purple one!" The young girl pointed to one that had caught her eye.

"Just wait," she said, pushing Claire away from the quilt. The mother turned to me and said, "I don't know if I want her to have a used quilt. We've been looking at new ones online. I'm sure we could find some in purple, Claire."

"No, Mommy, I want this one!" she insisted.

"If I may add, this quilt appeared to be nearly new when

I purchased it," I explained. "I think it dates to about 1950. I bought it because the workmanship was excellent, and it hadn't been washed."

"Well, she just went into a bigger bed, so it likely won't fit anyway," the mother said doubtfully.

"Actually, this size is perfect for a full-size bed," I replied. "It will give you a nice overhang on each side."

"Please, Mommy, please," the little girl begged.

"I think we'd better wait, honey," her mother decided. "It's pretty pricey for an old quilt. We'll keep looking, but thank you for helping us. I understand there is a Gracie's Quilt Shop in the area. Is that right?"

"Yes, but they only sell quiltmaking supplies," I explained.

Without another word, the mother took the little girl's hand and led her out of the shop.

"Well, I've heard everything," Betty said, coming out of the kitchen wearing the spare apron. "Why on earth would she pass up that quilt?"

"Some folks are just uncomfortable about someone else owning the quilt before them," I explained, shrugging my shoulders. "Some are all about new and perfect."

"That sweet little girl would have been perfectly happy with it. Okay, Lily, I just took three pie shells out of the oven and put three more in. Do you want me to roll out some more while I'm here?"

"No, you've done plenty. I'll finish this up today. I think twenty of these will be more than enough, don't you?"

She nodded in agreement and smiled. "I would hope so! If you run out, you run out. Most folks will have pie that day anyway."

"Thanks for everything," I said, giving her a big hug. "I

hope you'll stop by. Ted said he'd be around for whatever I need."

"Oh, he'll love it."

A couple was browsing in the front room as I began mixing up more dough. They were curious about the aroma, which led them to the kitchen so they could take a peek.

Chapter 33

By the time I took the last three pie shells out of the oven, it was nine o'clock. I was pleased but exhausted. I was walking upstairs when my cell phone rang. It was Carrie Mae.

"I'm not calling too late, am I?" she asked.

"No. I just crawled upstairs from a long day of baking. Betty came to help for a while so I could wait on some customers."

"That's Betty for you! I just wanted you to know that I'm collecting money for Snowshoes' funeral flowers. I know they're also wanting money for the cancer fund, but I think the shop owners need to show their own support to Snowshoes."

"Absolutely! Thanks for doing that."

"I hear he's taking it all pretty hard."

"Yes, Barney said he may not return to work."

"I guess we'll see. Well, you get some rest. Thanksgiving is at our doorstep. By the way, have you heard the forecast?"

"No. Please don't tell me it's going to rain."

"No rain, but they say it could be our first snow of the

year! They are usually not correct, but we'll see."

"That is just what I need!" I hung up and took a hot shower, which I desperately needed. I prayed that the weather would not spoil the pie party. When I crawled into bed, my phone rang. It was Marc, who typically always made me smile, but tonight was different. I was too tired to talk. After a brief conversation with him, I pulled the covers over my head and said a prayer for Snowshoes and my pie party. To my dismay, I got a text, so I took a quick look at my phone. It was from Alex. He said he'd be here after lunch tomorrow with the pies, in case the snow came. I couldn't stop thinking about it all.

The next morning, I thought about Ted. He was coming to string the lights. That would be fun and exciting. As I drank some coffee, I checked my emails. The first message in the group email was from Laurie. She attached a photo of her shop's Christmas decorations, which were very cool. She then asked us for Christmas present ideas. Loretta reported taking off from work to prepare for Thanksgiving dinner at her place. She also said a shopping day with Sarah was scheduled for Black Friday. They were going to be looking for a winter coat for Lucy. I responded to Laurie by saying I could use more lavender oil for Christmas and that her shop looked great, then wished Loretta a good shopping day and told her that I wished I could join them. I closed my laptop and looked outside to see Betty dropping off Ted. I greeted them at the door.

"Ready to have some fun?" I asked in jest.

"I sure am!" Ted responded. "Grandma said snow is on the way, so we'd better get busy."

"Not much we can do about that, I'm afraid. Here are the lights, and if we need more, I'll make a run to Johann's."

"Have fun!" Betty said as she went on her way.

"The ladder is on the back porch, Ted. If you get cold, I always have hot chocolate ready."

He flashed me a big grin. "Nice of you to offer, but I've been drinking coffee since I was ten years old."

I chuckled. "Well, then, help yourself to some anytime!" I donned my coat and gloves, hoping to be of some help. I had to admit, Ted was quite fun to be around. His grandmother had taught him how to respect others, and I appreciated that about him. I never really asked why Ted practically lived with Betty.

We continued our mission, with a frigid wind blowing against the strings of lights. We added more lights than we'd originally planned. I wondered how Doc would react to the big transformation to his office. Finally, we decided that we had enough lights. As we stood back to admire our work, we had no feeling in our fingers. It was time to go inside.

"We should do your shop next!" Ted suggested. "We have plenty of lights. Here comes Barney. Maybe he'll want to help."

I shook my head in disbelief as I shivered.

"Looks like Christmas is coming early at Public and Chestnut this year!" Barney touted. "It's beautiful!"

"Thanks, but we're not quite done," I reported. "You want to help?"

"No, thanks! I've got a ton of Christmas catalogs to deliver," he said. "Good luck, and Merry Christmas!"

"You too, Barney!"

He handed me an assortment of mail and went on his way.

Chapter 34

I kept the shop closed until I got all the fillings made for the pies. The Christmas music I turned on put me in a festive mood. When Alex arrived, Ted and I helped him unload his vehicle.

"The pie guy has arrived!" Alex announced.

"Oh, thank you so very, very much," I said, greeting him with a big hug.

"It's snowing in the city and headed this way, I'm afraid."

"Humbug!" I responded. "We can still have pie!"

"Lots of pie!" Alex joked. "Thanks, Ted. I hope you have a big appetite."

Ted nodded, smiling. "I'll be leaving now, unless there's something else you need," he said.

Since Alex and I were fine with no additional assistance, Ted was free to go.

"The lights look great!" Alex commented, giving Doc's office a quick look.

"Thanks," I answered. "We just need to get a Christmas

tree." I poured some coffee. The kitchen was a sight to behold! "I've put my pies on the back porch where it's cool," I told Alex as he counted them.

"So, I guess we're having pie for supper?" Alex teased.

"I guess," I said, giggling.

"You didn't think I'd leave The Hill without some goodies, did you?"

"Oh, Alex! I love you!"

The rest of the evening was quite fun as we traded the coffee for some good wine. Around seven, I glanced out the window and could see that snow had begun to fall. I couldn't believe it. Alex and I looked at each other and shrugged our shoulders, knowing our part was done. The pies were made. The snow didn't seem to matter.

We both awoke early the next morning in hopes that the weather would have improved. Alex had a sore back from sleeping on the couch, so he went to take a hot shower. I made coffee and prepared the enticing bagels Alex had brought.

"It's beginning to look a lot like Christmas," Alex sang as he came down the stairs. "I think someone got the holidays mixed up."

I had to agree. "What do we do now?"

"Life goes on! The weather prediction is that the snow should stop around early afternoon. I'll clear the sidewalk and we'll have coffee ready if anyone shows up. If anyone bothers to come, we'll be ready for them."

I loved his positive attitude. My phone rang. It was Carrie Mae. I knew she would be thinking of me.

"Lordy, girl! You sure know how to time your parties!"

"I know! Alex is here and the pies and coffee are ready, so let the party begin!" I teased.

"Well, that's great, but you'll have to save me a piece. I don't think I'm going to get out in this weather."

"Consider it done. I need to cancel Judy and Ted's help today."

"Your invitation was very generous, and folks will recognize that, even if they don't show. You two have fun, and don't eat too much pie!"

As I was calling Judy to cancel, I heard a knock at the door. "Oh, my! What are you doing here, Ted?" I asked in surprise.

"I came to shovel, of course," he said. "You're going to need a path to the pies, aren't you?"

"Indeed we will," Alex called from the kitchen. "Thanks for rescuing me, Ted!"

"Great, Ted. Don't get too cold. You know there's coffee and pie inside."

With that, Ted got to work.

Alex watched as I began cutting slices of pie. Every now and then, he would sing along with the Christmas music. When the shop door opened around noon, I was surprised to see Randal and Marge.

"Happy Thanksgiving!" Randal said. "We don't have family coming until dinner, and we just couldn't wait to have pie!"

I welcomed them with a hug and smile. "You are the first!" I said, feeling grateful to see them. "Thanks for coming. This is my friend Alex, who also helped make the pies."

They were excited to see all the pies. Marge chose

a slice of chocolate and Randal chose apple. I took a photo of the momentous occasion, just in case no one else came.

Chapter 35

It was about five minutes later when Gracie and her mother showed up. To my delight, as the afternoon continued, a few more visitors trickled in to get pie. Some walked around with pie in hand to browse, while some found a seat and settled in to visit and eat. Some knew each other and some did not. None of them stayed very long, which was fine with me. All in all, I was pleased with how it was going so far.

"You had a sweet little idea here, Lily," Vic from Gallery Augusta said. "I love pie, so this is a real treat. If you don't mind, I'm going to take a piece back to Ruth Ann. She's keeping an eye on our turkey for this evening. She will love it."

"Please do. Enjoy your Thanksgiving dinner."

It was interesting to see Ted and Alex working together. Alex tended to the pies while Ted made sure everyone had a coffee refill. The day felt as if it flew by. Ted was the first to leave, so I sent pie home for his family. Alex suggested that I lock the door at three since the crowd had dwindled.

"Hallelujah!" Alex shouted. "You should be pleased,

considering the weather. The snow kept most people away, but at the same time, you got your point across."

"Yes, I'm pleased. I liked that I could visit with everyone, too. I'm not sure that would have been the case otherwise."

"You were nice to send a pie home with Ted. He certainly is a pleasant young man, and he seems to appreciate everything you do for him. I could tell."

"I hope he doesn't disappoint me like Tom and Kip did."

"The way he treats his grandmother is very telling. Hey, we haven't had lunch or our Thanksgiving dinner. I think I can fix that."

"Alex, you didn't!" I protested as I watched him arrange some food on the counter.

"How about munching on a nice turkey sandwich with my homemade cranberry relish?"

"Oh, my! I'm in!"

We selected a bottle of wine and went out to the porch. I cleared a spot for us to have our food, and suddenly Alex threw up his hands and said, "Oh, I don't know what I was thinking. Do you have pie for dessert? What is Thanksgiving without pie?"

We burst into laughter. Pie was the last thing we wanted right now! My phone interrupted our laughter. It was Marc.

"Happy Thanksgiving, sweetheart!" he exclaimed.

"You too, Marc."

"How was the pie party? Did the snow spoil it all?"

"No, not really, but the crowd was smaller, of course. I couldn't have done it without the help of Alex."

"Well, I guess it's nice to have a man around the house."

"He makes a perfectly good wife," I joked.

Marc chuckled at my remark, and Alex gave me a dirty

look.

Meg got on the phone, and we chatted a bit about the day's happenings. She was delighted to have Marc with her and insisted that I come with him next time. I said my goodbyes and told Marc that I appreciated him taking the time to call.

By now, Alex was cleaning up in the kitchen, so I decided to call Loretta and wish her family a happy Thanksgiving. Fortunately, they had just finished dessert. Sarah put Lucy on the phone to get her to say a few words, but I couldn't make out what she was saying. I wished I could just squeeze her. I didn't tell Sarah that Alex was here, because she would have wanted to talk to him.

"Happy Thanksgiving, sis," Laurie said, taking the phone from Sarah. "We wish you were here, but I heard you had pie duty to attend to."

"With the snow and all, it turned out pretty well. If you ever decide to have a pie party at your shop, I highly recommend it."

"In your dreams!" Laurie replied.

We laughed.

"They're about to watch the football game here, so I'll probably head on home."

"Well, I'll see you at Christmas. It will be here before you know it."

"Indeed! Bill and the rest say 'happy Thanksgiving' to you!"

Chapter 36

When I hung up, I felt guilty about not saying anything about Ellen joining us for Christmas. Alex came from the kitchen with more wine.

"It's chilly out here. Let's go to the upstairs porch and turn on a fire," he suggested.

It was a great idea. I should have thought of that right away. Up the steps we went.

"You know that we're probably making Marc insanely jealous right now, don't you?" Alex mentioned.

I laughed. "He's probably glad he didn't have to help with pie duty. However, he did help me wait on customers last year during my Christmas open house."

"You know, Lily, he may ask you to marry him. He might even ask this Christmas. What would you tell him?"

"Oh, that won't happen. We truly have an understanding about that."

"You didn't answer my question."

"I'd have to turn him down. I'm too old to be anything but myself at this stage in life."

"I understand. Women are so bold these days. I don't even have to go looking for a relationship."

"Well, speak for yourself, Mr. Bachelor. It's a bit different in a small town."

"That's what I read in one of your articles. Actually, it's a great place to hide out if you're not looking for a serious relationship."

I looked at him strangely. Changing the subject, I asked, "Do you want to watch a movie?"

He shook his head. "No, thanks. I can barely stay awake after being a slave all day," he joked. "I'm dying to take another nap on that comfy couch of yours. But seriously, I need to get out of here early in the morning. I'm going to take a hot shower and get some rest. It's been a long day."

The rest of the night was silent as we turned in. Tomorrow would be Black Friday, an event merchants looked forward to. I could only hope to have a good day.

We both must have been out like a light, because the next thing I knew, I heard Alex stirring the next morning. I put on my robe to go down and make coffee. I could see crumbs here and there that reminded me of the pie party.

"Good morning, Lily Girl!" Alex announced, coming down the stairs. "I'll take my coffee to go, thank you."

"No pie?"

He grinned. "I think you can schmooze your way into giving the rest of the pies away."

"Thanks so much," I said, giving him a hug. I almost hated to see him leave when he walked to his vehicle. He was the very best friend anyone could have.

I went up and got dressed to start my day. I was just putting the rocker out when Betty drove up.

"Thanks for the delicious pie you sent home with Ted. He had a fun time."

"You're welcome!"

Just then, another car pulled up that looked familiar, but I couldn't quite place it. A woman got out and entered the shop.

"I'm here to get that purple quilt we looked at the other day. It's for my daughter," the woman stated. "Do you remember me?"

"Oh, sure! Your daughter loved that quilt."

"Well, it will be a delightful surprise for her at Christmas."

"I'll get it wrapped for you." I was thrilled to see her drive away so pleased. The sale was a wonderful way to start the day. Snow was also being cleared from the streets, which made me happy.

Susan came through the door as I was picking up more crumbs from the floor. "I heard about your great pie party, Lily. I'm sorry we couldn't make it. I still have out-of-town company."

"Would they like some pie? You can pick your favorite from the kitchen counter."

"You're kidding. Thank you. I'll take this pumpkin pie. I didn't make one this year."

"Tomorrow, I will deliver them to some friends who couldn't make it."

"Remember, we have quilt class coming up."

"If I still have pie, I will bring some."

"Santa is coming this week. I can't wait. I can't believe he's for real."

Before she left, Susan added to my Black Friday sales when she purchased a lovely glass cake stand. By the end of the day, I was worn out. In bed later that night, I knew I had to start thinking about Christmas. I needed a tree. Last year, I went with a small tree, but this year I wanted a big one to fill my upstairs porch. I also wanted to have some things for sale in Doc's office for the times that Santa wouldn't be there. I thought of the old sled I had for sale and some of my more rustic merchandise, like an old bench I had on the back porch. It was painted dark green, which would be perfect for Christmas. I still had a box of old tins that I hadn't unpacked from Rosie's inventory. I would take all those things to Doc's office tomorrow. I dozed off with visions of Santa sitting in Doc's office eating the leftover pies!

Chapter 37

The next morning, I was awakened by a phone call from Holly. She said she was calling from the hospital. Her voice sounded sad and a bit distant.

"What's happening now?" I asked, concerned.

"He's getting worse. They're running more tests today. He's driving everyone here crazy, so all I do is apologize. He demands that I stay here."

"Just leave when he behaves like that. What can he do?"

"I wish he would just…" Holly's voice trailed off.

"Don't say it, Holly. You'll regret it one day."

"At least I didn't have to go to all the trouble of fixing a turkey this year just so he could throw it away! I ate a pretty good meal here at the hospital."

After I listened to my dear friend and tried to comfort her, I had to get dressed to start the day. When I came downstairs, I decided which pies I wanted to deliver to which places. I put them in boxes and took them to my car. My first stop was The Cranberry Cottage. Karen had already decorated for Christmas, and her shop was adorable.

I saw Buzz loading some barn signs in the back of the shop, so I approached him. "I brought you a cherry pie, Buzz," I announced as I held it up.

He grinned. "I love you, Lily Girl!" he said as he gave me a gentle squeeze. "Karen won't be opening today. She had to go into St. Louis for supplies."

"Well, give her my thanks for what the two of you have done for me this year."

"This pie may be gone before she knows about it," he joked.

I waved goodbye and continued on to the Ashley Rose restaurant, which I knew would be open for breakfast. I made eye contact with Sally.

"Well, Lily Girl, I heard about that pie party," she stated. "I'm sorry I couldn't get there. Did you bring a pie for Anthony?" She gave me a mischievous wink.

"Sally, quit teasing me," I warned with a smile. "This is for you and your family. I hope you like blackberry pie."

"Love it!" she responded. "You are so sweet to think of me. No one has ever made a pie just for me."

"You've always been so nice to me. Ever since I moved here, you have made me feel welcome."

"You and Anthony are my two favorite customers," she explained. "Do you have any message for him if he comes in today?"

"You just don't give up, do you?" I teased. "Just tell him I said hello."

"You are the perfect couple. I just don't understand," she said, shaking her head.

"Well, we're not, really. I'm in a relationship with someone else. Enjoy the pie, okay?"

"Oh, I will. Thanks so much, Lily!" she said, blowing a kiss as I made my way through the door.

When I arrived at Johann's store, he caught my eye right away. His eyes then went right to the pie.

"You had pie left?" he asked in disbelief.

"I did, and this one has your name on it," I teased. "You seem like the kind of man who likes a good apple pie. Am I right?"

"Yes, indeed!" Johann happily responded. "All I need is a little of my vanilla ice cream. Say, help yourself to one of those poinsettias over there. I want my good customers like you to have one."

"How nice!" I said, taken by surprise. "I don't have one. Thank you! I'd like to get another for my apartment upstairs."

"I can't compete with this pie, but I certainly will enjoy it!"

I paid for my poinsettia and went to see Esther and Chuck at their B&B. I saw through the window that they were serving breakfast to their guests, so I handed the pie to Chuck when he answered the door.

"Enjoy!" I greeted him cheerily.

"Thanks, Lily."

My last stop was Carrie Mae's. She was thrilled to see me. I let her choose between a chocolate cream pie and an apple pie. She chose apple and said she would give the other pie to Betty.

"Ted is coming today to help me with some Christmas decorations," she informed me. "I think I'll just get out my old silver revolving tree and let it go at that. Younger folks sure get a kick out of seeing one of those. Of course, he'll string lights across the front of the shop like I do every year."

"It sounds like a great idea. I plan to take a walk in the woods today to find a tree for Ted to chop down. I guess I should get permission from the owner."

We chuckled, since the wooded area was owned by Carrie Mae.

"Chop down all you want. Thanks for the pie, Lily. Your party was a big hit, it seems."

When I got back to the shop, I put the rocker out with a bright, scrappy Nine-Patch quilt. I unlocked Doc's office so I could start filling it with some merchandise. The smell from all the cedar inside was awesome. Santa would just love this little place.

Chapter 38

"Moving into Doc's office?" a voice asked from afar. It was Barney coming my way. He continued, "Are you sure Doc's going to let you?"

"I think he'll love it," I said. "I just had it all redone for Christmas."

"I always forget to tell you that my neighbor, Mrs. Meyer, knows a little something about Doc's office. She said everyone in town called it 'the Office!'"

"Oh? I would love to talk to her. I think someone else referred to the building as the Office."

"Well, she's in her nineties now, but she remembers coming here with her mother when she was a young girl."

"Would I have to go to her, or do you think she would come here?"

"Good question. She's not in the best of health, but maybe her daughter could bring her by sometime."

"Oh, that would be great. By the way, I have a pie with your name on it! Don't leave." When I returned with a lemon pie, his eyes lit up in delight.

"Now, how do you suppose I can travel with that pie, young lady?"

"I'll keep it here until you're done today."

"Thanks. I hear they've posted arrangements for Pauline's funeral at the Lutheran church. The service will be next week."

"Yes, I heard. I hope Snowshoes is doing okay."

"It will take him a while."

When I walked back inside with Barney's pie, I thought about how nice it would be to give one to Snowshoes. I sure hoped he'd be back one day.

Between a few customers, I wiped down things for Doc's office and carried them out one by one. I may have been mistaken, but I thought I felt a presence with me as I arranged things. It was getting colder and colder, and the Thanksgiving snow wasn't melting at all. I had to admit that it made for a beautiful sight, however.

In the early afternoon, I decided to close. I wanted to gather more cedar to use inside the shop before it got dark. I bundled up as the wind howled outdoors. I took my clippers to cut the limbs, but the blades were dull, so I decided to just break them off.

As I ventured on, all I could hear was the wind and the crunching of snow as I walked. As I gazed across the wide sinkhole on the property behind my house, I saw the most perfect Christmas tree. I assumed I was still looking at Carrie Mae's property, which encompassed several acres. It would be a long way for Ted to drag a tree home, so I decided to keep walking.

It didn't take long to fill my trash bag with greenery. I turned around to walk back to the house and started to shiver from the cold. I passed a smaller tree that I could settle for, but the shape wasn't quite right. I stopped and stared once more at the perfect tree across the sinkhole. It had my name on it. Ted would figure it all out when I showed him.

Chapter 39

The next morning, I had to get ready for quilt class. I was looking forward to seeing everyone. Thinking of my secret sister, I wrapped a small antique Santa in tissue paper in case I could sneak it into Susan's car or handbag. So far, my secret sister hadn't left me anything.

When I walked in the door, to my delight, Susan announced that there was hot cider and cookies for everyone. There was lively conversation, and some were even talking excitedly about my pie party.

When Susan went into the kitchen to get more cider, I quickly dropped the little Santa in her quilting bag. When she returned, she announced that she would be showing us some embellishing ideas today. She mentioned beading, ruching, and braiding. She also had a jar of buttons that she planned to use in her demonstrations. On the table was a small quilt with a heart shape consisting of just buttons. I thought of Sarah and how she'd love all of those delightful buttons.

I watched Susan demonstrate various techniques, but

none appealed to me until she got to the buttons. Susan mentioned, "Gracie just got in a rack of buttons, by the way. You can buy them by color, and she also has mixed bags."

"Great!" I said as I remembered keeping the pearl buttons I had purchased from a woman when Sarah was visiting.

Heidi said she made napkin rings for gifts and put buttons on them. Marilyn said she liked to use buttons for tying quilts instead of using yarns or ribbons. Watching the others trying to bead was making me nervous. For that reason, I left the class a bit earlier than everyone else.

On the way to Gracie's shop, I decided I could either give Sarah my buttoned Civil War quilt or make her something with buttons as a Christmas gift. I was pleased to see Gracie working by herself at the quilt shop. "I came to see the buttons you just bought," I announced. "Susan was telling us about them."

She seemed pleased. "Yes, they are here by the notions. By the way, someone left a gift for you this morning. By the looks of the wrapping, she knows you pretty well." Gracie handed me a gift wrapped in white tissue paper and tied with a red bow.

"Well, I was beginning to wonder if I had a secret sister! Should I open it?"

"Yes, please," Gracie exclaimed.

As I pulled off the tissue paper, I saw a red journal with blank pages. I loved things like that, so my secret sister did know me well.

"How nice!" Gracie responded. "When will you know who your secret sister is?"

"I think next year, but I'm not sure. How was your Black Friday?"

"It wasn't as good as I had expected, but my mom reminded me that this is not a gift shop, which would do better at this time of year."

"After Christmas, everyone will get back to their quilting projects. I'm buying buttons to make some gifts, so don't give up. Is everything else going okay with you?"

She knew what I was referring to and hesitated before speaking. "Not really," she said, looking down. "Actually, you'll be glad to know that I broke off the affair. The financial tie to this shop and our relationship was really bothering me. Now that the business is up and running, I managed to secure a loan, and I've paid him back. I hope Glenda continues to be blind to all of this, because she means the world to me. I never meant to hurt her. I feel more pressure than ever before that I need to make this business successful, but it was the right thing to do."

"Gracie, I am so proud of you. I was so worried that things would have a bad ending. Family needs to come first. Even if your sister finds out that you were seeing her husband, she will respect and love you more for ending it." I reached over to give her a hug.

As I left her shop, I was glad to know that the affair was over. I couldn't imagine doing something like that to one of my sisters. I was enormously relieved that Gracie had stepped up and done the right thing.

Back at home, I finished up the last of the leftovers from the food Alex had brought from The Hill. I sat on the back porch thinking about what I could give everyone for Christmas. Alex and Marc would be the hard ones. I couldn't use the Cardinals theme with Marc every year.

I went back to the idea of making something for Sarah

that would be small and would fit into her apartment. I'd use red, green, and white fabric, and instead of a heart, I'd make a Christmas wreath in the center. I could write a message like "Merry Christmas" in the center and put the date on it. Giving something personal like that to Ellen would also be a clever idea. If I could get my other siblings to participate, it would be even more special. As a quilter herself, Ellen would be thrilled. Then I thought of Laurie—who would likely oppose that idea.

Chapter 40

The next morning, I wanted to decide on a Christmas tree before Ted showed up. I dressed in very warm layers and winter boots since the ground was still covered in snow. As I thought about a bigger tree, I knew that my few ornaments would not suffice. Simple white lights would be fine with me. I cleared a spot on the sun porch upstairs where I thought a tree would be perfect. I wanted it in front of the window so I could see it from outdoors. My thoughts were interrupted by a phone call from Ted, who told me he would be very late because his grandmother needed him for something. I told him not to worry about coming since the weather was still bad.

"Don't worry," Ted assured me. "We'll get it done!"

I hung up feeling frustrated by the delay and decided to enjoy an English muffin and coffee instead. Then I decided to take another look to see if there was a tree closer to the house that would make the job a lot easier. I also needed more cedar branches for Doc's office.

It was still early when I ventured outdoors. I took a bag

to fill with cedar limbs. I saw the same small shapeless tree I had seen last week, but still could not imagine it in my house. I walked closer to the large sinkhole so I could get another look at the tree that I knew would be perfect. There it was, just waiting for me. I decided to get closer so I could better describe to Ted where the tree was located. With my eye on the beauty, the next step took me by surprise. My right foot sank into a muddy hole and turned my ankle, which caused me to lose my balance. In a flash, I was rolling down the steep embankment! As I fought against the muddy snow, weeds and broken stubble pierced my skin. I helplessly continued to tumble. I was nearly at the bottom of the sinkhole when a small tree put a quick end to my frenetic rolling. I silently prayed that I had not reinjured my ankle from the previous fall I'd taken at Klondike Park. The pain that I felt at the end of the fall told me otherwise.

I felt completely dazed. What had just happened? What should I do? I tasted mud in my mouth, but trying to wipe it away made my muddy condition even worse. I hurt all over. I suspected that my ankle would never be the same. How foolish of me. I felt the need to cry, in hopes that it would help. However, knowing that I had to get myself out of this predicament kept my tears at bay.

I looked up and felt snowflakes landing on my face. I pulled myself up by holding onto a tree branch. There was my perfect tree, sitting just above me. If I called, would anyone hear me? I gave out a big yell, only to hear a small echo. I tried to stand and immediately fell on my side. It was not possible to put any weight on my right foot. I tested my hands and arms, and they appeared to be fine aside from some achiness. Perhaps if I carefully scooted myself up the hill, someone might happen by and hear, or see me.

Taking a deep breath that I hoped would also fill me with determination, I gave it a try and felt the moisture of the mud and wet snow penetrate my jeans. It was so very cold, and I was very wet. I had to ignore the pain. It would only get worse if I couldn't get myself to the top of the sinkhole.

The falling snow was becoming heavier, which made me slip every now and then as I pulled myself along. I prayed for my own safety, and to not freeze and die out here. After a while, I had to rest. I reclined back and let the snow fall on my face. I tried to wipe myself off, only to cover myself in more dirt. "Be calm, be calm," I said aloud. "Please God, help me. Help me do this!"

The top of the hill looked so far away, but I made myself envision reaching the top. I thought of the saying, "Inch by inch, life's a cinch. Yard by yard, life's hard." As I sat up to continue my arduous task, I felt warm moisture on my face. I realized that it was from my own tears. I wondered aloud, "Why didn't I bring my cell phone?" At this hour, no one would even be calling me. I could be here forever!

Chapter 41

I gave standing up another try. The steepness and grade of the hill didn't give me the stability I needed. I could no longer ignore the seriousness of the temperature. My fingers were numb as my fists pushed against the ground. With each large expenditure of energy, I gave a grunt. I had at least ten more feet to go. Maybe it was time to start yelling again. Barney was my only hope. He'd probably be coming through later than usual since the weather was bad. As I gave a loud call for help, I realized how weak I sounded compared to how I meant to sound. "Please give it one more try. Just one more try," I told myself over and over, quietly and between gritted teeth. Ten feet became four or five. I continued my slow and painful journey. When I got a foot away from a tree root and saw that I could pull myself to the top of the hill, I gave it everything I had. I grunted and pushed with all my remaining energy. Once I was on flat ground, I stretched out on my back to rest my aching and cold body. I was exhausted. Now that I was near home, I knew someone would find me. I thanked God. After taking a few minutes to collect some more energy, I again called for help.

"Ms. Lily? Where are you?"

I couldn't believe I'd heard Ted's voice. "I'm here! I'm here!" I replied.

"What are you doing out here?"

Grateful that he had reached my side, I could feel warm tears making their way down my cheeks again. "Ted, help me," I begged in a shaky voice. "I fell in the sinkhole and had to crawl up the side to get out. I've hurt my ankle."

"It's okay," he said, taking hold of me. "Hold onto me. Can you put your weight on the other foot?"

I nodded. "Don't let go of me. My toes and fingers are numb. I'm so cold. Just get me inside. Thank you so much!"

"Don't thank me yet. You're a muddy mess. I can't imagine how you did this! You shouldn't have been out here."

"Just get me to the back porch so I can get rid of these muddy clothes."

"We're almost there. Take it easy. Hold on! I tried calling you back to tell you that Grandma had changed her plans, but you didn't answer. I'm glad I decided to just come on over."

"I'm so glad to see you," I said, my teeth chattering.

Ted finally drug me the last few feet to the back porch and opened the door, where I paused, gasping to catch my breath. Ted tried pulling off my boots, and when he pulled off the one covering my hurt ankle, I let out a scream. I think my response surprised both of us.

"Get me the blanket in the kitchen so I can get warm and pull off some of these clothes," I instructed. Poor Ted looked like a scared rabbit, but he responded hurriedly.

"I'll call Grandma. You'll need a doctor."

"No, no, please don't. Just let me gather my thoughts. I just want to get warm."

Ted looked doubtful but did as I told him. I pulled the warm blanket over me and tried to remove my soaked jeans that were covered in snow and mud. It took me forever, but I didn't want Ted's help. That accomplished, I told Ted I wanted to go upstairs and take a hot shower.

"You're nuts! You can't even walk!" he argued.

"Hey, I scooted on my behind all the way up the sinkhole, so I can get up those stairs the same way. Turn up the heat on the thermostat and let me get cleaned up a bit. Now that I'm home, I'll be fine."

Ted shook his head in disbelief.

The stairs were easy compared to the hill, but it was my determination that got me there. A hot shower was my goal. "I'll be fine, Ted," I stated when I got to the top. "Just wait downstairs. Thanks again. I'll call you after I get cleaned up. We can still get that tree today, you know."

Ted shook his head and left me as I had requested.

I ripped off my remaining clothes and propped my body against the shower wall. The hot water took a while to warm my skin. I could have stayed in there for days, but I was too weak to stand much longer. The chill had penetrated to my bones. When I finally thawed, my body ached. I stumbled out of the shower and put on my robe. I threw myself across the bed and tried to reflect on what had just happened. How would Ted get that tree without going in the sinkhole? I then realized that I needed to take a break and stop thinking about the tree!

"Ms. Lily, can I bring you some of this hot coffee?"

"Yes, please!" I answered, reminding myself what a great

kid he was. "Ted, thanks so much," I said, taking the mug of coffee from him after he'd carried it upstairs. "Do you remember where I was when you found me?"

He nodded. "Pretty hard to miss," he noted. "Why?"

"Well, if you stand in that spot and look across the sinkhole, you'll see the big cedar tree I want."

"Today? You want me to go back out in this weather to get that darned tree?"

"No, of course not. I just want you to see it. You just need to figure out how to get it without getting yourself into trouble like I did."

"Sure, I'll look. You just rest. Don't try to go downstairs."

"I won't," I promised. "Oh, and Ted, there's a trash bag of cedar branches that I left out in that spot. I need those branches for Doc's office. Can you bring them back with you? Just put the bag on the back porch."

"Okay, okay. I'll try."

It was entirely possible that he wanted to kill me right then. "Wonderful! Will you stick around here the rest of the day?"

"Sure, now get some rest," he said as he went down the stairs.

Chapter 42

Hours later, I woke up with a throbbing pain in my ankle. I looked at the clock and reviewed all that had taken place.

"Lily," a voice called from the steps.

"Betty? What are you doing here?" I said, sitting up as she entered the room.

"Ted called me as soon as you began to nap," she explained. "I've just been listening for you to stir. Are you feeling okay? Do you realize that you could have died from frostbite out there?"

"Yes, the thought certainly entered my mind," I confessed. "I'll take some aspirin. I just turned my ankle and have a few scratches. I'll be fine."

Betty shook her head in disbelief. "I brought some tomato soup and corn bread for you and Ted. You stay put. I'll bring some up to you."

"Oh, that sounds great."

"Can I get you anything else?"

"Tell Ted to come up, if you would."

Betty gave me a questioning look.

"Yes, Ms. Lily?" Ted said as he reached the top of the stairs.

"Did you go out and see the tree I was talking about?"

He nodded his head. "Yeah, you got my curiosity up, so I went out and found your bag of limbs and brought them in," he confessed. "It's a dandy tree, alright."

"Great! It's perfect, isn't it?"

"It's a beauty! I think I figured out a way to get it here once I cut it down."

"How?" I asked.

"You know that sled you put in Doc's office?"

I nodded.

"I'll tie it to that and go through the woods as best as I can. It will take me longer, but I think it's the best way to keep from falling in the sinkhole."

"Brilliant!" I praised. "I can't wait!"

"Maybe tomorrow or the next day, okay?"

"Sure. In the meantime, you and Betty go on home. I'll be fine. Get me one of those walking sticks from the umbrella stand downstairs in case I need it."

Ted did just that. He chose one with a rubber tip at the bottom so it wouldn't slip. Betty said to call if I needed anything and ordered me to stay upstairs at all costs. Her soup and cornbread had certainly nourished me for the day. I told Ted where to find the key to Doc's office in the morning. I trusted him completely and realized that he may have saved my life. He sure was mature for being just sixteen years old.

After I ate the last bite of bread, I began to think about who I would need to tell about my injury. Holly was under enough stress, and I didn't think that my siblings needed to know. I would be good as new very soon. My cell phone rang.

It was Alex. Now there was a guy who would see the humor in today's antics!

"It's snowing here!" he said immediately. "How about there?"

"Yes, I've been closed all day."

"What have you been doing with your precious day off?"

I chuckled and began to explain how I had ventured out early in the morning and got myself in trouble. Alex tried to interrupt with different sounds and laughter, but I kept my horrifying tale going. As I went on, he began to realize that I had experienced a very scary situation.

"Was it the same bad ankle?"

"Yes, and that is a bummer. It was most likely weak, and it completely gave out on the muddy, wet ground. I am so angry with myself. I don't need this kind of nuisance this time of year, or anytime, for that matter."

"Before I join your pity party, what were you trying to accomplish?"

"I was just trying to get a closer look at the cedar tree on the other side."

Alex was silent. "You know I have many lines of sarcasm that I'd love to respond with, but seriously, what can I do to help?"

"Nothing. Absolutely nothing, but thanks. I can tell it's swollen, but it's not as bad as the last time. Ted brought me a cane from my collection that's for sale in the shop." I heard muffled chuckles from my friend.

"Well, you're all set, then! Too bad I can't see you. Sounds like Ted is a good guy to keep around."

"Yes, indeed!" I said as I hung up.

Chapter 43

The next day, with much care and awkwardness, I got dressed and told myself that this was not the time to baby myself. Christmas was coming! I went slowly down the stairs, holding tightly to the banister. I made a cup of tea and looked around to see where I could place the cedar branches. Out of the corner of my eye, I saw Rosie's rocking chair starting to rock. I smiled, hoping she was telling me that she was here giving me support. Carrie Mae's name showed up on my phone when it rang. I knew she would fuss at me, so I was hesitant to pick up. Carrie Mae and Betty had no secrets.

"Don't say anything, Carrie Mae!" I jokingly warned.

She laughed. "You're lucky that you didn't break every bone in your body!"

"I know. Accidents are crazy, and I wasn't watching my feet. I had my eye on the tree across the way. Thank goodness Ted heard me hollering!"

"So, what can I do?"

"Not a thing. I'm dressed and even have a cane if I need it. Ted said he'd come soon to cut the tree and set it up for me."

"Well, we haven't had a detective dinner lately, so maybe Betty and I could come and help you decorate it."

"Oh, that would be such fun! It would get my mind off this aggravating pain! Now, if Ted doesn't get it set up, we have a problem," I cautioned.

"Ted never disappoints!"

When I hung up, I continued to wonder how Ted could possibly handle the job. With the current weather, I didn't have to worry about opening the shop. As I managed to stumble about, my phone rang, and I saw that it was Susan.

"Will you be at quilt class tomorrow?"

"Probably not. I sprained my ankle. Please don't ask me how."

She snickered. "Lily, I'm sorry to hear that. I called to see if your Santa house is ready. Our Santa arrives soon, and I was going to have him start at your place. It will make for a great photo op."

"Sure! All I have to do is decorate with more cedar and add the rug and chair."

"I'll make sure he'll also be at your place during one of the nights of the Christmas Walk."

"Thanks so much. He is the best-looking Santa I have ever seen, if he's like the pictures."

Getting excited, I hobbled to the back porch to get some cedar branches. The smell was divine, and I couldn't wait to place them throughout the tiny room. I then opened a box of antique ornaments and put them in a large antique glass bowl that was sitting on a buffet. I also had two packages of old tinsel from the 1950s. The packages had never been opened, and the packaging was so quaint. Rosie had put a reasonable price on them, but they'd never sold. I remembered reading somewhere that early tinsel was made from dangerous metals. Now they use silver plastic strands to accomplish the same look. As a child, I always carefully placed each strand of tinsel on the tree for the last finishing touch. The more I thought about the vintage tinsel, the more I thought that it may be just the touch needed for my big tree, since I didn't have enough ornaments. I put the tinsel boxes aside, wanting to wait and see what Carrie Mae and Betty would think of the idea.

Toward nightfall, I was ready to rest again. I poured a glass of Vintage Rose merlot, which made me think about Anthony. Sometimes, I felt bad for not letting him be my friend. He was such a sweet man. Was I fooling myself by thinking there wasn't anything more? Of course not. I had Marc.

Chapter 44

Ted was at my door first thing in the morning to get the key to Doc's office. His idea of using the sled could possibly work. It would make my Christmas to get that tree on the porch upstairs. I patiently waited inside, drinking coffee as I kept my leg elevated on a chair. It was slowly starting to feel better, but there was still some slight swelling. I used this time to check my emails. The Tannenbaum Holiday Shop in Door County had me on their email list, tempting me with many of their Christmas delights. I took the time to purchase Door County ornaments for my siblings, which would please them. I needed to get serious about other gifts, including one for my new sister, Ellen.

A new email popped up from Karen. She invited me to a cookie exchange at her house. I was told to bring two dozen cookies if I wanted to participate. After my pie baking, I had no desire to bake cookies. I thanked her for the invitation but told her I thought I had a conflict. After scouting the news on my laptop, I was interrupted by someone at the kitchen door. It was Ted. I looked out, and there was my tree, wrapped tightly with rope and tied to the sled. "Ted, you did it!" I cheered.

He grinned triumphantly. "Do you have a stand ready?"

I nodded.

"Okay, I'll have to drag it up the steps, so it will make a mess," he warned.

"I'll lead the way! Don't worry about the mess."

Ted brushed off some loose snow, and the adventure began. I tried to help, but Ted did the lion's share while I enjoyed the marvelous aroma of cedar. The tree did make a mess, but I didn't care. The minute Ted stood it up, I knew it would work. It didn't touch the ceiling, but it was close.

"Do you want me to cut some off the bottom?"

"No, it's perfect. I don't have a tree topper, so it will be fine. I guess you know your grandma and Carrie Mae are going to help me decorate it."

He chuckled and shook his head. "I'm glad you aren't counting on me for that!"

I laughed aloud, proud of what this young man had accomplished.

"Is it straight?" he asked hopefully.

"A little to the right," I teased. "Actually, it's perfect."

"Good. I'll be on my way, and I'll put the sled back in Doc's office."

"That's not necessary, Ted. I need to get the office ready for Santa. Leave the sled on the back porch." I handed Ted some cash and thanked him once again. I knew that every time I paid him, he was thinking of his truck account. After Ted left, I stood back to admire the beauty that had become a beast. Would only a handful of folks even see this tree besides me? I would be with my family at Lynn's house for

Christmas. I had awkwardly begun cleaning up the debris when my cell phone rang. It was Holly, so I knew I had to take the call.

"Lily, they told me he doesn't have much time left to live." Her voice was quiet and shaky.

"I'm so sorry. Is it cancer?"

"Yes, it's everywhere, and he doesn't want any kind of treatment. It's his life. He surely won't make it until Christmas."

"I don't know what to say, other than that God has a plan. Try not to be hard on yourself."

"He doesn't want me to leave the hospital. If he were nicer, I wouldn't mind. I keep apologizing to everyone for him."

"Just go home and rest anyway. What can he do about it? They will call you if they think you should be there."

She finally agreed with me. Holly loved Christmas, just like I did. Even before he got sick, it seemed that Maurice took pleasure in making every holiday miserable for poor Holly. I wondered if he had enough left in him to do the same this year.

Chapter 45

Betty and Carrie Mae arrived around seven. I put on tea and took a pie out of the freezer from my leftover pie inventory. They marveled at how Ted had managed to get such a large tree up the stairs.

"I have to admit, Lily, you found a perfectly shaped cedar tree, which is hard to do," Carrie Mae said.

"Well, let's get the lights on and let it shine!" Betty declared.

"You sit there, Lily," Carrie Mae instructed. "Betty and I can figure out how to string the lights at the top."

As they struggled along, I announced that I didn't have enough ornaments for a tree of that size. I got strange looks from them, but when I showed them the tinsel, they began to share their stories from the past. We carefully opened the two boxes and separated the strands. I wanted to be the one to step on the small ladder and decorate the higher branches. They carefully held the ladder and steadied one side of me in hopes that I wouldn't have another injury. The tinsel was fragile, but once it was on the tree branches, it became magical.

Betty said her mother was the only one to do the tinsel on their tree because she wanted it done perfectly. Carrie Mae said it was like the icing on the cake and that she hated when she saw trees where people just threw the tinsel everywhere. As we worked, we talked and talked. Little by little, the whole tree began to sparkle. When we pronounced the decorating project complete, we ate dessert, admiring the neatness of our workmanship. I kept my foot up on a chair as we gazed at the beautifully-lit tree and the fireplace.

"I can't thank you enough, ladies," I said, feeling enormously grateful for their friendship.

"This sure was more fun than talking about Doc and that spooky basement," Betty quipped.

"I can't wait to talk to Mrs. Meyer, Barney's neighbor, to see what she might tell us about Doc," I commented. "However, right now, I just want to think about Christmas and the Santa house."

"Good idea!" Carrie Mae agreed.

I thanked the ladies and saw them to the door. It was only ten, but we were all a bit tired from decorating that huge tree.

I changed into a robe and came back to the porch to admire my tree in solitude. I was truly content. I liked the Lily Rosenthal I had created out here in this little wine country. Being happy with the birth of Jesus and at peace with oneself makes for a Merry Christmas and a Happy New Year. Thinking about my aspirations for the New Year, I thought that I should write a column with a positive holiday message. I could entitle it "Make Yourself a Happy New Year." I hadn't written a word, but I already had the outline in my head.

Content on the couch, I readily fell fast asleep.

When I awoke at three, I was startled to find myself covered up with a quilt. I sat up quickly, gathering my thoughts. It was the Christmas quilt that Butler had given me last year for Christmas. I knew that the quilt had been in my closet. Had someone else been in the room? Who had covered me?

I got up slowly to make sure I wasn't dreaming. I walked around the upstairs, turned off the fire and the Christmas tree, and headed to my bed. Had Rosie done it? As I did so many times when the supernatural happened, I took my pillow and covered my head, knowing all would be well in the morning.

Chapter 46

The next day, I didn't waste any time displaying my Christmas quilt behind the counter so folks could enjoy its beauty, but couldn't touch it. Somebody, somewhere had wanted to remind me that it was time to use it. My shop was turning red, green, and merry, which pleased me very much. My cell phone rang. It was Marc.

"Did you get your Christmas tree?"

"Yes, I did! Ted managed to bring it on a sled, and then he hauled it up the stairs. It looks great! I can't wait for you to see it."

"I'm sure I will soon. I'm thinking about getting a small live tree for my place. There's a tree lot close by that's been tempting me. The reason I'm calling is that I hope you schedule a trip into St. Charles to experience Christmas Traditions."

"I really want to do that. I've been there to see all the live decorations, but not when the characters and carolers have been out and about."

"Well, let me know what's good for you. I know you

have a lot going on there as well."

"Yes, Santa is paying me a visit tomorrow. I need to get a small heater hooked up for him. From what I've seen, he is perfect in every way. What's unique about this Santa is that he brings a quilt that he calls his quilt of wishes."

"Well, that sounds like a Santa I should see. Perhaps this would be a good time to bring my friend Will out to see you about those quilts that he wants to sell. I think that you have spoken with him before."

"Great idea! I'm trying to plan a quilt for all my sisters to sign to welcome Ellen into the family."

"Did you tell Laurie that Ellen would be joining everyone?"

"No, I haven't."

"I need to go, but schedule me in on your calendar."

"It will be my pleasure," I said, hanging up with a smile.

Marc's call was what I needed to motivate myself regarding my Christmas plans. I pushed Santa's chair and rug toward the door in hopes of finding someone who would carry them to Doc's office. If it weren't for the fall I had taken, I would have been able to do all these things myself. It was time to open the shop, but putting Rosie's rocker out on the porch was also awkward and painful. I managed to carry the small rug out for Doc's floor. As soon as I opened the door to the office, the delightful aroma of cedar greeted me. The rug on the floor made an enormous difference as I spread it out. As I locked Doc's office, Kitty and Ray drove up and parked.

"Merry Christmas!" Kitty greeted me. "When does Santa arrive?"

"This afternoon, if I can get his chair out here."

"I noticed that you're limping," Ray said. "What's up with that?"

"The simple answer is that I fell down a sinkhole attempting to get a Christmas tree."

"I'll accept that answer," Ray chuckled. "Can we do something to help you?"

"As a matter of fact, you can. I need Santa's chair carried from the shop to Doc's office. Would you do that for me, Ray?"

"No problem," he answered politely.

Ray retrieved the chair, and I reopened the door to Doc's office. Kitty followed behind.

"This is too cute for words!" Kitty exclaimed. "The red velvet chair is perfect."

"Thanks so much. How are things with you guys?" I asked.

"Well, we came by to tell you that we want to close the B&B and just rent to someone," Kitty shared. "If your niece comes back for good, she may want to rent it."

"Sorry. She's decided to stay put in Green Bay. If you need someone to look after your guests while you're gone, perhaps I could help."

"Thanks, but we really want to travel and don't want the hassle of worrying about it," Kitty explained.

"Kitty, I think we may have to come back later and check out this Santa," Ray suggested. "By the way, we sure hated missing your pie party."

"It was great! I'd be happy to give you a pie I have in

the freezer, if you can wait a bit," I offered.

"Seriously?" Ray asked. "That is an offer I would never refuse."

Kitty laughed and shook her head.

Chapter 47

At nearly two, Susan drove up in her van. I caught a glimpse of a chubby, white-haired man beside her. I felt like a child getting to meet Santa Claus for the first time. As the heavyset man got out of the car, he patted his belly and gave a hearty chuckle before speaking. "You must be Lily!"

"I guess there's no doubt who you are!" I responded with a nervous giggle. "Nice to meet you."

"Santa would prefer that you call him Mr. Claus," Susan instructed. "He doesn't want personal information out about him, as I'm sure you understand."

"Of course!" I said. "Would you like to see your little house for this evening?"

"Remember that I said you would be in a former doctor's office from the 1800s?" Susan reminded him.

"Indeed, I do!" he replied.

"I think this little structure has my name on it!" he joked as he looked at Doc's office.

"I have a comfy chair and a little heater if you should need it," I explained as I opened the door.

"Lily, this is splendid indeed," Santa said. "I am used to much colder weather than what you have in these lovely hills."

As I got closer, I noticed a small sprig of holly and berries on his hat. His red velvet suit fit him perfectly with its rich trim of white fur. His shiny black boots indicated that the ensemble might be brand-new.

"I'm sorry for staring, Mr. Claus, but your rosy cheeks and nose are incredible, and your white beard is amazing!" I said, completely mesmerized by his appearance and demeanor.

He emitted a jolly chuckle.

"Okay, Mr. Claus, I will leave you now," Susan said. "Here are your sack of goodies and your quilt."

"Thank you, Susan," he said.

"I can't wait to see your quilt," I commented. "As you can see from my sign, I sell antique quilts. I love their history."

"Ah, yes! This quilt has brought many joyful wishes," he claimed with another chuckle.

"May I take a closer look at it?" I asked. I observed a simple quilt of six-inch Star blocks that were alternated with plain white six-inch blocks. It appeared to be lap-sized and was hand-quilted. "This is very nice. Who made this for you?"

"It's been at the North Pole as long as I can remember!"

"Lily, I must remind you that Santa stays in character the whole time you're with him," Susan laughed. "I love the green light that just came on. It's a nice touch."

I couldn't believe what I saw. A green light was shining in Doc's office for the first time! Doc was evidently in the Christmas mood.

"I'll stay for a bit to make sure the people line up on this side of the sidewalk to see him," Susan informed me. "I see cars coming this way, and I want to make sure he's ready. I'll let you know when I leave. You can go back to your shop. Thanks again for everything. I'll be back to get him."

I watched from a distance as Santa sat down in the big chair. He took the quilt and placed it on his lap. Was it for warmth, or did it have another purpose? The children immediately ran toward Santa as soon as they got out of their cars. This was a photo opportunity for all.

"We're all set, Lily," Susan said as she waved. "This isn't his first rodeo, so he'll be fine. There may be some parents who want to come in your shop to stay warm."

I did go inside, but it was hard not to observe the instant crowd that Santa was attracting. Parking along the street was going to be a problem. I saw Vic coming toward me.

"You've certainly created quite an attraction here, Lily!" he said with admiration. "I just had to get a look at this guy. He's coming to our place tomorrow."

"He's the real deal!" I exclaimed. "How did we get so lucky?"

"I see that he has a quilt," Vic noted. "What's the story there?"

"Good question," I said as Susan came rushing in the door.

"You just won't believe it! When he asks them their name, he points to their name on the quilt!"

"I didn't see any names on the quilt when I looked at it," I responded.

"Nor did I!" Susan agreed. "He then asks them for just one wish for Christmas. Of course, they have many things they want to ask for, but he says to just ask for one wish."

"Oh!" I responded. "That would be hard for anyone."

"He puts something in their hand when they leave," Susan went on. "It's not a candy cane, that's for sure. I hear someone crying, so I'd better get back out there."

"Thanks, Susan!" I called after her as she made a quick exit.

"Has anyone come in the shop?" Vic asked.

"Not a soul," I said, shaking my head.

"I was afraid of that," Vic responded. "I was going to put him in the back of our shop so people would have to come through."

"Vic, you will have a big traffic jam. You'd better put him on your front porch."

"You may be right. I'm going to go out and watch this ordeal."

Chapter 48

A few of the dads came into the shop to warm up while the mothers stayed with the children. One of them bought a couple of vintage cigar boxes I had for sale. Around eight thirty, Susan came in to tell me they would be closing for the night.

"I thought it was a wonderful first night, didn't you?" I asked.

"Yes. Everyone is very impressed. He must be a magician, because I still don't know how he does those names on the quilt."

"Did you see what he's putting into their hands when they leave?"

"Yes. It's a gold-wrapped chocolate star. No one knows quite what to make of it."

"I don't either! Well, we'll do it again next weekend. Thanks for helping, Susan."

When I ventured outside after everyone left, the green light had also gone out in Doc's office. It had been a long day and evening. I almost felt the need to say goodnight to

Doc. The green light had been a nice touch! Thank goodness he hadn't done anything to scare anyone. When I got into my pajamas, I decided to call Alex and tell him about this mysterious Santa. As I explained, I wasn't sure Alex was listening.

"A green light went on?" he finally asked.

"Yes, and it wasn't flashing like the other light. Everyone thinks I planned it that way."

"That's good! Hey, for all you know, Doc may be getting a kick out of this. Did you think that maybe this mysterious Santa may be Doc himself?"

"Now that's a little too crazy! When he comes back for the Christmas Walk next weekend, I'm going to watch him more carefully. Why don't you come out?"

"We'll see. That place of yours is getting spookier and spookier."

When I hung up, I realized that only Alex, Carrie Mae, and Betty would really understand the craziness that was going on here. Would Doc always continue to be a mystery?

I woke up to a marvelous Monday. The sun was shining, and since the shop was closed, I decided to go to quilt class. I was moving around better and better, but now and then my ankle hollered at me. I put aside Sarah's block so I could show the others at quilt class. To proceed with anything for Ellen, I felt I needed to first talk to Lynn about it. Lynn wasn't an early riser, but I decided to call her anyway.

"What is it, baby sister?" she asked in a groggy voice.

"Don't you work? Are you still in bed?"

"The gallery is closed on Mondays, so I decided to

sleep in until someone woke me up."

"I'm sorry, but I'm going to quilt class this morning, and I wanted to talk to you first. I've got an idea I want to pass by you."

"Let me get some coffee. Hold on."

"It's about what to get Ellen for Christmas."

"What about it?"

"I think we should give her something together, so she feels welcomed into the family. Lynn, are you listening?"

"Yes, yes. Go on."

"I'm making a little quilt for Sarah that has buttons on it. It's turning out pretty cute."

"I'm sure it is."

"So, what if each of us sisters signed a block that welcomed Ellen into the family? I don't mind completing the quilt."

"Including Laurie, right?"

"Of course! I'm sure she'll be more receptive by Christmastime. We can't do anything about the past, but it would be a nice gesture for the holidays."

"As a quilter herself, do you think Ellen would really appreciate it, or would she think it was goofy?"

"I think she will like anything from us, frankly."

"Well, then, go for it. Count me in. I'm sure Loretta will be fine with it as well."

"Great. I'm going to discuss this idea with my quilt teacher and see if she has any ideas."

"Good idea."

"Have you or Carl seen Marc lately? I haven't heard from him since Friday."

"No, sorry. Carl is out of town. I wish you could

come in to have lunch. I think The Hill is calling your name."

"Oh, I wish! You have to remember that I'm now a retailer, and Christmas is at our doorstep."

"I know, I know."

Chapter 49

I rushed to get ready for quilt class. I wanted to get there early to talk to Susan about my quilt for Ellen. The weather was nice, and nearly all the snow had melted. I decided to take one of the few pies left from the pie party out of the freezer to share with the class. I was pleased to see Susan's car there when I arrived early.

"Lily, you're early for a change, and even bringing dessert!" Susan observed with a big smile. "What's up?"

"It's a thank you from the pie party, and I have a favor to ask you."

"Sure. What's that?" she asked as she took the pie to the kitchen.

I started from the beginning, telling her that we had discovered a new sibling and that this was going to be her first Christmas with us.

"That's pretty cool!" she said, smiling. "How can I help?"

I explained to her that I wanted all my sisters to write something on fabric to wish her well and welcome her to the family, but didn't have any ideas as to how to make it into a quilt. I also shared that Ellen was a professional quilt artist, and that I didn't want it to look too juvenile.

Susan listened intently as she put the coffeepot on for all of us. "Can it be a wall instead of a bed quilt?"

"Absolutely. I don't really have time to do anything bigger."

"So, you want it to be really personal, right?"

"Yes, of course."

"Did you know that you can put photos on fabric?"

I nodded.

"I've done it for myself here at the library with our printer. I can see something where each of your sisters would have a block with their baby picture on it and then leave plenty of space where they can write a personal message. Do you have a photo of this new sister?"

"Not that I'm aware of, but I could probably get one. If I brought you the photos, could you put them on fabric for me?"

"Sure. Bring me white cotton. It will be best if the photos were all black-and-white or all color."

"I agree. I really like this idea, Susan."

Candace and Heidi arrived, so I didn't want to take up any more of Susan's time. As I filled my coffee cup, I began to think about who would have which photos. I really wanted to avoid asking Aunt Mary for one of Ellen's baby pictures.

Susan's focus today was on choosing quilting designs for our quilts. She had samples of markers and pens from Gracie's quilt shop and demonstrated how they worked. She cautioned us about the pencil markings that the church ladies like to use. Marilyn fussed at her mother, chiding her about her group still using pencils. When Susan started to talk about designs for longarm machine quilters, it went well over my head.

"This pie is delicious!" Edna raved.

"Thanks. My friend made all the fruit pies, so I can't take any credit," I explained. "He is a longtime friend I used to work with, and he loves to cook and bake."

"Now that's a good friend!"

"I've never told you, but Marilyn and I enjoy reading your column," Edna said.

"Thank you," I responded.

I left the class feeling excited about making Ellen a Christmas quilt of our good wishes.

Chapter 50

Knowing that Lynn was on board with my idea, I could move to the next step and make a call to Loretta. I waited until five, when I knew she'd be off her shift.

"Boy, this must be important to get a call from you instead of a text," Loretta responded.

"Well, this is an urgent conversation, because it involves something I need to do before Christmas."

"Okay, I'm listening."

I began by telling her what I was planning for Ellen for Christmas. She listened patiently until I got to the part about needing baby photos to enact my plan.

"You certainly have the creativity to do this, Lily, but what about Laurie?"

"We can't worry about her, as you said earlier. I may have a baby photo of Ellen, but if I don't, I can use one I know I have of her as a toddler."

"So, you'll proceed in the hopes that Laurie will sign it before we give it to Ellen?"

I paused. "That's my plan, unless you say I shouldn't."

"I would say asking her before Christmas Eve would be better than asking right before we give it to Ellen."

"I really can't, or we'll risk her not coming to Lynn's at all."

"You're right. I'll try to do more on this end."

"Thanks, sister. How are Sarah and Lucy?"

"All is well, but I don't always ask."

"Good. Love you all!"

Learning Loretta would help with Laurie was comforting. Now I could think seriously about how I envisioned the quilt.

At about seven that evening, I finally heard from Marc. "Good to hear from you!" I greeted him cheerfully.

"I'm certainly paying the price for being gone so long, but it was good to see Meg."

"Do things slow down for lawyers during the Christmas season?"

"Yes, they do, but we're not there yet. I also want to remind you about Christmas Traditions here in St. Charles. You said you wanted to come."

"I'd love to. I just have to pay attention to Santa's schedule so I can have his house open."

He chuckled. "Wednesday would be a good day to come. You could spend the night and still be home in time to open the shop."

"I like that idea."

"Wonderful! I've got to go. Love you!"

I was pleased that as busy as he was, he wanted to see me. I was also interested in the Christmas event in St. Charles.

The day was long, so I went to bed early. I prayed that Laurie would have a change of heart toward Ellen so we could all be united as a family at Christmas. Of course, I thanked God for Marc, who continued to keep me on his radar despite my living so far away.

The next morning, as I moved slowly, I could still feel some slight pain in my ankle, but it truly was improving. When Barney showed up with the mail, he reminded me that Pauline's funeral was that afternoon. It would mean closing the shop, but I wanted to be there for Snowshoes.

"Oh, Lily!" Barney said as an afterthought. "I think Bernice will stop by fairly soon with Mrs. Meyer, her mother."

"Oh, that would be great!"

"Bernice lives with her mother. She never married."

"What is Mrs. Meyer's first name, or does it matter?"

"I don't recall. She's always been Mrs. Meyer to me," Barney chuckled.

"I really appreciate your telling her about my interest in Doc's office. Any little thing she can remember would be helpful."

"I don't know how sharp she'll be at her age, but they say you remember things from the past more than you do things from yesterday!"

Chapter 51

Christ Lutheran Church was more sizable than some of the other churches in wine country. I passed this lovely church on the hill quite frequently and had always admired its beauty. As I parked, I noticed there was a fellowship hall on the property, but there were very few cars there today. I hoped I had the correct time.

I walked into the charming church and saw a few familiar faces. I saw Betty sitting alone, so I sat next to her. She said Carrie Mae was feeling under the weather. She also noted how few people came to funerals of the elderly. Many of their friends and family were no longer living. It was very sad.

The pastor was a nephew of Pauline. He received the casket as it was slowly brought down the aisle. Snowshoes followed behind it, as did a few other relatives. The large single cross on the stone wall behind the alter drew my attention as we listened to the short sermon. I had hoped there would be more personal information about Pauline instead of only scripture. I guessed that every church performed funeral services differently. Afterward, the family headed to the cemetery, which was on the church property on the hill. There was no mention of any kind of reception or dinner.

Once outside, I followed Betty to her car and told her about the possible visit from Mrs. Meyer. Betty seemed to recall who she was. I decided to head home, but feeling hungry, I stopped at Kate's Coffee to get a sandwich to go. As Randal prepared my order, he asked me about the funeral.

"I hope Snowshoes comes back to his job," I said.

"I have my doubts about that," Randal said as he took my money. "By the way, I heard your Santa house was an enormous success."

"It was!" I responded. "I think Doc would have been pleased."

When I got home, I took my food upstairs and turned on the gas fireplace. I then turned on the tree lights and thought about the funeral. Would Pauline have been pleased about her sendoff from this earth, or would she have been disappointed? I supposed she didn't care in the least, because she was now with her Lord and Savior. I smiled, then checked my laptop for any emails from my sisters. There was nothing. I then looked at my column's website, and one of the comments from a reader suggested that the magazine include photographs with my columns. She had a good point, and I supposed I should consider it if the magazine management approved. Just then, I received a text. I was surprised to see that it was from Ellen.

Hope you had a good Thanksgiving. I thought I would show you the latest quilt that I'm entering in a show. I look forward to seeing you at Christmas!

The photo was of a striking contemporary wall quilt in black, red, and white. Another of Ellen's photos showed the ornate quilting design she used. Susan would have loved to see these. I responded right away.

> That is stunning, Ellen. It looks like a winner! Thanksgiving was very good. I look forward to Christmas as well, sis.

I couldn't believe I signed off in that way, but it felt right at the time. It made me feel good that Ellen was comfortable sharing her quilt with me. That's what sisters do. Lynn frequently did the same when she completed a painting. I couldn't help but wonder if Ellen would ever be accepted enough to be included in our group email. I decided to be brave, so I forwarded Ellen's quilt photos to the rest of my siblings. I figured it would be a start. They all had an appreciation of the arts. I hoped for good responses.

Chapter 52

The next morning, I focused on rearranging my quilt room. I needed to refold some of the quilts and display them in different places. I enjoyed this exercise because it was like visiting friends that I loved, and something about their texture was comforting. It was sad how some quilts got more attention from customers than others. Some quilts really didn't shine until they were completely unfolded so one could see all of their beauty.

"Hello! Is anyone here?" a voice called from the front door.

"I'm here! Good morning!" I greeted the two women who came in the door.

"Are you Lily Rosenthal?" one asked.

"Yes, I'm Lily."

"I'm Bernice Meyer. This is Alberta, my mother."

"Yes, Barney told me about you and said that you may be stopping by. Why don't you have a chair, Alberta?"

Alberta nodded and seated herself in an antique chair by the counter. "Thank you," she responded. "What a lovely shop you have."

"I am so pleased to meet each of you," I began. "Barney said you remember coming to see the doctor with your mother when you were very young."

Alberta smiled and nodded.

"Now, Mother's memory isn't what it used to be, but she surprises me sometimes by recalling things from way back," Bernice explained.

"Alberta, did you see Doc's office when you drove up to see me?" I asked.

"It doesn't look quite the same," she replied. "It seemed bigger before."

"You have it decorated for Christmas, I see," Bernice added.

"It is," I agreed. "We are using it for Santa Claus while he's here in Augusta."

They smiled.

"I have it all cleaned out. Would you like to see inside?"

Alberta looked at Bernice for direction as to how to respond and then said, "I suppose."

"I'm really anxious to know more about the doctor," I said as we went outdoors. "Do you remember his name?"

Alberta was silent. "I'm not really sure," she said as we slowly walked toward his office. "I think it started with an S."

"Alberta, what do you remember most about coming here?" I said as I opened the office door.

She smiled. "I always got candy," she said simply.

"Candy?" I asked with a smile. "Why did you get candy?"

"It was so I would be good while my mama visited with the doctor."

"You waited in this room?"

She nodded as she looked up and down, seeming to take in every detail. "I remember getting scared sometimes when my mama took so long," she said more seriously.

"Do you remember what room she was in?" I asked.

"They went over to his house," she stated.

"My house?" I asked, and she nodded.

"Downstairs," she reported.

"Downstairs?" I repeated.

"In the basement," she explained. "She wouldn't let me go with her."

"What was the matter with your mother?" I asked with more interest. "Was she sick all the time?"

"I guess." She shook her head like she didn't remember. "She always brought him a cherry pie. That was his favorite."

"Yes, my grandma made the best cherry pies," Bernice added. "My guess is that she didn't have money to pay him, so she'd bring him a pie. They didn't have much money back then."

"When you waited, were there other folks who came to see the doctor?" I pressed.

"Sometimes. I was always glad when there would be other kids," she recalled.

"Alberta, did dads ever come to see the doctor, or was it just moms?"

She paused. "I think just moms."

"Was the doctor a sweet, gentle man?" I continued.

"He had candy, so that was pretty nice, I guess," she decided.

"What kind of candy?" I pushed. "Do you remember?"

"Peppermint, but I remember that around Christmas, he'd have little chocolates that were wrapped in gold," she said. "That was a real treat, and it's the only time I remember getting chocolate."

"Did your mama eventually get better?" I felt had to know.

"I guess," she answered, as if she couldn't remember.

"Mom has her good days and bad days with her memory," Bernice reminded me.

"I do remember that here is where I sat on a bench," Alberta volunteered.

"So, there was a bench along this wall?" I asked, hoping to jog her memory.

"Yes, and Doc had a desk right there," she described. "I know that next to that desk was his spittoon. I hated when he'd spit into it." She made a funny face. "Should we go, Bernice?" she asked, probably getting impatient from standing too long.

"Sure," Bernice said. "I hope this was helpful in some way, Lily."

"Yes," I responded. "I can't thank you enough for telling me what you did remember, Alberta. I hope it will be okay to call you if I have any further questions."

She nodded as she walked toward their car.

"As soon as we can find a name for him, I can research more on my own," I explained to Bernice. "I can't thank you enough for bringing her."

"No problem," she said politely. "I hope you have a Merry Christmas."

"You too!" I said as they got in their car.

Chapter 53

I watched them leave and then went back into the house. They were such nice folks, but I hadn't learned a lot of new information. I could just picture a little girl sitting on a bench waiting for her mom as she enjoyed the candy that was given to her. The Doc taking the mother out of his office explained what Betty, Carrie Mae, and I witnessed when we ventured into the basement. Betty and Carrie Mae would be amused by Alberta's story, and I was sure their imaginations would take it from there. I poured another cup of coffee and checked my group email, thinking that surely I would have some comments about Ellen's quilt by now.

Loretta was the first to respond with lovely compliments on the quilt. Lynn talked about Ellen's artistic ability. Laurie responded, but said Ellen was just trying to influence me with her interest in quilts to earn her acceptance into the family. Maybe she was right.

Gracie entered the shop, taking me by surprise. She had a package in her hand. I turned away from the computer.

"I have a special delivery for you, Ms. Lily," Gracie jokingly announced. "It's from your secret sister."

"Well, why should you be delivering it?"

She snickered. "I think your secret sister thinks you come into my shop frequently, and she decided to leave it there for you."

"I see. I'm sorry I don't get in there more, but I have a shop to run."

"Don't be silly. I understand. Open it! It's rather heavy."

"Oh, and it makes a little noise!" I unwrapped the heavy tissue and found a wonderful glass jar full of antique buttons.

"I think word got out about your needing buttons."

"I'm needing some for a quilt I have in mind for my new sister. Susan is helping me design one with my siblings' baby pictures in each block. I'd thought about using some buttons on it as well."

"New sister?"

"It's a long story. The buttons I bought from you are going on my niece's quilt for Christmas. She adores buttons. These buttons are really old. It must have been a collection from someone's family."

"It appears that way, but I don't know anything about them. By the way, I love how your Santa house turned out. Did Santa approve?"

I chuckled. "Yes, I think he was impressed. I'm sure it was better than the strip malls he was probably used to."

"Another reason I stopped by was to invite you to a girls' night out Christmas party at my place. I especially want to thank Susan and all the quilters for being such good customers this year. I'll add a few other friends to the guest list as well. I don't have much space, but I know everyone has expressed interest in seeing the part of the log cabin where I live."

"Oh, it really sounds like fun, Gracie."

"Glenda is a master at party food, so she volunteered to take care of most of it and help me with the drinks."

"Well, we could all bring something."

"No, I want this to be a thank you, just like you insisted with your pie party."

That made me smile. "I'll be there with bells on. The thought of it being just the girls sounds comfortable. I seem to be out of place among couples."

She winked, nodded, and then said goodbye before heading back to her shop.

So far it had been an interesting day, but with almost no customers. Everyone who came in was more interested in Doc's building than shopping. I finally closed the shop and felt a tad lonely as I went upstairs. I thought about Marc and wondered if I should call him. After thinking about it for a while, I made the call, but it went to voicemail.

I took a shower and put on a robe, then turned on the Christmas tree and fireplace to enjoy a glass of wine. It was only eight, so I decided to call Carrie Mae and tell her about my visit with Mrs. Meyer.

"She said the doctor's name started with an S?" Carrie Mae asked with interest.

"Yes, but I don't know how much to make of it. She's losing some of her memory. What little she revealed she did so on her own. I could just see her as a little girl sitting on the bench with her candy. At least we now know that Doc made a practice of going into the basement with his patients."

Carrie Mae giggled. "Wait until Betty hears that!" She said. "Well, it sounds like Alberta may be a valuable resource in the future."

"Perhaps, but she's not getting any younger," I lamented.

"Neither are we, my dear!"

Chapter 54

When I awoke the next morning, I realized that Marc had not returned my call. Was he avoiding me?

By the time I went downstairs to have coffee, I saw that the mail had already arrived. When I saw a padded envelope, I hoped it would be something from Loretta. It was indeed a baby picture of Ellen! She looked to be about six months of age and had a lot of hair. As much as I didn't want to admit it, I could see a resemblance to my dad. Perhaps that would convince Laurie.

It was a cold, windy day. When I opened the shop, I placed a scrappy red, green, and gold patchwork quilt on the back of Rosie's rocker, hoping it looked festive. It was noon before I got my first customer.

"Hi, Lily!" the gentleman greeted me. "I'm distributing maps for the Christmas Walk. Your little house out there sure looks festive."

"Thanks. It was a pretty big hit last week."

"I heard. Say, we could sure use your help on the committee next year."

"Thanks, but I'm still a newbie to all of this. I really appreciate all of the hard work you do to make these things happen."

"We enjoy it, and most of us have been participating for many years."

I was interrupted by a call, so the man left. I was pleased to see that it was Marc responding.

"Sorry. I just saw that you called," he said apologetically. "I had a dinner meeting last night. Hope all is okay with you."

"I'm fine. I was just missing you and decided to call."

"That's a good thing. I'm planning to get out to your walk. Will is showing some interest in coming with me."

"I'm sure Santa will be glad to see both of you."

"Well, I'm not sure I've been a very good boy," he joked.

"I guess Santa will have to be the judge of that."

"Can you come on Wednesday for our Christmas Traditions."

"I'm hoping to be there."

After talking to Marc, I felt relieved that nothing was wrong. I guessed I would never feel totally secure in our relationship.

Around noon, I decided to put a note on the door saying I would return soon. I knew Susan would be at the library, and I wanted to give her all the baby photos to transfer onto fabric for me.

Chapter 55

After Susan finished helping an elderly woman make a copy on the copy machine, she came over to see what I had. "Lily, this will be so sweet. You'll want to leave plenty of room for them to write their messages to her."

"I agree."

"Did you get an invitation to the girls' night out event at Gracie's?" Susan inquired.

"Yes. I'm excited. I keep telling myself I need to socialize more."

"It's nice that her sister is helping."

I watched Susan as she carefully began the process of putting the photos onto my white fabric. It took a while due to several interruptions, but it was worth the wait. As I left the library, I saw Vic putting out a sandwich board by his gallery, so I pulled up to say hello.

"Come on in, Lily," he suggested.

"No, I need to get back to the shop."

"Your sister Lynn sent another painting for consignment that you may want to see."

"Really? She didn't tell me. Sure, I'll take a quick look."

The gallery was empty as Vic pointed out a large watercolor of a vineyard that could have been anywhere in wine country. I stared, wondering how my sister created it.

"It's really wonderful! I wish I had some of her talent. I think her visits here to wine country have influenced her."

"Well, you're a talented writer, Lily. Artistic abilities show up in many ways. I wish I could afford to buy this painting of hers."

"Me too!"

We chuckled.

"I could give you a discount if you're serious about it," Vic offered with a wink.

"First of all, it's too big for any space that I have, but a miniature would be precious." Out of the corner of my eye, I saw some unusual wine racks. "Vic, tell me about these."

"This is the work of Pete Newsome. He's a wonderful woodcarver who works with natural pieces of wood to create something that is useful."

Pete had taken assorted wooden boards and stood them upright to create a way to store and showcase wine bottles. There were different heights of boards, all polished to perfection. Most of the racks had a contemporary look, which appealed to me. The longer I looked at the larger one, the more I could picture it in Marc's condo. The smaller one would be perfect for Alex. I realized I had two gifts decided on.

"These two will be perfect for two great men in my life," I announced to Vic.

"Great! I'll be happy to give you the merchant's discount. Let me wrap them up."

"Thanks," I said, checking my watch. Vic gave me a big hug as I left.

After I unloaded my precious gifts, I made a plate of cheese, crackers, and grapes to eat at my counter, hoping that some customers would come through the door. Eventually two young ladies came in, greeting me cheerfully.

"How can I help you today?"

"Well, we've never been out here before," one of them confessed. "We just had a wonderful time at the Blumenhof Winery. Delicious wine, by the way. We thought we'd check out a few shops before heading back to St. Charles."

"St. Charles?" I asked between their giggles. "Do you know a lawyer by the name of Marc Rennels?"

They looked at one another. "No, sorry," one finally said.

As they continued to browse, I knew from their behavior that they had consumed a lot of wine. Suddenly, I heard a loud crash. I turned around and saw them looking down at the floor, where a Royal Doulton china teapot was strewn in pieces.

"Oh, no!" one girl squealed. "I am so sorry. I just turned around and my purse knocked it off the shelf."

"It's okay. Large purses will do that if you're not careful," I consoled her.

"Well, pick it up, Angie," the other girl said, sounding aggravated.

"No, no, I'll take care of it," I insisted. "We don't need you getting cut."

"I'll be happy to pay for it," Angie offered, sounding remorseful.

"That's not necessary," I responded. "Accidents happen."

"Well, let's go before we get in more trouble," her friend

commanded.

"Be careful going home," I said as they left. I had to wonder who the designated driver was.

After they left, I happened to notice three twenty-dollar bills on the counter. The price tag on the teapot was $39.95. I couldn't believe Angie's generosity. It certainly was an encouragement to me. The teapot had been here without selling since I'd purchased Rosie's inventory. Perhaps Rosie had had something to do with this little encounter...

Chapter 56

I hadn't heard from Holly in days. I decided to call her before any more time passed.

"I was about to call you as well," Holly reported after I said hello.

"Well, I wondered if things are any better."

"Maurice's health continues to get worse, but he's really changed these last few days," she remarked. "He's become much nicer and has even apologized for the many years of difficulty I've endured."

"Wow! That is different. What changed?"

"He told me the hospital chaplain has been visiting him every day. Maurice seems to like him and said he's confessed to the chaplain how he's made so many people's lives miserable."

"If that's true, it's a miracle."

"I agree. He's been open to talking to me about his death, which he's come to terms with. He said God is a forgiving God, something he has never been able to accept before. He actually admitted that he has been very afraid of the hereafter until talking to this chaplain."

"Praise the Lord, Holly. Have you been able to get some rest now?"

"Yes, he even sent me home early last night."

"Good to hear."

"I never thought I would see the day that this would happen."

"God works in mysterious ways, and I personally believe in miracles."

"He had an old friend stop by who he hadn't seen in years. It made him feel so good that someone cared enough to come see him."

"I'm sure!"

"He's an accountant, so Maurice asked him if he would mind helping me with the finances after he's gone. Can you believe that?"

"He's been so secretive about all of that, so you're going to need it, my friend."

"The accountant seems like a really nice man. I'd never met him before. I couldn't believe some of the pleasant things he said about my husband. I certainly didn't know that person."

"I am so happy to hear all of this."

When we hung up, I wondered if I had been dreaming! Maurice's change had to be such a relief for Holly, especially since he could die any day. I supposed he'd come to his senses and wanted to settle up with his Maker. As I thought about this turn of events, I wondered if any of this would be useful in one of my columns. Since I had the time and the inspiration, I began to put my thoughts on paper.

Life is full of disappointments for everyone, but it has its surprises and miracles as well. In just one moment, life can change on a dime. Holly thought she knew her husband so well and had given up hope that things would ever change. I could very well experience the same thing. I may think I've got everything figured out, and then something comes along—like an additional member of the family! It could also apply to running a store. One good sale or catastrophe could make or break a business. Once I started writing, the words flowed naturally. The title became "Embrace Life's Changes."

Time had gotten away from me. When I looked out the window, snow flurries were gently falling. It was past closing time, so I brought in the rocker and quilt. I dusted off the light snow that had already accumulated on the folds of the quilt. I was sure this antique quilt had suffered more than a few winter snowflakes in its lifetime.

I went upstairs to turn on the fireplace and Christmas tree. The view out the back window was winter perfect. I sat on the couch and worked on my quilt. Just being able to gaze at the baby photos was a constant joy. I knew my siblings had experienced a happy childhood, but as I worked, I wondered about Ellen's.

Chapter 57

The next day, I was pleased to see that the snow had only amounted to a dusting, especially since I had agreed to drive into St. Charles. I was really looking forward to experiencing the Christmas Traditions I had heard so much about. I sent a text to Marc, telling him that I would be there around noon. He told me to be careful and said that there had been a dusting of snow there as well.

Missing the morning traffic was a blessing. I was so bundled up for the cold that I could hardly move. I packed an overnight bag in case Marc was open to me staying until the next morning.

When I arrived in St. Charles, I decided to take a drive down the entire Main Street before going to Marc's place. The street was lined with fresh greenery on the light poles, which were wrapped with red velvet bows. Coordinated live green wreaths were on each door, also sporting red bows. Each building was decorated with live green garland, some with twinkling white lights and some without. When I got to the corner of Main Street and 1st Capitol Drive, I saw a giant

Christmas tree with a red sled poised for a perfect photo opportunity. Children and their parents were already lined up to take advantage of the postcard-like scene. I couldn't help but notice all the shoppers carrying bags. Oh, would I love to have this kind of traffic in Augusta!

I turned around at the end of the street to drive along Riverside Drive, which lined the park and the Katy Trail. Many lit trees and the Katy Depot caught my attention as I slowly drove along. As I took in the sights, I kept considering why we could not do more in Augusta. Glancing at the time, I realized that Marc had to be questioning where I was by now, so I headed in his direction. I was ready for lunch and couldn't help but wonder where we would eat.

"It's about time you got here!" Marc greeted me with a nice kiss on the cheek. "Did you have any problems?"

"Not at all. I just took a little time to drive around here a bit. The street and park look amazing!"

"What did I tell you? I made reservations at a cute little restaurant called Magpie's Café. It's right on the street. Are you hungry?"

"It sounds great, and yes, I'm starved."

Small and charming it was. The stuccoed building looked quite old. The waiter took us to a table for two right by a window overlooking the street. I couldn't help but notice a sign by the counter that read, "The witch is in!"

"What does that mean, Marc?"

He chuckled. "This building has historic significance, but it became more famous in the 1970s when the building became the residence of two witches who had a school of Wicca. When publicity became too much, they moved away. They say there is evidence on the third floor that they would hold some sort of ritual, but who knows for sure?"

"Most of the buildings on this street are known for their history, aren't they? I see that many have plaques on them."

"Yes, but St. Charles is mostly known for being the starting point for the Lewis and Clark expedition."

"I did know that," I admitted.

"Keep in mind when you place your order that this café is known far and wide for its baked potato soup. Now, some would argue that it's more famous for its desserts, but you can decide."

"Well, I already looked at the desserts, and I could start with the Hershey chocolate pie."

He laughed. "I'll have the bread pudding, which is spectacular!"

While we enjoyed our soup, salad, and dessert, I filled Marc in on Holly's latest phone call. He said he had a friend who had also had such a change of heart. He then asked if I believed what she had reported.

I paused. "I hate to say it, but it's hard to believe. I'm hoping it's true."

Suddenly, we heard the music of the Fife and Drum Corps coming down the street. Everyone in the restaurant got out of their seats to go witness the wonderful experience. The Corps were playing the Christmas carol "Oh Come All Ye Faithful." Behind them paraded Santas from various countries, each carrying the flag of the country they represented. Other Christmas characters followed, like Scrooge, Tiny Tim, and the Sugar Plum Fairy. They were interacting with the crowd, and everyone loved it. Marc and I enjoyed every second and even sang along with the music.

"Here comes Santa!" a little girl next to me shouted.

She was correct, because in a beautiful white horse-driven carriage were Mr. and Mrs. Claus. They were waving to everyone as we heard Santa's loud "Ho, ho, ho!"

Santa was decent-looking, but compared to the one we had in Augusta, this one looked fake. I couldn't believe how so many of the spectators followed behind the carriage and continued to sing Christmas carols while going down the street. I could tell that many of these folks had made this event their own Christmas tradition.

Chapter 58

"Can you believe your office is on this street, so you can enjoy all of this every day?"

Marc laughed. "I'm a bit used to it, and for the most part, I enjoy it very much. Having my own parking garage is helpful, though, because parking in the area can be difficult."

After lunch, we walked slowly down the street. The snow had stopped, but what remained gave the greenery the touch it needed.

"I know you'll want to visit the quilt shop, but is there anywhere else you'd like to go?"

"Yes. I hear a lot about the spice shop. I would like to pick up something there for my secret sister."

Marc smiled and led the way. The Olde Town Spice Shoppe consisted of two small rooms filled with delightful aromas and spices. I could hardly move with all the customers shopping shoulder to shoulder, and I couldn't help but wonder how a shop like this would do in Augusta. I loved the gift baskets. I bought a small spice sampler for Susan and then picked out two baskets for Betty and Carrie Mae for Christmas. Most of the baskets held a wide array of soup mixes I knew they would enjoy. Marc was a trooper about carrying the large bags, so I scrapped the idea of stopping at the quilt shop.

As darkness set in, Marc suggested stopping at Lewis and Clark's Restaurant to have a cocktail. Marc knew Dan, the owner, so after a brief conversation with him, we shared a bottle of cabernet that Dan recommended.

"Do you like Mexican food?" Marc asked. "There's a wonderful restaurant down the street on our way back to my condo, if that sounds appealing."

"I'm in! That's something I rarely get to eat. I like how you think!"

Marc winked at me.

The charming place was full of Mexican décor. Marc suggested the chicken taco salad, and the recommendation did not disappoint. When we finally got back to Marc's condo, he turned on his fireplace to take the chill off the room. We sat on the floor by the large coffee table and enjoyed the fire. I turned down another drink, as I just wanted to settle in. Marc lit a candle nearby.

"Have you always been such a romantic?"

He paused. "I don't think of myself as being romantic."

"I know. That's what I love about you. It's your nature to be kind, thoughtful, and sweet."

"I love you, too, Lily Girl. Come closer and whisper some of those sweet things in my ear."

I smiled and got closer.

My dreams that night were mixed with the sounds of the Fife and Drum Corps playing as I ate pie after pie from my pie party. I woke up feeling queasy. I could smell coffee coming from the kitchen, so I knew Marc was making breakfast. I quickly got dressed, not knowing what time it was. I did know that I needed to get home.

"Good morning, sleepyhead!" Marc greeted as he offered me a kiss on the cheek. "How about some coffee?"

"Yes, please!" I agreed, not really wanting much conversation. "I guess I need to get on my way soon. I'll pass on that omelet you're making."

"You don't know what you're missing!"

"I eat too much food when I'm with you," I joked.

"I know you're thinking of getting back to that shop of yours, so I won't try to talk you into staying."

"It was such a perfect visit, Marc. I loved everything about it."

"So, what are you wishing for for Christmas? I'm at a loss as to what to get you."

"Not a thing! You're entirely too generous as it is."

"How is the quilt that you're making for Ellen coming along?"

"Slowly, because I'm doing it all by hand, which I enjoy. I'm still concerned about Laurie's reaction to it. I hope my concern is resolved before Christmas."

"Giving her a surprise like that after she's already at Lynn's may not be the right thing to do either, but you know your sisters better than I do. I'm looking forward to meeting this Ellen."

"You'll like her."

"Here's a cup of coffee to take with you. Be safe, and text me when you get home."

"I will. Thank you for everything, sweetheart," I said, giving him a hug and kiss.

Chapter 59

I was in seventh heaven while driving home. There were visions of sugar plums dancing in my head. I couldn't imagine the team it must take to pull off the St. Charles Christmas Traditions event. When I got home, I put away my purchases and noticed that I had a reminder text from Gracie. Tonight was the girls' night out gathering at her place. I put a bottle of Vintage Rose merlot aside to take as a hostess gift. I wished I had thought of getting Gracie something at the spice shop.

As the rest of my day went along, my sales were mostly intended to be Christmas gifts. No one was looking at quilts, but the sales of a spool cabinet and an old trunk made my day. I was also pleased to sell a cameo pin I still had from Rosie's inventory.

I closed at four to get ready for the party. It was cold, so I chose to wear my red cable turtleneck sweater with black pants and black boots. When I arrived, I parked across the street. Marilyn was also getting out of her car. "Marilyn, wait up!" I called. "Where's your mom? I don't think I've ever seen you without her."

"I do have a life away from quilting," she joked. "She was invited, but she felt this was for younger women."

"Well, Edna doesn't seem old to me. I'm sure there will be others here her age."

"Welcome!" Gracie greeted us as we walked into a room full of laughter. "If you don't know someone, please introduce yourself. You can hang your coats over here, if you like."

"Thanks!" I responded, doing just that. "I brought you some good wine."

She smiled, accepting the gift from me.

"And I brought you some of Mom's homemade fudge," Marilyn added.

"Yum!" Gracie responded. "Please thank her for me."

As I walked into her small living room area, it was as charming as I had imagined. I recognized many familiar faces. Glenda, Gracie's sister, was pouring wine for nearly everyone, but there was also a bowl of punch. My eyes immediately took in the Christmas décor in Gracie's primitive log cabin. She had a small loft with stairs that likely led to her bedroom. In the corner of the room was her lit Christmas tree, which was hung upside-down from the ceiling. It was very attractive in the small space. The ornaments hung downward.

"How clever it is to hang a Christmas tree like that," I said to Heidi, who was also checking it out.

"It's actually a German tradition, and a great idea if you have pets around," Heidi explained.

I walked over to the food table, where there were tiers of appetizers and delicacies. Live greenery and berries were displayed between platters.

"Hi, Lily!" Esther said as she helped herself to the refreshments. "Try some of my family's ravioli. I make it every Christmas."

"You made this?" I asked, taking her up on her suggestion. "Oh, how I've missed good Italian food since I left The Hill."

"Well, it's the next best thing to the kind you get at Charlie Gitto's, if you're familiar with that restaurant," Esther bragged.

"Yes, it's the best!" I exclaimed. "I haven't been there since my sister had her birthday dinner."

I continued to fill my plate with ravioli, canapés, fresh shrimp, and strawberries. I wanted to try everything before I left.

"Well, look who's here!" a familiar voice said next to me.

"Lisa! How are you?" I asked, surprised. "Merry Christmas!"

"I'm great, and am now a single woman," Lisa informed me.

"Are you still living in Marthasville?" I asked, remembering her fabulous estate.

"No, I bought a new house in Augusta Shores from a couple who had just built it and then had to move because of a job transfer," she explained. "It's way more room than I need, but it's quite fun to decorate it to my own taste."

"I'm so happy for you!" I smiled. "Did you keep all of your quilts?"

She nodded. "Yes, they have their own room as they did before," she assured me. "I'm sure I could still part with some of them if you ever want to buy more for your shop."

"Thanks!" I responded eagerly. "I may just take you up on that."

"Well, I have another party to attend, so I'll be leaving," she said, excusing herself. "It was so good to see you."

"Merry Christmas!" I said as I watched her get her coat.

"So, you know Lisa?" Judy asked as she joined me.

"I've purchased some quilts from her that she was anxious to get rid of," I explained.

"That reminds me, Lily. I have another one that I would like to put on consignment," Judy stated. "I came with Marge, by the way. Have you seen her?"

"No, but I need to say hello to her. There's Chris from Wine Country Gardens! Do you know her?"

"I know who she is, but I haven't met her," Judy replied. "I love that place!"

Chapter 60

"May I have your attention, please?" Gracie said as she tapped her glass. "I hate to interrupt your happy chatter, but I first want to thank you for coming out this evening. My initial reason for having this gathering was to thank Susan and her quilt class for supporting my shop, just as many of you have. It is nice to welcome you into my new home. I also want to thank Glenda, who knows how to entertain when it comes to food. Esther, thanks for letting us experience your wonderful ravioli. It was delicious!"

A round of applause came from around the room.

"Now, I want to call on my friend Chris from Wine Country Gardens, who also brought us something special for the holidays. Chris, take it from here!"

Chris smiled and said how pleased she was to be at this fun party. "I asked Gracie if she had ever heard of Eiswein, and she said she hadn't," Chris began. "I told her I'd be happy to bring some this evening so you could have the opportunity to taste it. Years ago, German winemakers discovered how to make this wine because many of their grapes would freeze in the vineyards during the winter. Winemakers in Germany, Austria, and Canada were the first to produce it. The state of Michigan soon followed, and then the Finger Lake region of New York. It is very difficult to produce because it's aged in very rare oak with tropical fruit. It is a rather sweet wine that is often used as a dessert wine. Tonight, I brought some Riesling Eiswein that I would like you to try. We'll serve it to you in small glasses, much as you would an after-dinner drink. You'll want to drink it slightly chilled to get the full effect. Glenda will come around with samples for you to try."

"Thanks, Chris," Gracie said. "I'm anxious to try it."

"Well, I'll bet someone, somewhere is making ice wine tonight, it's so chilly," Karen joked as she joined me. "Are you going to try it?"

"I think I'll pass," I said. "I really like this red wine I'm drinking."

"Is it the Vintage Rose I saw you bring?" Karen asked with a smile. "You know that's Anthony's favorite."

"How is the barn quilt business these days?" I asked, hoping to change the subject.

"Winter is production time and not particularly good for sales," she explained. "Our best sale time is summer and fall. Are you ready for the Christmas Walk?"

"I am," I responded. "Santa will return."

"Hi, Lily!" Ruth Ann said as she joined us.

"Ruth Ann came with me tonight," Karen shared. "The gallery had a great response as well from our fine Santa Claus."

"Oh, Ruth Ann, did you put him outside like I suggested to Vic?" I asked.

"We were going to, but it was terribly cold with snow flurries predicted. But Susan kept the line moving pretty well, so it wasn't too bad."

"Did he have his quilt?"

"Yes!" she said, nodding. "It's quite something how he shows the children their names."

"I've decided that he has got to be using tricks like a magician," I said. "I'm going to pay more attention this weekend."

"Hi," Susan said as she joined us. "Isn't this a lovely party?"

We responded affirmatively.

"How is your photo quilt coming along, Lily?" Susan inquired.

"It's coming along very slowly," I reported.

"Bring it to class next time, okay?" she requested.

"I will, if you promise not to look very closely at the hand quilting," I warned. Before I left, I wanted to sample a couple of desserts as I said hello to Candace and Marge. There were just a few women that I didn't get to meet. I glanced toward the door and saw that Sally from Ashley Rose was about to leave, so I decided to leave as well.

"Good to see you, Lily!" Sally said, putting on her coat.

"You too. I'm so glad I came. I didn't see you here earlier."

"I was pleased to be included," Sally commented. "Will I see you in the restaurant for dinner soon?"

I smiled, thinking of Anthony. "We'll have to see," I answered. "It's a busy season."

"Merry Christmas!" Sally said as she exited.

I echoed her wishes as I walked over to Gracie to thank her for a wonderful party.

"You're welcome," she said, giving me a hug. "We'll have to party like this more often!"

When I arrived home, I had a smile on my face. Gracie's Quilt Shop had brought a variety of women together. It was nice to celebrate with Gracie and see so many women in one place.

Chapter 61

The day of the Christmas Walk seemed to attract a crowd earlier and earlier, despite it not officially starting until six. Roads were blocked off so there would be room for parking. The luminary committee was already working on placing bags of candles all over town on each road. Vendors of beer, wine, and food were also seeking out their assigned locations. The railroad depot vendors had already set up the night before. Demonstrations were popular, especially the glassblower located on the main road. If anyone planned to eat in a restaurant during this event, a reservation was a must.

This year I hoped to get a limited-edition ornament with one of the historic buildings painted on it. A new one was for sale each year, and they made wonderful gifts. Perhaps I could also still purchase some from previous years. My wonderful Santa would be arriving at four, but I wouldn't be surprised if children lined up to see him much earlier.

Last year, Susan had been nice enough to drop by to mind the shop while I got some food at the Ebenezer Church hall. This year, however, Susan was preoccupied with Santa. Ebenezer Church had ongoing Christmas caroling led by members of their choir. Many people used my shop as a place to get warm after becoming chilled at the outside activities. I was very pleased that the carriage rides went by my shop so that people could get off if they wanted to. If they'd parked far away, the carriage rides certainly came in handy.

Judy entered the shop. "Well, it appears that you're ready for tonight."

"I think so. All we need is Santa."

"I get off at the coffee shop at five if you want me to help you for a while."

"Really? If you could, that would be great. I don't know what to expect this year."

"Unless Randal makes me stay longer, I'll be by."

"Thanks so much!"

A large family came in as Judy left.

"Why isn't Santa in his house?" one of the little boys asked.

"He'll be here later," I said as cheerfully as I could. That news didn't go over well. The children showed their disappointment by running around the store. The youngest, being held by her father, started to cry for Santa. The mother tried to comfort the child while also shopping around in the front room.

"Kevin, put that back," the father yelled at one of the boys, who had pulled an antique Belsnickel figurine off the counter. Startled by his father's reprimand, the child immediately dropped the figurine, and it landed on the floor. Thankfully, it did not break.

"Kevin, pick that up and apologize," the father instructed

sternly.

"It's okay," I said, collecting the Santa. "It's not broken."

"Let's go, honey," the wife insisted. "We'll come back when Santa's here."

As they gathered up the unhappy crew, I drew in a breath of relief. My cell phone rang, so I went to answer it. It was Marc.

"Ready for Santa?" he teased.

"I am! Are you calling to tell me you'll be out to see him?" I asked.

"I am! Will is coming with me, and if you're not too busy, he'd like for you to look at those quilts that he wants to sell."

"Sure! My friend Judy said she'd stop by around five to see if I needed any help."

"If you're busy, Will said he'd leave the quilts with you, and you can contact him later."

"What time are you coming?"

"Around six if traffic is light."

"Sounds good. See you then."

Chapter 62

Knowing Marc and Will were coming to visit made the night much more exciting than Santa's visit did. I quickly went upstairs between customers to change and freshen up my makeup. As I came down the stairs, a woman arrived who was looking for vintage lanterns. Fortunately, I did have a red one, which I was using as a display with Christmas greenery. She loved it.

"Oh, I hate to ruin your display," she said apologetically.

"Not to worry. It's for sale, and I'm pleased that the display helped."

"Great, I'll take it."

The crowds trickled along until it got closer to four, when Santa would be coming. Those who did come into the shop to browse were killing time waiting for his arrival. At last, Susan drove up with St. Nick, so I went out to unlock Doc's office. "Welcome back!" I said to them. "I'll turn the heater on for a bit to take the chill off."

Santa gave one of his hearty laughs and a nod, not uttering a word. I noticed he had the patchwork quilt and a green bag of goodies for the children.

"Will you stick around to help him, Susan?"

"Oh, yes. He'll be very busy tonight," she assured me.

"Let me know if you need anything," I said as I was leaving. "There's hot cider or hot chocolate if you'd like some."

"Thanks, Lily," Susan replied. "I'll get this line organized."

People started to crowd around the building. Just like clockwork, the green light went on in the office. Doc was on it, and it made me smile. To my surprise, when I came back into the shop, a woman was standing by the checkout counter, waiting to purchase an antique baby quilt.

"Oh, I've always loved this little quilt," I said. "These sweet little prints of bubblegum pink and madder brown tell me that it's quite old."

"I love the size of the Nine-Patch," the woman said. "Do you know exactly how old it might be?"

"The colors and prints have a range that I would estimate to be from 1860 to 1870."

"Oh! Maybe it shouldn't be used. What do you think?"

"Even though it's in good condition, I'm sure it was made to be used," I explained. "You should enjoy it, but be cautious of its age."

The customer left feeling excited about her purchase. It was close to six when Marc and Will arrived.

"Lily, you won't believe how far away we had to park!" Marc said with disbelief. "The crowd is amazing. Will, I believe you and Lily have met."

"I'm so glad to see you again," Will said, giving me a hug. "It's good to be back in wine country. You really know how to draw a crowd!"

I smiled. "Having Santa Claus on your property kind of

helps," I joked.

"I guess Marc told you I'd be bringing some quilts for you to look at. I can see you have plenty of other things to do, so just look at them another time."

"Okay, I will," I agreed. "I can't wait to see what you have."

Just then, Judy entered the shop. "I'm sorry, Lily, I tried to get here sooner."

"Well, I'm just glad you're here. Judy, this is Marc. I've mentioned him before. This is his friend Will."

"Nice to meet you, Marc," Judy said as she took off her coat. "Will, it's nice to meet you as well. Lily, is there anything I can do for you?"

"Yes, please check on the customers in the other rooms," I instructed.

As she proceeded to do so, Marc whispered in my ear, "You look marvelous, Lily."

I blushed.

"No secrets," Will commented with a grin.

"We'll let you get to your business while we get something to eat, and then we'll check out the Santa you have out there." Marc informed me. "Should I put in a good word for you?"

"Yes, please do!" I laughed. "Enjoy the food, sights, and sounds!"

"We will," Marc said as he waved. He and Will then turned and pushed through the crowd.

Chapter 63

When I saw a break in the crowd, I told Judy I wanted to go outside to observe Santa and take him a cup of hot cider. The air was brisk, but everyone was in a festive mood with a beverage of some kind in their hands. I managed to squeeze into the little office and handed Santa a cup of cider. When I placed it on the table, he just gave me a "ho, ho, ho" and nodded in approval.

A small boy had just gotten up on Santa's knee when Santa asked him what his name was. The boy looked rather frightened and softly said his name was David.

"Well, David, I see your name right here in this quilt. Is that how you spell David?" he asked.

The boy gave a feeble smile.

"So, what does David wish for this Christmas?" Santa asked.

He hesitated. "I want a Mr. Spike," he blurted out.

"Why, sure!" Santa chuckled. "Santa knows all about Mr. Spike. Have you been a good boy?"

David nodded as he looked into Santa's eyes.

"That's good, so ho, ho, ho, off you go!" he said, pushing the boy off to his dad.

Susan quickly placed a little girl in place of David. The mother excitedly pushed me away to be closer for a photograph, so I got out of the office. I was freezing and was anxious to get back into the shop.

"Did you get to make your wish?" Susan teased.

"Afraid not, Susan," I said, shivering. "How does he magically have their names?"

She laughed. "Don't you know that there are a lot of things you are not supposed to know at Christmas?" she joked. "You do believe in Santa, don't you?"

"Okay, whatever Santa has is working, so I'm going in," I surrendered. "Do you want something hot to drink?"

"Sure! By the way, I met that Marc of yours, and he sure is handsome."

When I got back inside, I saw out the window how Susan continued to keep the line moving. I asked Judy to pour her a mug of cider.

"I'll take it to her," she offered. "Did you notice that when the kids start to cry, they stop when they get on his knee? I've never seen that before. Susan makes sure their photos are snapped quickly. This would not run smoothly without her assistance."

"I realize that. Before you go, do you know what a Mr. Spike is?"

Judy giggled. "No, I can't keep up with all the silly stuff kids want these days," she admitted.

It was nine before Marc and Will came back from their adventure around town. "Did you miss us?" Marc asked, giving me a wink. "We first headed to the Silly Goose for something to eat, and then we picked up a beer as we walked around town."

"How did you get in the Silly Goose without a reservation?"

"Who's going to turn away two good-looking guys who appear to be good tippers on a night like this?" Will joked.

I laughed. "You were lucky!"

"I bought you something," Marc said as he handed me a paper bag.

I immediately opened it up. To my surprise, it was one of the collectable ornaments I had been wanting. I was even more pleased to see that it had Carrie Mae's Uptown Store painted on it.

"Thanks, sweetie," I said, kissing him on the cheek. "I've been wanting one of these."

"Okay, you lovebirds, we need to get on our way," Will urged.

"Agreed, my friend," Marc concurred.

"Let me know what you think about the quilts," Will said.

"I will. Thanks for bringing them out," I said with a smile.

"It was nice to see you," Will said as he watched Marc give me a goodbye kiss.

Judy decided to go home as soon as Susan and Santa left.

"Here's a little Christmas bonus for you," I said, handing her some cash. "I really appreciate your help."

"I would have done this for nothing, but thank you! Will I see you at quilt class on Monday?"

"Probably, if I can use the time to sit there and work on my photo quilt. Every bit of time counts these days."

"Good idea. I may bring the sampler I'm stitching."

I was happy to end the day and bring in the rocker. The air seemed to be even colder, so I couldn't wait to crawl into bed. Right now, it felt as if Christmas would never arrive!

Chapter 64

After checking my emails, I got ready for quilt class. I put my photo quilt in a tote bag with my thread and needles in hopes that I would get something done in Susan's class. When I arrived at the library, Susan and a few of the ladies were in one of the side rooms, admiring some sweaters that were arranged on a large table.

"Lily, I want you to meet Amy Britan," Susan said. "She is exploring Augusta and is considering opening a knitting shop. Wouldn't that be grand?"

"Yes!" I responded, putting out my hand. "It's nice to meet you. Did you knit these wonderful sweaters?"

She nodded and smiled. "Yes, thank you. They are for sale, so take a look."

After everyone had arrived, Susan said, "Ladies, please get your coffee and be seated."

I sat down next to Judy and Marilyn with my cup of coffee. I was pleased to see that a few others had brought things they were working on.

"It's almost Christmas, so I know some of you wanted

to work on your projects today," Susan announced. "If any of you need assistance, I'm here to help. Heidi, thanks for bringing some Christmas cookies. As some of you know, our guest today is Amy Britan from Washington, Missouri. She brought some gorgeous sweaters to show us, as well as some small accessories. I know I've spotted one I need to have. We're all hoping to entice her to find a place here in Augusta where she can open a shop. Tell us more, Amy."

"Thanks for having me," Amy began as she stood up. "I've had a home-based business for many years, and I'm bursting at the seams from lack of space, so it's time to expand and offer more opportunities, like classes."

"As you should, Amy," Heidi said. "I know a lot of quilters who also knit. When and where do you think you can open?"

"Not anytime soon, I'm afraid," Amy explained. "I asked Susan if she thought there was enough traffic here in Augusta. I also know it's hard to find a place to rent, and I don't want to purchase anything at this point."

"You can build up your business here with no problem!" Candace assured her. "I know I would like to learn. You mentioned that you'll have classes?"

"Absolutely!" Amy answered. "I've looked at the Cottage Guest House, which is now for rent, but it's way too expensive for me."

This news disturbed me a bit because I still wanted it to remain a guest house. I knew why Amy was concerned with the volume of traffic here because I had the same concerns regarding selling quilts. At least I had antiques, which added to my shop's appeal.

"If you don't open in Augusta, where will you go?" Marilyn asked.

"I'll most likely stay in Washington," Amy admitted. "There are some decent places for rent."

"Amy's handiwork is made from Italian and Irish yarns," Susan informed us. "You have to feel them before you leave. If any of you hear of a place for rent, please pass it on to me or Amy."

It didn't take long for me to get up from my seat and examine the sweaters. They were expensive, but I could see why. I loved the heavy cable-styles for cold winters like we were having now. Sweaters would be perfect gifts for my sisters, Laurie and Loretta, who had horribly cold Wisconsin winters. I also noticed some of Amy's children's sweaters and sock caps. Those would be perfect for little Lucy. When I saw a cream-colored vest, I thought of Holly.

"Your timing for Christmas gift-giving is perfect, Amy," I commented. "I'll take all of these things in this stack, and that will finish up much of my Christmas list."

Amy's eyes lit up in delight. I paid her, put the things in my car, and then rejoined the others at the table. They were stitching, eating, and gossiping all at the same time. It seemed that the topic was the Christmas Walk.

"Susan is doing a fantastic job with Santa," I bragged.

"Thanks, Lily." Susan blushed. "It's been more work than I'd thought. It's fun to watch the little kids, however."

"I think it's neat the way he asks them for just one wish," Judy mentioned. "Most kids have a wishlist a mile long."

"Yes, it is neat," Susan agreed. "Some of them take a while to decide which wish is most important. What about each of you?"

Chapter 65

"That would be tough," Heidi confessed. "I'd really have to think about it. It's like having Aladdin's lamp and only getting one wish."

"It is!" Susan agreed. "Let's go around the table and hear everyone's Christmas wish. Keep your ears open for some secret sister gift ideas."

Everyone laughed and agreed.

"Well, I don't have to think twice about what I would wish for," Edna began. "I'm wishing for a new knee as soon as possible."

"I'm sorry to hear that, and I hope all goes well," Susan said kindly.

"Of course, I wish that for my mom as well, but I really just wish for good health. Without your health, you have nothing," Marilyn said.

Everyone agreed.

"That's hard to top," Judy said thoughtfully. "I thought about this very thing when I watched Santa with the children last weekend. I think my first wish would be to pay off my mortgage so other wishes could come true."

I thought that was a very wise wish. I didn't know too much about Judy's personal life.

"I have enough stuff," Heidi declared. "If you asked my husband what I'd wish for, he'd say that new refrigerator I've been hounding him about. They are so expensive!"

"This is tough," Candace lamented when we turned to her. "I could wish for peace on earth—or a new makeover like you see them do on TV!"

Her answer made us giggle.

"What about you, Lily?" Susan asked.

"I think about my family and what they would wish for first, but for me personally, I just wish and hope that my little business will survive."

"Lily, you'll be fine," Judy consoled me. "People love your shop."

"Thanks, Judy. What about you, Susan?" I inquired.

"Call me silly, but I think that if I reveal my wish, it might not come true," she confessed. "Remember your mom telling you that when you made a wish before you blew out your candles?"

We smiled as we remembered.

"So, my answer is that I don't think I'm going to jinx myself!"

"But I guess you could look at it in another way," I said. "If you don't tell Santa what you want, how is he supposed to know what to bring?"

"That's the perfect answer from a liberated woman like Lily," Heidi joked.

"Perhaps," I said proudly.

"So, are you going to Wisconsin again this Christmas?"

Marilyn asked.

"No. My family is going to St. Louis to stay with my sister Lynn, so I'll stay there a couple of days," I explained.

"How nice for you," Marilyn said. "Will your significant other join you?"

"I think he'll make an appearance or two," I said, smiling.

As the others left, I stayed behind to ask Susan a few questions regarding my quilt.

"Make sure you have everyone use the same marking pens on the quilt if you can," Susan advised. "It sounds like they're not all quilters, so you don't want them using just any kind of pen."

"Good to know." I nodded. "I'll get each of them their own pen. I bought mine at Gracie's."

The library was getting much busier, so I left because I didn't think I should take up much more of Susan's time. I went by Johann's to pick up a few groceries. As always, Johann appeared happy to see me.

"That pie of yours really hit the spot," he said.

"Thanks, but I can't take all the credit."

"You know, Lily, I keep hearing that Doc is still hanging around your place," Johann said. "Now you have a magical Santa occupying his office! How's that working out?"

I laughed. "You are pretty well-informed. It appears that all is well, and I don't know quite what to make of it myself! I recently met a Mrs. Meyer who remembers going to Doc's office with her mother when she was a little girl."

"Well, I'll be. Could she tell you much?"

"Yes and no," I reported. "Her memory is failing, so I didn't know how much to believe. She's in her late eighties. I hear everyone in town always talked about 'the Office.'"

"I've heard the same thing," Johann agreed. "You've done an impressive job with the place, so I'm sure Doc would be pleased."

I smiled. "I hope so."

"Every Christmas, I give folks some of these tangerines," Johann said, pointing to a bushelful nearby. "It's not Christmas without them. We used to get one of them at church at Christmas when I was a kid." He reached into the basket and pulled out a tangerine, offering it to me.

"Nice! Thank you. I haven't had one of these in a long time."

"Have a Merry Christmas if I don't see you before then."

"The same to you, Johann!"

Chapter 66

Being closed on Mondays gave me time to work on household tasks and my photo quilt. I made myself a salad for lunch and took it to the porch upstairs. As I ate lunch, I checked my laptop for any emails. I first responded to Sarah. The recap of her trials indicated to me that she was asking for some funds to help her make ends meet. I had helped her out previously. With Christmas coming up, I would have to think about it.

Laurie's email sounded quite chipper for a change. She was delighted to be reducing her inventory due to healthy Christmas sales. She said she'd also had a good follow-up checkup with her oncologist last week. Loretta complained of working longer shifts at the hospital because of so many people having the flu. Lynn said she was knocking herself out to have the fabulous Rosenthal family at her house for Christmas. She was excited about getting a real tree for the first time, to the dismay of her husband, who said she was just trying to be more Rosenthal-like.

I couldn't resist responding to Lynn's comments first.

What was "more Rosenthal-like?" I would be interested to know exactly what Carl meant! I also congratulated Laurie on the good report from her doctor and told Loretta that she'd better not bring the flu to us!

I then checked the comments on my magazine articles. Two of the three were complimentary, but the third one questioned the quilt care advice I had included in a past issue. She thought I was entirely too conservative in my care since many quilts were made for utilitarian purposes. I responded that she had a good point, but that they should be respected according to their condition. I also recommended that she check other sources for additional information.

I finally returned my attention to my quilt. At about two, I remembered I hadn't taken the time to look at the quilts that Will had brought out for me to see. I went downstairs, hoping I would have some lovely surprises. The first one I pulled out was a Lone Star quilt in yellows and golds. I knew right away it was a kit quilt, and that I may have even had one like it before. They still were desirable for a lot of folks because they came from kits that had coordinated colors and all the quilting lines designed on the fabric. The workmanship was wonderful, and the quilt appeared to never have been washed.

The second one was a typical Bow Tie pieced quilt that was likely made in the 1930s. The scrappy prints of indigos and shirting were a nice complement to the light blue background. This quilt had been washed but remained in good condition.

The third one was a gorgeous wholecloth quilt made from cream-colored cotton sateen, which was popular in the 1920s. I couldn't wait to open it up to see all the fancy quilting designs. I wished Susan could have shown this to our quilt class when we talked about design. There were many feathers, hearts, and grapevines throughout the quilt, but the center was a basket of flowers. I was sure that this quilt was likely made for a special occasion like a wedding and never used.

The quilts were wonderful. I could use them for my shop. The challenge would be in deciding on a fair wholesale price to offer Will. He seemed to be an honest person, and I did not want to take advantage of him. I folded the quilts back up and wrote my prices down, then decided to call Will and explain the values.

He answered right away. "What a fun night Marc and I had in Augusta," he said. "You have a wonderful shop in a great community."

"Thanks, Will. I enjoy meeting Marc's friends, and I'm pleased that you thought of me regarding your quilts."

"Are they worth anything?"

"Indeed, and I love every one of them." I then began to explain how I came up with each price, and he seemed impressed.

"Wow, I didn't think they would be worth that much, so it sounds fine to me."

We chatted for a few more minutes before I asked for his address so I could send him a check.

Chapter 67

I took a moment to celebrate being the owner of three wonderful quilts. If they had been red-and-white, it would have been even more delightful. There wasn't any doubt that people were hanging onto their red-and-white quilts.

When I got back to my stitching, I considered what I wanted to write on my quilt block for Ellen. I wanted it to be welcoming, sincere, and maybe even somewhat humorous. I'd have to give that more thought. I looked down at my stitches and had to admit that they had gotten better with time and practice. I found the repetitious movement relaxing and therapeutic. My mind seemed to wander as I stitched. I wanted to keep going and going. By late evening, I turned on the fireplace and Christmas lights. A frozen pizza would have to do for dinner. I had just finished the pizza when I got an unexpected call from Holly.

"Hey, girlfriend! Glad to hear from you," I said.

"He's gone, Lily, he's gone!" she stated in a shaky voice.

"Holly, I am so sorry. When did it happen?"

She paused. "This afternoon. When I arrived at the

hospital, there was a lot of confusion coming from his room. I waited in the hall because I figured something had happened. Not for one second did I think he had passed."

"That is so sad. How are you doing?"

"I'm in disbelief, to be honest, like this may be a cruel joke or something. When they let me in to see him, he looked so peaceful, like he was just taking a nap. I haven't seen that kind of look on him in years."

"What are the plans?"

"I have them all written down. I've made this list many times, wondering what I would do. He wants to be cremated and have his ashes taken to Texas, where his mother is buried."

"So no funeral?"

"No. I gave some thought to a memorial service, but who in the world would come? The only friend I'm aware of is that Clete guy who stopped by."

"How sad. Do you want me to do anything or come to be with you?"

"No need. It's all pretty simple. I just came home, and it feels very odd."

"I'm sure that it does. Your life will change dramatically from this moment on."

"I do honestly think he came to terms with his Maker before he died."

"I hope he was sincere. You must believe he was. Are you going to be okay?"

"Sure. I wanted you to be the first to know. I'll keep you posted."

"Sit and relax with a glass of wine while you digest all of this," I advised.

"No, I have a lot to do, but thanks for offering to come. It means a lot."

"Of course. I love you!"

"Love you, too!" she said as we hung up.

I had knots in my stomach just thinking about what she was going through right now. Her call was so matter-of-fact. She used to love him. Was she thinking of the good times or the many bad times?

As I got ready for bed, I kept thinking about how Holly would adapt to this change. Would she really take the ashes to Texas? What would her Christmas be like? Would she want to move from that house? Would she get any surprises when Maurice's will was read? Nothing from that man would surprise me. I was still awake at one, praying for a friend who had gotten relief and pain at the same time.

At three, I finally got up, went downstairs, and made myself some hot chocolate. I looked out the window to see a very quiet and still Augusta. When I came out of the kitchen, I saw Rosie's rocker moving back and forth. I walked over to the chair and settled myself in it. In the stillness of the wintry night, I began to weep. I wept for Holly. I wept for Maurice, a tortured man who had made my sweet friend's life miserable. I wept for the brevity of life itself. I wondered what new direction Holly's life would take now that she did not have to follow Maurice's commands. Death is always sobering. What a poignant reminder to live each day with purpose, loving and caring for others.

Chapter 68

It was later in the morning when I opened the shop. At that moment, the phone rang.

"Lily, it's Mary Beth."

I hadn't heard from Mary Beth in quite some time. She and Holly had become friends at the gym. "Oh, I'm so glad you called. I guess you've heard from Holly."

"She called this morning to say she was too busy to swim because her husband had died. Just like that. She was so calm and matter-of-fact about it. She wasn't emotional at all. I hate to say it, but I'm so glad that creep is out of her life!"

"I know, I know. I got the same reaction from her, but you know it's got to be a shock, even though she's wished for something to happen to stop his madness many times."

"So, what shall we do?"

"I'm letting her digest this. I'll do whatever she wants, but she seems to want to be alone."

"Well, if you think of any way I can help, let me know."

"I will, and you do the same."

When I hung up, I thought about what should be done

when you received news like this. Who did you tell, and what came next? You couldn't pretend it just didn't happen. Many of my friends knew I had a friend named Holly, but only I had met her crazy husband. I had to tell someone, so I called Alex. He'd heard me express my frustration regarding Maurice more than once.

"Good morning, Lily Girl!" Alex answered. "What's happening?"

I wasn't sure where to start. I had such mixed reactions about this death. I also wanted to know from Alex what he thought of Holly's reaction to it all.

"Wow, the poor girl doesn't know whether to cry or celebrate," he said.

"It makes me want to cry for her."

"I say you do what you've always done and just listen, because she's going to be all over the map with her emotions."

"You're right—as always!"

"Did I hear you correctly? It is so gratifying to hear you put that truth into words."

I laughed.

"Say, how are you and that Santa doing?"

"Just great! Oh, and I didn't tell you that I went to a girls' night out party last week. It was really nice."

"That's cool! So, how is lover boy doing?"

"Oh, please! I did go in to see him for Christmas Traditions on Main Street. It was truly awesome, and it put me in the Christmas spirit."

"You'd better be careful this Christmas, or he'll be putting a ring on your finger."

"Enough of that talk. I have to get this shop open."

"Okay, give me a holler if you want to meet up. I think

The Christmas Wish Quilt

Richard wants to have a little party for the contributors to the magazine, so stay tuned."

"That would be really cool!"

"Okay, go get 'em, Lily Girl!" he said as we hung up.

As always, Alex knew how my head worked, and I felt better after talking with him.

"Good morning, Lily," a voice said from outside the door.

"Korine! How good to see you! How have you been?"

"Pretty good. How about you?" She gave me a hug.

"What have you been doing?"

"I got a pretty good paying job taking care of Agnes Moor until she passed away. Her family didn't want to put her in a nursing home, so I practically lived with her for a while. They paid me well."

"Did she live here in Augusta?"

"Near Dutzow. She was the sweetest thing. I miss her. She was eighty-seven. Her body just gave out on her."

"I can imagine. Caring for her in that way will be an experience you won't forget."

"For sure. So, I thought I'd just stop by and say hello. I don't suppose you need any help here, do you?"

"I suppose I wouldn't mind you coming to help me clean every now and then. Things haven't changed as far as paranormal activity, just so you know."

"Oh, I wondered."

"When Santa is in Doc's office, a green light comes on and no one knows why. It's pretty bizarre."

"Yikes! Doesn't that scare you?"

"Actually, it's pretty cool. I think Doc likes the festivity!"

"I don't know, Lily. Let me think about it."

"I understand."

"When I stopped by Carrie Mae's shop, she had quite a few people, so maybe they will head this way."

"I hope so. I'm glad you stopped by. Merry Christmas, in case I don't see you again."

Chapter 69

Unexpected snow fell overnight, and it looked like it could turn into a significant amount. The hazardous road conditions meant having to depend only on local traffic for the day's customers. For that reason, I decided to keep the shop closed. I watched Ted outside clearing what he could on my sidewalks despite the snow falling as he worked. He was so determined to make every dime he could to buy his truck. I finally opened the door and motioned for him to come in and warm up. "It looks good enough, Ted," I shouted. "I won't be opening today, so it will do for now."

He was happy to oblige. He put his shovel on the back porch and came in the kitchen door, where I offered him some hot chocolate.

"I think I told you that I've been drinking coffee since I was ten years old," he hinted with a smirk on his face.

"Ted, I forgot."

"I love hot chocolate, so thanks," he replied, happy to find a way to tease me.

"Here's some cash for today, and for last week when you

came over," I said as I handed him an envelope of money. "Do you know exactly how much more you need to get the truck you have your eye on?"

He grinned and nodded excitedly. "Yes. I'm getting close. It's just so hard to find work in the winter."

"Do you mind sharing with me how much you need?"

"To the dime, without what you gave me today?"

I nodded.

"Four hundred and fifty dollars and fifty cents."

"That's it?"

"Well, I have to also figure in expenses like the license plate and all. Grandma may help me a little with that."

"Ted, I would like to give you five hundred dollars for your Christmas gift."

His eyes widened.

I continued, "You have helped me so often and may have even saved my life. Without you I might still be wallowing in a sinkhole."

He laughed.

"You are so dependable, and I know how much that truck will mean to you."

"I don't know what to say! You don't owe me anything. I'm grateful for the work you provide. I'm certainly willing to work it off."

"No, Ted, it's a Christmas gift. Go buy your truck!"

"I don't know what to say, other than thank you so much." He gave me a hug.

"You enjoy that hot chocolate while I write you a check."

"Sure enough!"

I got my checkbook from under the counter and wrote out a check. When I returned, I managed to get another hug before Ted left to go to Carrie Mae's. I was about to check my emails when I thought of Holly. I called her, and she took quite a while to answer. She sounded groggy when she said hello.

"I hope you're okay. Have you been able to sleep?"

"Not really. I have too much to do."

"Like what? Did you decide to have a funeral or some kind of service?"

"Not really. I have Maurice's ashes in my possession, so now I have to make arrangements to get them to Texas."

"Is there any hurry?"

"The sooner I get these ashes out of the house, the better. Well, I mean I just don't want anything to happen to them."

"I understand. Can I help with anything? Do you want me to call anyone?"

"I did call his friend Clete, who had been nice enough to visit him in the hospital. He offered to help me with any financial stuff. I also called Ken."

"Ken?"

"Yes, is that bad?"

"No, I guess I just thought he had gone by the wayside."

"He was nice and was attentive to me when I needed it. He knew what a monster I lived with. My neighbors have now heard the news, and they have been very kind. I'm sure they know it will be a much more peaceful neighborhood with Maurice gone."

"That's great. That should make you feel good."

"I called Goodwill this morning, and they're coming over this afternoon to pick up his clothes."

"Already?"

"It all has to be done."

"You have the rest of your life to deal with some of these things. Would you like me to come up and have lunch with you? The roads are bad today, but how about tomorrow?"

"No, just let me get organized here first."

"Very well, but give me a call. You are not alone."

"Thanks, Lily."

I hung up feeling so sad for Holly. I was sure her bad memories of Maurice were making her get rid of things faster than most widows. Why did she think of Ken? Did she want to let him know she was free now? I hated to think of all that must be going through her mind.

Chapter 70

The snow was getting lighter, but it continued to fall. I took my laptop to the porch upstairs and turned on the fireplace and the Christmas tree lights. I was pleased to see that my first email was from Sarah. She thanked me for the very small check I had recently sent her. She said Lucy was almost walking on her own and that she was looking forward to having a little birthday party for her on Christmas.

The only sister email was from Laurie. She had attached a cute photo of Santa stopping by her store. She was pleased with her Christmas sales and told us that she would close for the season when she left for Christmas in Missouri. She ended by saying it was the last call if we needed any oils and that she would be happy to bring them when she left for the holidays. I complimented her photo, but couldn't resist bragging about our Augusta Santa. In closing, I told her she could bring me more lavender oil.

I was surprised when my landline rang.

"Lily, this is Lisa."

"Hey! How are you enjoying the snow?"

She moaned. "Well, it's kept me home and busy with domestic duties. I was doing some organizing and thought of you once again regarding my quilts. I've put aside some that you can check out if you're interested."

"Great. I will."

"I don't know when these roads will clear, but if you manage to come out, I'll cook for you."

"Now that's an offer I can't refuse!"

"I just need a little notice."

"I can't wait to see your house."

"It has an amazing fireplace, which I haven't ventured very far from in the last few days."

"Stay warm, and I look forward to seeing you soon."

I pictured Lisa organizing her many, many quilts. Putting things in order was always gratifying to me, especially when it came to my quilts. I liked folding and refolding them as if they were my friends. I recalled when I'd had to do inventory at Rosie's shop before I brought everything here. I'd liked touching and examining each and every item. I remembered how Korine had seemed to enjoy washing all of Carrie Mae's glassware. It was an opportunity to enjoy their beauty.

I was ahead of schedule on writing my column, but the more I thought about Lisa organizing her quilts, the more convinced I became that it could be turned into a column that most readers would enjoy. It would be a positive message that I knew Richard would like. If I called it "Falling in Love Again," it would certainly get people's attention. People may think I was referring to a partner, but I would focus on quilts and people's belongings. While I had the time, I started writing down my thoughts from my own personal experience.

I wrote into the night, stopping now and then to look out the window at the accumulating snow. It was creating a lovely crystal blanket that covered the landscape perfectly. Part of me wished everything could stay this way. There were quiet times like this when I wished Marc were here. I wondered if he felt the same way. He had very little downtime, so he was likely glad to be left alone. His schedule allowed little time for leisure. Our lives were quite different, yet we continued to be attracted to each other.

It appeared to me that it all came down to balance. Yes, everyone could function alone and be perfectly happy most of the time, but some wanted it all. I wanted someone to share a personal relationship with as long as it allowed me to be myself. That was the beauty of the relationship between me and Marc. We understood that marriage was not where this relationship was heading. I supposed that all would be perfect until one of us wanted more; then there would be trouble.

Chapter 71

Since I wouldn't be seeing Carrie Mae and Betty on Christmas, I decided it might be nice to invite them over for tea so I could give them the baskets I had bought for them from the Olde Town Spice Shoppe. There was still snow on the ground, but if Ted could drive them, they would likely come. I made the call to Carrie Mae.

"Lands, girl," Carrie Mae said. "I've been enjoying the luxury of not being open."

"Well, since I won't be able to see you at Christmas, would you and Betty want to come to tea? I have a little something for you, and you just have to see this Christmas tree of mine!"

"How sweet! Yes, I would really like to see the famous tree that got you in the sinkhole."

We both laughed.

"Perhaps we can get Ted to drive the two of us over. By the way, Betty told me about what you did for Ted. He will be your slave forever!"

I smiled. "In that case, I'll count on the two of you

coming. How about tomorrow afternoon? I hope we don't get more snow like they say we may."

"I'll call Betty after we hang up," Carrie Mae offered.

"Wear that really ugly Christmas sweater you have. I just love it."

I did some cleaning and wrote a few Christmas cards. My card list got shorter and shorter each year. There were a couple of visitors who tried to get in the shop despite my closed sign. Like Carrie Mae, I felt it wasn't worth opening. Around four, Betty called to tell me that Ted had agreed to bring them over for tea and thanked me for the invitation.

"I'm so glad to get out of the house. Lily, how can I ever thank you for what you did for Ted? He picked up the truck a couple of days ago, and I know he's anxious to show it off to you."

"Great! I think the world of him, and I'll look forward to seeing you tomorrow."

While it was on my mind, I pulled one of the last pies out of the freezer. It was cherry. The red color would be festive. I also put out a plate of cookies that I had purchased from Grandma's Cookies. They were so delicious!

In a party mood now, I started to set a fancy table for our tea, right in front of the fireplace and Christmas tree. I went downstairs and brought up a Nippon tea and coffee set that wasn't selling because of the hefty price that Rosie had put on it. The pattern included a red rose, which gave it a nice holiday touch. Over my red tablecloth, I put a square white Battenburg tablecloth set on point. It was perfect. I had small white napkins that I could tuck in a crystal water glass.

Pleased with the results, I thought of Rosie. I sensed she would be pleased to see me use her things. I poured myself a cup of tea and turned on the TV while I quilted on my photo quilt. The news was on, and a report of a fire on The Hill caught my attention. Would I recognize the place? When they showed and described more, I began to realize that it was the building where Rosie had her antique shop. I turned up the volume in disbelief. How did that happen? What else could happen to destroy her memory? I wanted to cry. At the end of the story, the reporter said the fire would be investigated and that no one had been hurt in the blaze.

"I'm so, so sorry, Rosie," I said aloud to her. I got on the phone and quickly called Lynn. "Lynn, you've got to find out more for me," I insisted. "Could you drive by and check it out?"

"Sure, Lily. It's awful! All of the buildings in that neighborhood are so old. I wonder if any others got damaged as a result. Try not to let this upset you too much."

"I'm so glad I have her things and that someone else didn't buy them. Her rocking chair is a daily reminder of her."

"I'm sure many others in the neighborhood cherish their memories of her as well."

I hung up in frustration as I sat all the way out in Augusta. There wasn't a thing I could do! When I'd done the inventory for the sale, I had gotten to know the building and its contents very well. First Rosie died a violent death, and now her building had burned to the ground! I sure hoped it wasn't the result of arson.

Chapter 72

After a poor night's sleep, I decided to get up early, knowing the Christmas tea was taking place that afternoon. I was pleased that it had stopped snowing. Unfortunately, it would be another penniless day for Lily Girl's Quilts and Antiques.

Ted didn't disappoint. He showed up early to clear my snow. I admired his red truck as he cleaned off my snow-covered car. Of course, Ted's truck looked like it had been in the garage and didn't have a trace of accumulated snow on it. I opened the door and motioned for him to come in.

"Good morning!" he said with puffs of smoke coming out of his mouth from the cold. "I hear you're having a party today!"

"Yes, and I hear you're the chauffeur! Do you want some coffee?"

"No, thanks! I've got to get this done and then head over to the Watsons' house."

"Okay. Thanks for coming by, and I'll see you later."

My cell phone rang. I saw that it was Alex.

"Did you hear about Rosie's building?" he asked.

"Yes, and I'm so upset about it. Lynn is going to drive by to see the damage."

"It's a terrible way to end her life on The Hill. They barely mentioned her in the news report. Well, I just wanted to make sure you knew. Try not to think about it. I'm on my way to do an interview for an article I'm writing."

"Thanks for calling." I hung up and got some coffee before checking my emails. Marc called as I opened my laptop. "Are you calling to tell me about Rosie's shop?" I asked him.

"I am. I figured you knew. Apparently, the building next door burned as well. I think it may have been vacant, from what they said."

I mentioned the fond memory I had of Marc helping me with the inventory there. A storm had come, the lights went out, and I found a candle to burn to give us some light. We ended up having pizza and wine on a tablecloth I'd spread out on the floor of the shop. Marc agreed that the night had been pretty romantic.

"I'll never forget it," I sighed.

"Nor will I."

"The Dinner Detectives are coming for tea this afternoon since I won't see them at Christmas."

"Sounds good. By the way, Will was very appreciative of you taking the quilts off his hands."

"I was happy to oblige. The quilts were great!"

"So, will I see you before Christmas Eve?"

"Not likely with this weather. Absence makes the heart grow fonder, remember?"

"Even fonder?"

"Much fonder!" I replied.

I hung up and proceeded to check my laptop. I had no emails. I wasn't in the mood for chitchat anyway, as I was still thinking about Rosie's building.

At two, I heard a knock on the door that told me the detectives had arrived. I ran down the stairs and opened the door. I was shocked to see them both wearing fancy hats.

"Look at you two!" I greeted them with a laugh.

"Well, when you're invited to tea, there is a bit of protocol to follow, even if it doesn't go with your favorite Christmas sweater," Carrie Mae teased.

We giggled. I waved Ted on so he could enjoy the afternoon until it was time to don his chauffeur's hat again.

"Come in! Let me take your coats. I'll hang them here by the door." After they each got a hug, we headed up the stairs.

"Lily!" Betty exclaimed. "This is a lovely tree! Look at this table setting! What a treat for two old ladies!"

I smiled. "I love doing this," I said proudly. "The English breakfast tea is hot, so I hope you enjoy it. If I remember, neither of you take cream."

They nodded.

"My daughter takes cream, and she insists that the English put the cream in before pouring the tea," said Carrie Mae.

"Yes, I know." I grinned.

Chapter 73

"So, do we need to do a little detective work today?" Betty asked with a laugh.

"I suppose Carrie Mae filled you in on my visit with Mrs. Meyer," I replied.

"Yes." Betty nodded. "I thought her memories fit right in with what we had suspected so far."

"Did you hear about the green light coming on in Doc's office when Santa was here?" I asked.

They nodded.

"It was all over town, like it or not," Carrie Mae informed me.

"I think Doc enjoyed having Santa here," I shared.

"Thank goodness that all went well for Santa," Betty said. "Word would have spread quickly if there had been any more activity."

"Well, let's enjoy the goodies I have for you," I said. "These cookies are from a great cookie shop on Main Street in St. Charles. I have a pie as well. I've become the pie lady, I'm afraid."

They chuckled.

"I could think of something worse," Betty joked. "What kind are we having?"

"Cherry with vanilla ice cream. Remember, Alex did all the fruit pies, so I can't take any credit for it." I went into the kitchen and was stumped to see that the pie I had put on the counter was no longer there! I didn't want to have an impulsive reaction, so I looked in the refrigerator, on the stove, and then downstairs, in case I hadn't brought it up. There was no sign of that cherry pie. I joined the others with a look like I had seen a ghost.

"What is it, Lily?" Carrie Mae asked, concerned.

"My cherry pie has disappeared," I admitted, perplexed.

The two looked at each other quizzically.

"You've looked everywhere?" Betty asked.

I nodded.

"Well, these cookies are certainly adequate," Betty assured me.

I sat down and poured myself some tea. The others knew I was upset.

"Lily, don't worry about it," Carrie Mae comforted me. "There must be a reason Rosie or Doc doesn't want us to have some."

"Why not?" Betty asked, taking another bite of her cookie.

"Good question, but trust me, there is always a reason," I said flatly.

"My, these cookies are delicious!" Carrie Mae exclaimed.

"I know. Grandma's Cookies has become an institution on Main Street," I explained. "The shop owners have said that their customers use a visit to the store as a bribe to get their children to go shopping with them."

"I keep looking at your wonderful tree," Carrie Mae said softly. "I can see why you were determined to get this one. The shape is perfect, which is hard to find in a cedar tree."

"Nothing like that smell at Christmastime," added Betty.

"Okay, so I have something for you ladies that I purchased in St. Charles," I said as I presented their baskets to them. "There's a shop on the street that has wonderful fresh spices and herbs. It's such a unique store. They also have a wide selection of soup mixes. I don't cook much myself, but I went crazy seeing all the goodies. I hope you enjoy these soups during the winter."

"Thanks so much, Lily," Carrie Mae gushed. "I'm sorry, but we didn't bring anything for you."

"You know I have to bake you something," Betty reminded me. "That's my thing!"

"Ladies, you do enough for me," I interrupted.

"Thanks, Lily," Betty said, looking at each item in the basket. "I can't wait to try some of these things."

"I'm glad you're pleased." I smiled. "More tea?" I filled their cups, and our conversation got a little more personal. They brought up Marc's name and wondered if we were getting serious. "All is well, ladies," I shared. "I'm not keeping anything from you."

"These are wonderful years right now," Carrie Mae sighed. "Art and I shared many precious years together."

"Lily, did you know that Art was once mayor of Augusta?" Betty asked.

"No, I did not, but that doesn't surprise me," I responded. "I know how the Wilsons were pillars in this community."

Chapter 74

An hour later, after many topics had been discussed, Betty and Carrie Mae asked for their coats so they could be on their way. Ted had arrived only minutes before. When I opened the door, Betty commented about how well I had decorated Doc's house.

"Can we peek inside?' Betty asked with a smile.

"Of course!" I said as I reached for my coat. "You can then visualize what Mrs. Meyer was describing."

The ladies gathered their baskets while I unlocked Doc's office. When I opened the door, I stood there in disbelief. I waited a bit so Betty and Carrie Mae could see.

"No way!" Carrie Mae was the first to respond.

"How did the pie get in here?" Betty asked nervously. "Are you playing with us, Lily?"

I shook my head. "That's bizarre! I'm telling you that it was on my kitchen counter."

"Didn't you say that Mrs. Meyer's mother would bring Doc a cherry pie every time they visited?" Carrie Mae asked.

"You're right, she did say that," I recalled. "I don't know

what to say!"

"Well, you can't leave it here," Carrie Mae stated. "You wanted us to have it, so I'll take it home. Do you want half, Betty?"

"No, please take it all!" Betty insisted. "This is downright spooky."

"Good idea, Carrie Mae," I said, handing her the pie.

"Good luck and Merry Christmas!" Carrie Mae called from their vehicle after they had joined Ted.

I waved to the three of them. At that moment, I wanted to run away with them. When I got back into the shop, my cell phone was ringing. It was Holly.

"Holly, it's so good to hear from you."

"I just wanted you to know that I'm leaving for Texas, where I plan to leave Maurice's ashes."

"That's good," I said with relief.

"He has an uncle who will meet me at the airport. I'll just give him the ashes and then head back home."

"No service?" I inquired.

"The uncle can do whatever he wants."

"Well, if you think that's best. It will be good to get all of this behind you. Just be brave and be safe, okay?"

"I will."

"I don't want you to be left alone for Christmas, so call me when you get back."

"Celebrating Christmas is the last thing I have on my mind right now."

"I understand." I hung up feeling so sad for my friend. I prayed for her to have a peaceful trip. Before I went to bed, I emailed Lynn about Holly's husband dying. I said that I might invite her to some of our festivities if that was okay. It didn't take long for Lynn to respond.

"Of course! Everyone is welcome. That poor girl deserves some happiness. Just so you know, I sent Ellen an email to find out when she is arriving. She will get here on Christmas Eve during the day and will stay at the Ritz Carlton nearby. She will then come over on Christmas morning when we open presents. Our time is running out on when to tell Laurie. Would you do the honors, since it was you who invited Ellen?"

I was a bit irritated by Lynn's request, but I bit my tongue. The whole scenario brought up so many unpleasant memories, but now was the time to start healing. "I will be proud to tell Laurie that she has a half-sister who will be celebrating the holidays with us. She'd better react properly like a good Rosenthal. Even Mother would certainly approve of what we are doing."

"Whatever, Lily. Thanks for taking care of this awkward situation."

I went to bed feeling sad for Holly and wondering when and how I should chat with Laurie about Ellen spending Christmas with us. I was thankful to have a healthy, happy family that could embrace others and offer kindness and friendship to them. That was what everyone should be doing at Christmas.

Chapter 75

The next morning, I greeted Barney as he brought the mail.

"Are you planning to open today, Lily?"

"I am! This snow is isn't going away, and its Christmastime. I could use some customers."

"Is your Santa coming back again?"

"No, but it sure was great having him here."

"Well, I'll be on my way. Thanks for having your walkways clear."

I went inside and sifted through the mail as I drank my morning coffee. I had a few Christmas cards and something from *Spirit* magazine that didn't look like my usual paycheck. I quickly opened it and saw that it was an invitation to a Christmas party. It was beautifully done in green and gold, and the party date was the twenty-third of December. I would have to go to Lynn's house early and then go with Alex if he didn't have a date. What would I wear? I needed to do some serious shopping.

My schedule was getting tight before Christmas, so I

called Lisa and told her I would have to visit her after the first of the year. I didn't want to add more merchandise to my inventory at the end of the year anyway. I got the answering machine when I called, so I told her my plan and wished her a Merry Christmas. My next step was to text Alex about the invitation I had just received.

> Can I be your date for the magazine party? Please?

It was thirty seconds later when he responded.

> Not Marc?

> You and I would have more fun! Did you plan to take someone?

> ????? Let's just plan on it.

> You sure?

> Sure!!

Well, that was settled. I would be seeing Marc two days in a row, so I shouldn't feel bad, right?

A customer walked in, so I put my phone aside.

"Brr! It's cold outside!" she said.

"Come on in. It's warm in here. What can I help you with today?"

"I need a gift for my friend who is a quilter."

"I have antique quilts in the next room if you'd like to look."

"I will, but I don't think I can afford to buy her an actual quilt."

"I'll look around as well to see if there is something else that would be appropriate," I assured her.

A young man entered. He quickly said hello and seemed to be in a hurry.

"I need a quilt for my wife for Christmas," he announced.

"I think I can help with that," I answered. "My quilts are in the next room. Follow me."

We joined the first customer, who was pulling quilts off the rack like she was actually going to buy one.

"How much is this blue quilt?" the young man asked.

I found the corner of the quilt and looked closely. "Four hundred dollars."

"Okay, that one will do," he said with certainty.

The other customer's look was priceless as she witnessed the easy sale.

"Great!" I responded as I took the quilt to the counter. "If she should ask what this pattern is called, tell her it's an Irish Chain."

"That's cool," he replied. "She's part Irish."

When he left, I smiled to myself. That was the fastest and easiest sale I'd ever made.

"What's this?" the woman asked, coming out of the quilt room.

"Oh, that's a spool holder, and in the center of it is a place to put your scissors," I explained.

"I also see that you have several quilt stands around with quilts on them," she noted. "Are they for sale?"

"Yes, they should have tags on them."

"I really like this one, if it's not too expensive."

"The tag says one hundred and twenty-five dollars."

"Okay," she said. "I'll just get her that and forget about the spool holder. I know she will use this."

I was so excited about the two sales that I could hardly contain myself as I carried the rack to the car for her. Christmas was indeed in the air, or else neither of these sales would have taken place. Merry Christmas to me!

Chapter 76

As I was closing the shop for the day, I got a call. It was Butler. My first thought was that it might have something to do with Carrie Mae. "Butler, how are you?"

"Very good. How is the Christmas season going?"

"It's been decent, considering that the snow kept me from opening on some days."

"It's been a nasty winter compared to some. The reason I'm calling is to ask you to dinner."

"Dinner? How nice." That was unexpected.

"I decided I needed some Christmas cheer, and I thought of you."

"How sweet! I'll check with Carrie Mae and see when she can go."

"No, I'm just asking you."

"Oh, I see. Well, when did you have in mind?"

"Tomorrow night, if you're free. I have a friend who invested in a restaurant in Washington, Missouri called The Blue Duck, so I thought it might be fun to check it out. Have you been there?"

"No, but I've heard good things about it. I'd like to get to Washington more than I do."

"Well, here's your chance. How about I pick you up around seven?"

"Okay, I'll be watching for you."

"Marvelous!"

When I hung up, I wondered what I had done. Had I just agreed to go on a date with Butler? This was different than our usual business lunches. The evening would certainly be interesting enough. He was charming and full of information regarding quilts and antiques.

In bed that night, I wondered what Marc would say about this date. I had managed to keep my fantasy relationship with Anthony a secret, but this was an evening with a single man. I had to admit I was flattered that he'd thought of me. After all, Carrie Mae and I had shared in his grief after he lost his nephew. When he surprised me last Christmas with the special quilt, I should have known he was fond of me in some way. He also knew how much I loved that exquisite quilt.

Getting little sleep, I woke up early to raid my closet, looking for something to wear to *Spirit's* Christmas party as well as to my dinner with Butler. I looked at my row of black clothing because there were no other choices. My accessories would have to add some color. It would be chilly, so I thought of what I might use for a shawl. It was then that I remembered the piano shawl I had for sale in the shop. It was gorgeous, with six-inch fringe, and was quite expensive. Rosie must have known something I didn't about it. Oh, how I wished there was a boutique close by where I could shop. Carrie Mae had said they had come and gone in the area.

I went downstairs for coffee and rescued the shawl. It

felt wonderful as I swung it around my shoulders. I waltzed around and noticed that my live greenery was getting dry. Christmas had better be over soon! I then received a text from Holly.

Arrived in Houston at the Hyatt hotel. The uncle was very unfriendly. He nearly snatched the ashes away from me. Is that whole family nuts?

Oh, be careful, Holly.

Will do.

Chapter 77

The day seemed to plod along at a snail's pace, and I felt as if I looked at the clock every hour. As it got closer to seven, I could tell I was getting nervous. I pressed the shawl, and when it was time to put it over my black dress, my outfit came alive. The red design matched my lip color perfectly. My dressier black boots were a good match for the ensemble. I felt attractive and sexy. At seven, I went downstairs to watch for Butler. When I saw his car, I got my coat. I opened the door, and the pleasant aroma of his cologne greeted me.

"Lily, it's good to see you," he said, giving me a slight hug.

"You too! Something told me you would be right on time."

On the twenty-minute drive, we covered several topics. He wanted to know how Carrie Mae was doing, and as we visited, I could finally feel my nerves calming down.

The Blue Duck was a contemporary-style restaurant located along Front Street on the river. It was near many historic structures, like the Missouri Meerschaum corn cob pipe factory. I remembered Alex telling me that he had written an article about them. The river side of the restaurant was all glass and offered a splendid view. In the summer, it would be wonderful to be seated on their patio. When I took off my shawl, I was acutely aware of Butler's eyes on me. I hoped I wasn't overdressed.

"You look stunning, Lily! That shawl is Indian, circa 1900. Where did you find such a lovely piece?"

I smiled. "From my own inventory." I blushed. "Do I wear it better than a piano?"

He chuckled and winked. "You have a flair for the unique."

After we ordered drinks, Butler asked the waiter if one of the owners he knew was in this evening. He was not. We ordered a spinach salad and some Greek flatbread, which was a perfect pairing with the wine we were drinking. I'd never noticed Butler's face up close until tonight. His salt-and-pepper hair was dramatic, and his eyes were deep blue. They danced around as he spoke. I wondered about his age. How had he managed to get through losing not only his wife in an accident, but his nephew to suicide?

"So, Butler, what are your plans for Christmas?" I asked between bites.

He looked down. "Nothing planned," he said quietly. "If I feel up to it, I may hang out with a couple of friends. Holidays are pretty quiet for me."

"Do you have family in town?"

He shook his head. "My wife had some family here, but I've lost contact with them. It was too painful to be with them without her, and then we just drifted apart."

"Why aren't you trying to get together with your brother?" I asked. "I thought you two had worked things out."

"Oh, we stay in touch, but he has a life out there," he

explained.

As I described my plans to spend Christmas with family, I felt guilty not asking him to join us.

"How is your relationship with your baseball man?" Butler asked.

I smiled. "He's fine and very busy."

"A pity he's too busy to give you the attention you so deserve."

I wasn't sure how to respond. "We're both busy, and I'm at a disadvantage living in Augusta. It takes an effort to get together with my sister as well as with Marc." As we consumed more wine, our conversation got easier. I hadn't realized what a sense of humor Butler had. Before long, signs of the restaurant closing got our attention.

"This is the most fun I've had in a long time," Butler admitted as he put his hand on mine.

"It's been a great evening," I agreed. "I wanted to give you a little Christmas gift, but I didn't know what to give you."

"You agreeing to see me this evening is quite enough, Lily. Will you promise that we can do this again when you return?"

I smiled, not knowing what to say.

"You are confused as to my intentions, aren't you?"

I smiled again. "You are a wonderful and interesting person, Butler. I feel so privileged to know you."

"That is a lovely answer, but I'm too old to play games at this stage in life. You must know how attracted I am to you. I wish you would agree to date me. I would like to get to know you better."

I couldn't believe what I'd just heard. "Oh, Butler, I can't agree to that right now. I'm in a relationship, as you know. I

ANN HAZELWOOD

don't want to lose you as a friend, because I admire you so much."

"Perhaps I've said too much," he said, looking down. "I also don't want to lose you as a dear friend. We should go. Are you up for a nightcap somewhere? There are some great bars down here on the river."

"Thanks, but I'd better get home," I responded. "You could get me into a lot of trouble, I'm afraid."

The drive home was a bit tense. I could tell Butler had a lot on his mind and may have been sorry that he revealed his feelings. Most women would give their eye teeth to be out with a man like Butler.

Chapter 78

Butler insisted on walking me to the door as he wished me a Merry Christmas. I was caught off guard when a simple hug goodbye turned into a kiss on the lips! He knew I was immediately taken aback by the aggressive move. "Thanks for dinner," I said as I backed away.

He smiled. "I'll call you again, Lily. Merry Christmas!"

"You too, Butler." As I got inside and removed my coat, I thought I must be dreaming. What had happened this evening?

As I dressed for bed, I folded the piano scarf carefully on a hanger to take with me to Lynn's house. I wondered if Marc ever found himself in a similar situation. Did one of his female friends ever suggest a more romantic relationship? I wanted to stay friends with Butler, so I hoped that my rejection would not spoil it. Should I tell Carrie Mae about what happened?

To my surprise, I slept very well. The next day would be the day to connect with my family, so packing would have to be completed. I tried to put Butler out of my mind for the moment. As I began packing, I wondered if I should wear my shawl to the magazine's Christmas party. Certainly no one else would have the same look.

All my gifts were wrapped and put in a big box. The wine racks for Alex and Marc both had light tissue wrapped around them and were tied with red bows. Hopefully, Marc and Alex would not realize they each got a wine rack, even though the racks were very different.

After lunch, I opened the shop and turned on some Christmas music. As I put out Rosie's rocker, I was pleased to see Carrie Mae drive up. A couple was coming in at the same time.

"What are you doing here?" I asked Carrie Mae jokingly.

"Well, I wasn't going to let you leave town without a little Christmas gift from me," she announced cheerfully.

"You didn't have to do that. Let me check on the couple that went to the back room." When I returned to the main room, I saw Carrie Mae take a chair. She seemed out of breath. "Are you okay?"

"This old gal can't stand for very long anymore," she complained. "Now open this gift."

I took the gift bag and pulled out a lot of tissue. At the bottom was a small box. "What's this?" It looked like a ring box. I opened it up, and it was a gorgeous emerald ring surrounded by diamonds. I stared at Carrie Mae in disbelief.

"Go ahead and try it on," she encouraged. "It belonged to my mother, and I never wore it. I really want you to have it, and I'll bet it fits your finger perfectly."

"You have got to be kidding me. Wouldn't your daughter love to have this?"

"I have a treasure chest of beautiful jewels the girl will

never wear, so you just enjoy it."

She was right. The ring fit the first finger I put it on perfectly. It was stunning! "Thank you so much! I will cherish this forever!"

"I'm glad you like it. I feel better now about your leaving. I need to get back to the shop."

"Now, just sit for a minute. I'd like you to stay seated while I share something with you." I briefly told her about the dinner with Butler. She didn't react until I told her that he'd said he'd like to date me. Her look changed completely.

"How do you feel about that?"

"I'm as shocked as you are," I admitted. "I don't want to lose his friendship."

"You know I think the world of Butler, but it surprises me that he would ask you out when you are seeing someone else," Carrie Mae said. "I could tell he was attracted to you, but after his wife's death, I didn't think he'd ever date again."

"I think he's very comfortable with me and doesn't care if I'm seeing Marc."

"Well, you're going to have to come to grips with that situation," she warned. "It really wouldn't be fair to Butler or Marc if you didn't. Butler's a pretty good salesman."

We were interrupted when the couple came to the counter to purchase a small lamp. Carrie Mae wished me a Merry Christmas, and off she went.

Chapter 79

I couldn't believe the day had finally arrived for me to see my family. A bonus for the day was the *Spirit* magazine Christmas party. I went over my schedule as I had my morning coffee. The weather was clear, and I tried not to think about how much business I may be missing by being closed for the next couple of days. As I was loading the car, Barney arrived to deliver the mail. "I'm glad I saw you before I left, Barney. I left a little something for you in your Christmas card."

"Thanks, Lily. You didn't have to do that. I actually have some good news to share with you."

"You do?"

He nodded. "Snowshoes will be back on this route after Christmas."

"How wonderful! What about you? I'll miss you."

"Oh, I'll be over yonder by Marthasville. I'll miss all you good folks in the neighborhood."

"Well, have a Merry Christmas!"

"You too. I'll be checking on you every now and then."

"Thanks for everything, Barney."

The news put a smile on my face. Everything was in the car, so I took a deep breath and said Merry Christmas to Augusta as I headed toward St. Louis. I wondered when everyone would arrive that night. I hoped to see everyone before Alex picked me up to go to the party.

I arrived on The Hill with mixed feelings, bracing myself as I drove down my old street. I turned the corner to the ruins of Rosie's shop and saw the yellow tape surrounding the ashes, just like it had been when Rosie was murdered. The damage was significant, and the wall that had been attached to the building next door had fallen. I pulled into a parking spot across the street to look closer. Others were doing the same as I walked across the street.

I could identify the shape of Rosie's counter. Only half of it remained as piles of ashes surrounded the room that once had been her main retail space. I wanted to run toward it to see if there was anything left of her shop. There was still some snow that covered the dark ashes, which made it quite surreal. I was shivering from the chilly air. Taking a deep breath, I realized I needed to move on.

I got in the car and drove down the street to get some bagels at Tony's. The aroma was as wonderful as I'd remembered, but there was not a familiar face in sight. How could things change so much in such a brief time? I traveled on to Lynn's house, which was not too far from my old neighborhood. I was glad to see her car in the driveway. She came out of the door as if she were waiting for me.

"It's about time you got here!" she shouted as she gave me a hug.

"I'm sorry. I had to make a couple of stops."

"Rosie's place?" she asked.

I nodded. "Yes, and I had to stop at Tony's for bagels!"

"Let me help carry your things."

"No peeking inside my car," I warned. "A couple of things need to remain there."

"That's fine. My goodness, your purse weighs fifty pounds or more!"

I laughed.

A cup of hot tea was handed to me as soon as I entered the door. I immediately picked up the scent of Lynn's large cedar tree. "Lynn, you outdid me with this tree. I thought mine was big. This is really beautiful!"

"Thanks. Sit and enjoy while I put your things in the guest room."

"What time is Ellen coming tomorrow?"

"Sometime in the afternoon," she said as she joined me for tea.

"Okay, that means tonight or tomorrow morning, we have to break the news to Laurie that Ellen is coming."

Lynn took a deep breath.

"I know, I know. I agreed to be the one to tell her. Can we let her have a couple of cocktails first?"

Lynn chuckled. "I can't wait to see our little Lucy," she said with a smile. "I borrowed a nice crib to put in the room with Sarah, and I have the birthday cake ordered."

"Lynn, remember last Christmas day when Sarah's water broke while she was mashing potatoes for our dinner?"

We giggled.

"I'm curious, have you received a Christmas card from Aunt Mary like we usually do?"

"No. Have you?"

"No, and she likely has mixed feelings about Ellen being here with us this Christmas."

"Frankly, Aunt Mary is the least of our concerns."

Around five, Carl arrived home with an assortment of delicious appetizers from various downtown restaurants near where he worked. I could smell the toasted ravioli. After giving him a hug, I decided to take a shower and get ready for the party. When I returned to the living room, Carl and Lynn gave me a whistle.

"Hubba hubba," Carl teased.

"Where did you get that gorgeous shawl?" Lynn asked with envy.

Chapter 80

After Carl and Lynn boosted my ego, I was ready to party when Alex picked me up. He looked so handsome in his casual yet classy ensemble that included a fashionable bow tie.

"What a pair you two make!" Lynn exclaimed.

"Lily Girl will steal the show," Alex bragged. "She's made quite a name for herself at the magazine, so there will be lots of people who are anxious to meet her."

I blushed and pushed Alex out the door as Carl wished us an enjoyable time.

"When is the rest of your family arriving?" Alex asked on the drive.

"Anytime now. That means that either tonight or tomorrow morning, I have to tell Laurie about Ellen coming."

"Hey, it's Christmas. Everything will be fine."

When we arrived, we walked into a crowded room where someone checked our coats. I immediately noticed the elegant silver Christmas décor throughout the venue.

"Lily, Lily," Richard said as he greeted me with a kiss on

the cheek. "Merry Christmas!"

"Merry Christmas to you as well!"

"In case you hadn't noticed, I brought Lily with me," Alex teased as Richard shook his hand.

"There are people here who have asked about you!" Richard informed me. "By the way, you look simply gorgeous!"

"Thanks, Richard," I responded.

Alex gave me a funny look and told me he'd get us a glass of wine.

Richard interrupted several attendees who were chatting and introduced me. Some complimented my work and others wanted to know more about Augusta. I was pleased to see Alex coming my way with two glasses of wine.

"Having fun yet?" he whispered in my ear.

I was about to respond when an attractive blonde interrupted us.

"Alex, it's so good to see you!" she gushed. "I've missed you terribly!"

Alex winked at her, and I turned my back to the other folks so he could handle her as graciously as possible. Richard likely interpreted that as an opportunity.

"Lily, let's go out to the patio where it's a little quieter," he said as he slid his arm around my waist. "Didn't I tell you that everyone would love your column? I hope it's helped your business some as well."

"The exposure has been helpful. I don't know about increased sales, but I have signed an autograph or two."

"Just wait," he assured me. "It will get better. I wanted to hand this to you in private to let you know how much we appreciate you."

As he handed me what I presumed was a bonus check,

Richard kissed me on the cheek, which I hadn't expected.

"Hey, boss!" I heard Alex say as he came to join us. "Are you stealing my date?"

"Well, it got a bit noisy in there, so we came out here to discuss business," Richard replied in a serious tone.

"Sorry," Alex responded. "Lily, can I get you another drink?"

"No, thanks," I replied. "I'm anxious to try some of that delicious food I saw in the dining room."

"Well, let's get to it," Richard said as he once again put his arm around my waist.

Alex followed. He knew me so well that he had to know how much I wanted him to stay close by. I filled a small china plate as if I had a huge appetite. Alex managed to squeeze in behind me. Richard got called away and left the food table to join a small group of people nearby.

"Want to get away?" Alex whispered in my ear.

I smiled. "Not until I eat some of this heavenly food, but I'm ready when you are."

"Little Miss Blondie got a little too aggressive," he explained. "I told her you were my date, so you'd better start acting like it."

I gave him a wink and laughed. "Oh, honey, thank you!" I said as I gave him a kiss on the lips. I thought Alex was going to choke on his drink. "Would you like a shrimp?" I asked, popping the appetizer in his mouth and looking at him adoringly.

"Uh, yeah, yum!" he said, taken a bit by surprise.

"You'd better watch it, or I'll take you out to the dance floor," I teased.

"Too late, here comes Richard," Alex warned.

"Lily, would you give me the pleasure of this dance?"

"Sure," I said, handing Alex my drink. Alex's face turned red. I knew Alex would be watching every move as I danced the slow dance with Richard. Fortunately, the song was brief, and Alex was there to greet me with my glass of wine.

"Richard, Lily has out-of-town family coming in tonight. I promised to get her home early," Alex explained. "This party has been awesome. Thank you so much."

"It truly was!" I agreed. "Thank you for the generous surprise."

"My pleasure, sweetheart," he said, kissing my cheek. "Enjoy your family and have a Merry Christmas."

"Thanks," I said, giving him a slight hug. I took a deep breath when we got outdoors. Alex asked the valet for our car, and we felt like a couple of kids who had just made a great escape!

Chapter 81

"I was afraid Richard would be his old self," Alex said, shaking his head in disgust. "Are you okay?"

"I'm a big girl," I said with a wink.

"Right! I saw your eyes begging for me to rescue you."

I burst into laughter. "Hey, I'm going home with a bonus, are you?" From the look on his face, I knew the answer.

"Man, oh, man," he said, frustrated.

"I'm sure your check is in the mail," I teased. "Richard said he wanted to give mine to me in private."

"I'm sure he did! Did he also ask if you wanted to see his paintings?"

I laughed again.

"Hey, you want to get a nightcap at Rigazzi's?"

"Sounds good, but we're a little overdressed."

"Who cares? I need a beer!"

An hour later, we left Rigazzi's, still laughing. It was so good to be around Alex again. He had a delightful sense of humor.

"I think my shawl must be an attention-getter. What do

you think?"

"It's a dramatic statement, which means you're sure of yourself. Men like that."

"Really? Hmmm," I murmured as we arrived at Lynn's house. "Hey, don't drive away. Your Christmas presents are in my car."

"That's just great! You know I don't do my shopping until Christmas Eve," Alex explained. "I don't have anything for you."

When he saw the odd wooden shape of his present, I had to explain what it was.

"This artist's work is very cool! Here's his card." I watched his eyes get big with admiration.

"This is darn cool for sure! You did well! Thanks!"

"Don't tell Marc, but you both got a version of the same thing."

"Well, I'm glad I rate with the main man."

I also gave Alex the baseball cap I had purchased for him earlier in the season. With a sigh, I said, "I'd better get inside. Thanks for saving my life tonight. We'll see you for dinner, right?"

"Planning on it," he said, giving me a hug.

I was glad he didn't make any comment about me kissing him on the lips. I was hoping he would just forget about it.

Lynn had left the door unlocked for me, so I quietly entered the house, noticing that everyone had arrived. I could see their things scattered throughout the living area. As I was going down the hall to my room, Laurie peeked out of the first guest room.

"Laurie! You made it!" I gave her a hug.

"I tried to stay up for you, but Carl served me too much

wine. Did you have a good time tonight?"

"Shhh! Come into my room so we won't wake anyone."

She followed me while putting on her bathrobe.

"Did you all have a good trip?" I asked.

"We did! Lucy got a bit cranky because she was confined."

"She's walking, right?"

"Yeah, she took her first steps this past week. I think Sarah wanted it to be a surprise for everyone, but Lucy had different ideas. It's really great to be back in St. Louis. It's been a while for me."

"I'm trying to think straight, because Alex and I went for a couple of beers after the party."

"Oh, I want to hear about everything! Doesn't Marc care that you went out with Alex tonight?"

"We're like brother and sister. Marc knows that, and Alex looks out for me, like he did tonight when things got a little uncomfortable. He's the best."

"This shawl is awesome! Was it really a fancy party?"

"Thanks. It was beautifully done, with fancy food and Christmas decorations. I'm so glad we got this time for the two of us to talk, because I need to tell you something."

"You're going to marry Marc?"

"No... no! Just settle down!"

"Then what?"

"Promise you will not overreact, okay?"

Her face got serious. "Look, I just beat breast cancer. What could possibly upset me?"

I took a deep breath.

Chapter 82

"Ellen is joining us for Christmas," I blurted out. "She came to visit me, and I invited her. It just felt like the right thing to do. She didn't ask to come."

"Why didn't you tell me?"

"I was afraid you wouldn't come, and I couldn't risk that. Look, I'm not saying you need to embrace her, but just think for a moment about what her life was like and how Aunt Mary wasn't honest with her." I studied Laurie's face, but could not read her expression.

"Does everyone else know?"

I nodded. "Please don't be angry. Ellen has been a cousin we have long neglected, for one thing. Imagine how that felt. I'll admit, when she told me about our father being her father as well, I had a multitude of reactions. I finally prayed about it and hope you will, too."

"Lily, I just don't know what to say. I think I'm more bothered by you all not telling me about it sooner."

"I'm sorry. I just couldn't risk all of us not being together at Christmas."

"I'd better get some sleep," Laurie said as she got up from the bed. "I'm too tired to respond right now."

"I understand. Sleep tight. I love you!" I was too tired to analyze her reaction. As I undressed, my mind was on overload. Richard made my head spin, and Laurie made it go in reverse! Fortunately, I fell quickly into a deep sleep, waking when I heard Lucy crying in the hallway the next morning.

"Knock, knock," Sarah said. "Can we come in?"

"Hold on, Sarah," I said, feeling somewhat disoriented as I hurriedly put on my robe. I opened the door.

"Good morning!" Sarah said cheerfully as she greeted me with Lucy in her arms. "I'm sorry she woke you. She's been fussy all morning."

"Hey, sweet Lucy. Come here to Auntie Lily," I said, taking her in my arms.

Lucy was not having it and turned to Sarah, who stretched out her arms to receive her.

"I'll get you some coffee," Sarah offered. "I want to hear all about last night."

"That's a great idea!" I said as cheerfully as I could. I made myself presentable and quickly brushed my teeth.

"Good morning," Loretta said as she tapped on my door.

"Good morning to you," I replied as I gave her a warm hug.

"There's no sleep when you have a baby around," Loretta warned.

"No problem," I said with a smile. "She is so darned cute!"

"Here you go, Lily," Sarah said as she handed me a mug of coffee. "How is Alex?"

"He's fine, and he really looked after me last night with some of the people I didn't know," I revealed.

"Does he have a girlfriend?" Sarah asked.

"Not that I'm aware of. There were plenty of women there who certainly tried to get his attention."

Just like they'd always done over the years, it didn't take long for Laurie and Lynn to join us as we sat on the bed. There was always so much to laugh or gossip about. Laurie didn't appear to be upset. Carl and Bill were making pancakes, so we all got dressed and met up again at the kitchen table.

"Church is at five thirty tonight," Lynn reminded us. "You'll like hearing Pastor Ron."

"Pastor Ron?" I questioned. "Is that what they call him?"

Lynn nodded.

"Bill is going to stay home with Lucy," Loretta said. "She'll be a handful if we take her."

"Is Marc coming to church?" Sarah asked.

"We'll see. I really don't know," I said. "While you are all here, I want you to sign Ellen's quilt." I pulled it out.

Laurie looked puzzled.

"I got everyone's baby pictures, including Ellen's, to transfer onto the quilt," I explained. "I'd just like everyone to write a short wish for her. As a quilter, I know she will love this."

Everyone looked at Laurie.

"Where did you get my photo?" Laurie asked, looking at me.

"Don't you recognize it? Mom had our photos done when we each turned a year old."

Chapter 83

"It's fabulous, Aunt Lily. Did you do all the quilting?" Sarah asked.

I nodded and smiled.

"I wasn't very cute like the rest of you," Loretta complained. "This is a sweet idea, Lily. You have turned into a real quilter."

Each sister took turns writing a message on the quilt. I was excited to see my project completed—just in the nick of time.

"Okay, ladies. I could use some help in the kitchen for tonight's dinner," Lynn announced.

When Laurie went to her room, I told the others that I thought she'd taken the news about Ellen very well. I was then assigned to make spinach dip, which didn't seem too hard. Working in Lynn's large, modern kitchen was a pleasure! Around three, the doorbell rang. My stomach took a turn, and I prayed to God that all would go well with Ellen's visit. Carl answered the door.

"Come on in, Ellen. Did you have any problems finding

us?"

"Not at all," Ellen responded. "My GPS and I are pretty good friends."

"Ellen, please come in," Lynn said as she gave her a hug. "Let me take your coat."

"How good of you to join us," Loretta said. "You may not remember Sarah, my daughter. Her daughter is napping right now."

"Good to see you," Sarah chirped. "I do remember you somewhat."

"You look just like your mother," Ellen replied.

"You're right, Ellen," I agreed. "I never looked like anyone. I'm so glad you made it. Did you run into any snow?"

"None, thank goodness," Ellen sighed. "You know, it's a little warmer in that part of Kentucky than you are here. Laurie, it's been a while," she said as she walked over to where Laurie was standing.

We watched for a reaction.

"Yes, it has been," Laurie finally responded.

"Lily tells me you have a darling shop in Fish Creek," Ellen said. "I'm friends with someone in Paducah who has a similar shop. She's gotten me hooked on so many oils. I don't know how I managed without them."

Laurie smiled politely.

So far, so good.

"Fish Creek is quite the tourist attraction when it comes to specialty shops," I added. "I think most people would say that Laurie's shop is one of the most popular."

"I'd love to visit sometime," Ellen stated. "Someone I went to school with lives on Washington Island. I'd love to go visit her when it isn't so cold."

ANN HAZELWOOD

"You're welcome to head north anytime," Loretta chimed in. "Green Bay is best in the spring and fall. We have a lot of snow on the ground right now."

I watched Laurie take in the conversation.

"Ellen, would you like some coffee, tea, or wine?" Lynn offered.

"Coffee would be great," Ellen replied. "By the way, the hotel you recommended is quite beautiful. The decorations there are amazing, just like they are here. I noticed the real tree right away. I could smell it as soon as I walked in the door. It's beautiful!"

"We'll see how long it lasts," Carl said.

"I wanted to have a real one since we were all going to be together this year," Lynn explained. "I'm not sure whether we're starting a new tradition. Carl was not at all pleased about it."

"Thanks for letting me join you for church this evening," Ellen said as she looked at me.

"Lynn said we'll like the pastor," I offered. "Ellen, how is your mother?"

"She's fine," she answered, looking uncomfortable with my question. "I think she'll be with friends tomorrow for dinner."

"Well, that's good," I said, dropping the subject.

Laurie remained quiet as the conversation continued. At around five, everyone freshened up for church. I volunteered to take Ellen with me in my car. On the way to church, she asked something that was rather observant on her part.

"Do you think Laurie is okay with me being here?"

I smiled. "Why? Did you sense something?"

"Oh, I could feel something different with her."

280

"Laurie has always been the most sensitive. By the way, a family secret you should know is that Laurie recently had breast cancer. She's fine for now, anyway. It scared us all to death, because there hasn't been any cancer in our immediate family before."

"Oh, I'm so sorry to hear that. Life changes after a scare like that. I'm glad she's okay."

"Just be patient with all of us, Ellen. You were the cousin we never knew, and now you're our half-sister."

"I totally understand. I'm having to examine my feelings as well."

Chapter 84

The historic church was stunningly beautiful, with two gigantic Christmas trees placed on each side of the altar. The red carpet made the whole church look like a Christmas card. In one corner was a very realistic manger scene.

Ellen sat between me and Carl, where she would feel most comfortable. I didn't know how spiritual Ellen was, but when the children's choir sang some traditional Christmas carols, she seemed to join in. Pastor Ron didn't disappoint. His sermon was to the point and not too long, and the topic was the gift of love at Christmas. At the end of the service, the lights went dark and we carried small white lit candles. It was a touching service, full of the true meaning of Christmas.

When we got back to Lynn's house, Bill and Carl built a fire in the fireplace. Carl had filled the dining room table with an elaborate array of finger foods. I couldn't wait to sample them!

Lucy was happy to have a large audience who adored her. Her wobbly new steps were so fun to watch as she made her way to Sarah. I occasionally got a smile from Lucy, but I knew better than to force my desire for hugs and kisses onto her.

Ellen pitched right in as she helped Carl pour glasses of wine for everyone. My cell phone rang. It was Marc.

"I'm sorry I didn't make it to church, Lily," he said apologetically. "Is it okay if I stop by?"

"Absolutely! Carl just offered us our first glass of wine."

"I'll be there in thirty minutes."

I hung up and informed the others that Marc was on his way.

"I'm anxious to meet him, Lily," Ellen commented. "How did you two meet?"

I smiled. "He asked me for directions to a famous baseball player's home on The Hill," I explained. "I call him my baseball friend because we both love the St. Louis Cardinals."

"How special!" Ellen responded.

"Do you have a significant other?" I asked. She shook her head and smiled as if she couldn't care less.

After a short time, I heard the doorbell. Carl went to answer. As soon as Marc entered, Carl put a drink in his hand like he knew exactly what Marc would want.

"Merry Christmas, sweetheart," Marc murmured softly as he gave me a kiss.

I grinned with pleasure. "Marc, I want you to meet Ellen," I said as she observed the two of us.

"Welcome, Ellen. I've heard a lot about you."

"I've heard a little about you as well. I'll bet you will be glad for the Cardinals' spring training to start soon."

He smiled. "How did you know?"

She returned a smile. "We have many St. Louis Cardinals fans in Paducah, Kentucky, where I live," she revealed. "They think nothing of driving three or four hours to go to a game."

Carl tapped his glass to get our attention. "I want to welcome everyone to our home this year. Lynn and I have looked forward to hosting you. We especially want to welcome Ellen into the family. I wasn't sure if the world could handle another Rosenthal sister, but I'm sure everyone will manage. Sarah and Lucy, we are thrilled to have the next generation here to take over for all these older folks. Everyone, please raise your glasses to good health, love, and family. Merry Christmas!"

We cheered and clinked our glasses as we all echoed the toast. Ellen happened to be standing near Laurie, and they made a toast together, which warmed my heart. *Thank you, God.*

Chapter 85

We attacked the food table like we hadn't eaten all day. I did observe Laurie avoiding Ellen to some extent, but I understood. I thought things were going well overall.

"Attention, everyone!" Lynn called out. "I just want to tell you that brunch is scheduled for nine sharp tomorrow. No sleeping in! You won't want to miss Santa's delivery!"

We took that as a signal that the day was ending. Ellen said her brief goodbyes to everyone and said she'd see us in the morning. Marc asked if we could have a little time alone while I was in town. I suggested that the best time would be after dinner tomorrow. Minutes later, Sarah was putting Lucy to bed. Marc, Bill, and Carl were in front of the TV watching a hockey game. It was just us sisters now sitting in front of the fire.

"More wine, anyone?" Lynn offered. "By the way, Lily, congrats on easing in Ellen as one of us. Thanks, Laurie, for making her feel welcome. We've each had to deal with this change in our own ways."

Laurie didn't say anything.

"Nothing will come between us," I assured everyone. "This is us!"

"To us!" Loretta cheered, raising her glass. "Did you all make a Christmas wish for Santa?"

"Susan, my quilt teacher, asked that question last week at our class, and the answers were all over the map," I reported.

"I find I am making more wishes for my granddaughter than for myself these days," Loretta shared.

"Thanks, Mom," Sarah said as she joined us in the room.

"What's your Christmas wish, Sarah?" I asked.

She paused. "I didn't think I would ever wish for a complete family with a white picket fence living in a small town like Augusta, but it sounds perfect," she stated wistfully.

"Ahhh, how sweet!" I replied. No one asked for any details.

"My wish is to remain cancer-free forever," Laurie said more seriously.

"Hear! Hear!" Loretta responded.

"I'm just thankful that Carl and I have kept this marriage together," Lynn confessed. "I guess it would be nice for the two of us to get away more often."

"That's wonderful," Loretta said. "What about you, Lily?"

"As I told my quilter friends, I just wish to keep my head above water with my business. Thank goodness that my freelance writing helps out."

"Lily is so famous," Lynn bragged. "We can all say we knew her when."

That comment made each of us giggle.

"Well, to my surprise, I got a nice bonus last night from my boss at the magazine. I can use it for many things—like a new water heater."

"Our parents would be so proud of you, Lily," Loretta said quietly.

"So, what would Dad think of Ellen being here with us tonight?" Laurie asked in a sarcastic tone.

"We really don't know for sure, Laurie, but he should be grateful that we looked beyond his poor judgement regarding his affair," I retorted. "We did what's right for Ellen, which is more than he did. The way Aunt Mary kept Ellen away from the rest of our family was just wrong."

"Don't you understand that, Laurie?" Loretta asked.

"I don't know," she responded. "I never did like Aunt Mary like the rest of you did. I don't care if I ever see her again."

"We may not," Lynn replied. "None of us got Christmas cards from her like we always have."

The guys joined us now that the hockey game had ended. Marc said a sweet goodbye, and everyone else turned in for the evening.

Chapter 86

I couldn't believe I was waking up to another Christmas morning. Before I joined everyone else, I took some quiet moments to thank God for a house filled with love and family. I ran through the day's schedule in my mind. First, we would enjoy a light brunch and then open presents. Lucy's birthday party with cake and ice cream was at two. At seven, a turkey dinner was planned. After that, Marc and I would leave to celebrate Christmas at his place. I would have to say goodbye to my family tonight and would leave for Augusta tomorrow morning.

I showered and dressed before joining the others already gathered around the Christmas tree. Lucy was squealing in delight at the unwrapped toys sitting under the tree for her.

Lynn's brunch menu was carefully selected, and each dish was beautifully presented. On our glass plates we enjoyed muffin-sized breakfast casseroles, pastries from The Hill, and glass goblets of yogurt and fruit. Carl made eggnog and mimosas for us to try. I craved my usual hot cup of coffee to get me started.

Lucy had already acquired a baby doll that Laurie had given her. She was clutching it tightly as she toddled around the room. Marc and Ellen arrived at the door at the same time. They were all smiles and came bearing gifts.

"Merry Christmas morning!" Marc said as he kissed me on the cheek.

"And a Merry Christmas morning to you as well!" I responded. "We've already had food and drink, so help yourselves. It will have to last until the big birthday party at two."

"Well, you won't have to tell me twice," Marc said, patting his stomach. After filling his plate, he joined me on the couch to watch all the action.

"Good morning, good morning!" Carl called above the noise. "Keep on eating, but as you can tell from this Santa hat on my head, I will be the one passing out gifts this morning. From the looks of things, we may be here quite a while!"

"I'm so glad Aunt Lynn didn't hire a professional Santa like she first talked about doing," Sarah said, sounding relieved. "Lucy freaks out when she sees one."

I thought of our cool Santa in Augusta and how the children loved him. I also wondered what my Augusta friends were doing this Christmas morning.

"In addition to Lucy, we have a new guest this year. I think Ellen should receive the first gift," Carl announced.

Her eyes widened in surprise as if she hadn't expected to get anything. "Well, this is special!" she said as she began to unwrap her gift. Lucy made a beeline to help her, so Ellen took the pretty ribbon and draped it over Lucy's shoulders. I kept my eye on Laurie as Ellen opened her gift. "A quilt?" she questioned. "Seriously? Oh, my God. Look at this!" She carefully unfolded the quilt. "How did you get my photo? These pictures are adorable! Who made this?"

Everyone looked at me.

"Lily, this is really special," she said before reading anything on the quilt.

"Read each of the wishes!" Lynn urged.

Ellen slowly read each block aloud with emotion in her voice. "I don't know what to say, other than thank you so very much!" she finally responded. "I can't tell you how much this means to me."

"Well, things are getting way too serious, so how about this big box here that has Lucy's name on it?" Carl suggested, placing it in front of Lucy.

Everyone cheered. The gift was a darling white rocking chair. Lucy immediately sat in it with her new baby doll. I couldn't help but think of Rosie and her rocking chair.

Suddenly, it was as if gifts were being passed in every direction. I told Carl that my siblings' presents had to be given out in unison so they could all be opened at the same time. He happily obliged, and their reactions to the hand-knitted sweaters were priceless. Sarah looked a little disappointed that she didn't receive one, but I told her to be patient. Evidently, I chose the proper color for each one, and Loretta admitted that she'd tried to learn to knit but had failed. Ellen commented on how rare it was to find hand-knitted sweaters these days. My sisters were also very touched when they opened the Door County ornaments that I had purchased for them. I noticed that my family had generously included Marc on their gift-buying lists and that he was receiving gifts of wine and Cardinals memorabilia.

Chapter 87

Ellen got up from her seat and handed each of us sisters and Sarah a gift bag.

"Now, I don't know everyone's tastes, so you're not going to hurt my feelings if you trade with one another," Ellen explained.

"Okay, okay," I agreed, as did the others.

We each opened our bags and pulled out wallhangings that were about thirty inches square. They were gorgeous! There was no question that I was keeping mine, since it was done in red and white. It was a modern version of a Basket block and had buttons here and there for embellishment. How Ellen knew Laurie loved aqua was beyond me. I could tell Laurie loved her gift without her saying a word. Loretta's quilt was more traditional, and that was so like her. Lynn's was black and white, which was a color scheme she often used in her artwork. Sarah's was very colorful and was adorned with buttons, which was perfect for her. I watched Ellen's face, and I thought she was pleased with our reactions.

It was Sarah's turn to open my gifts to her. She loved

the knitted items, but couldn't stop admiring the button wall quilt. She then shared with everyone the story of how I'd bought her a jar of buttons when she'd visited me in Augusta.

"Aunt Lily, you know me so well," Sarah said, giving me a hug. "I love Lucy's little sweater set. Thank you so much."

"The maker of these sweaters wants to open a knitting shop in Augusta," I shared. "I think she'll do very well, judging from everyone's reactions."

"I do, too," Sarah agreed.

The gifts I received were delightful and personal. Lynn gave me hand-painted wine glasses that depicted the wine country. I told her she needed to make some to sell. Loretta made me a wonderful red-and-green Christmas table runner. Laurie brought my lavender oil as I had requested, and also gave me a darling little shelf to put in my bathroom for all my oils. In between the excitement, Lucy kept stealing the show with her sweet antics.

"Is it my imagination, or are you wearing a new, very expensive ring?" Lynn asked.

I smiled. "Carrie Mae gave this to me before I left," I explained. "It was her mother's. Can you believe it?"

"That has got to be worth a pretty penny," Loretta remarked.

"It is very wowsy!" Sarah laughed. "Please tell her hello for me."

"I will." I nodded. "She's always asking about you and Lucy."

When the excitement calmed down a bit, Carl and Lynn went into the kitchen to do prep work for dinner. Marc and I were pretty comfy right in front of the fire.

"Are you wondering why you haven't gotten a gift from

me?" Marc asked as he squeezed my hand.

"Well, I guess you're wondering the same thing."

He grinned. "It makes for a pretty exciting rest of the evening, doesn't it?" he teased.

"I can't wait!" I said, squeezing his hand.

I was pleased to see that Ellen was pitching in by helping Lynn set the dining room table. Laurie was busy entertaining Lucy, despite Sarah wanting her to take a nap before her little party. My phone rang. It was Holly. "You're back?" I asked immediately.

"Yes, this morning. I am so glad to be home. I can't wait to tell you all the details of my weird experience."

"Would you like to come over and join us this evening?"

"No, thanks. I just want to go to bed and forget everything. I'm going to fix myself a gin and tonic and wish myself a Merry Christmas."

I burst into laughter. "Merry Christmas to you, my friend. I love you!"

"I love you too, Lily."

I hung up and looked at Marc. I shook my head in disbelief.

"She'll be fine, Lily." He paused and then said, "So tell me all about the magazine party."

Chapter 88

I didn't want to go into a lot of detail, but I told Marc I'd gone with Alex so I'd feel more comfortable with some of the people I didn't know. Marc didn't react. I then told him about receiving a bonus, and he seemed very pleased about that. As if on cue, Lynn interrupted us to say that she had taken the liberty of inviting Alex to dinner.

"I'd assumed so," Marc replied with a smile.

I went to the kitchen to refill my coffee cup and noticed that Laurie and Ellen were no longer around. I went over to Loretta, who was feeding Lucy, and interrupted her. "Did you notice who is missing here?" I asked quietly.

"Yes, let's hope that's a good thing," Loretta said with a sigh. "I don't think they've left the house."

I could tell that Sarah was trying to get some time alone with me, but it was nearly impossible with so many people around. Loretta brought out Lucy's cake and put it on the kitchen table.

"Due to the scheduling of a desperately-needed nap, we're going to celebrate a little early," Loretta announced as she tied balloons on the back of Lucy's highchair. That was the signal for everyone to gather around.

"Is everyone ready to sing?" Sarah asked. "Okay, on the count of one, two, and three."

We all joined in, and I noticed Ellen and Laurie were now with us. Lucy was quite amused and clapped her hands as we sang. Out of nowhere, more presents for Lucy appeared. This really increased her determination to get out of the chair. When Sarah put a small chocolate cake on her highchair tray, her right hand immediately grabbed the top layer for a healthy bite. From there, her hand went to her hair and cheeks. It was a sight to behold, and we laughed heartily. Everyone pulled out their phones and began taking pictures. Sarah was a good sport, and I was pleased that Loretta was letting her be the mom.

Marc went over to Lucy to playfully snatch a bite of her cake. Lucy moved quickly to smear a gob of chocolate on his hand. Marc grinned and looked at me. As he walked my way, he dipped his finger into the chocolate on his hand and put it to my mouth. Everyone laughed, including Lucy.

Sarah wiped Lucy's hands so she could open her presents. I was impressed that even Marc had showed up with an assortment of bath toys in a plastic tub-like basket. I teased him about his choice, and he said a salesperson had suggested that he purchase some fun bath toys.

Loretta was slicing a bigger cake for the rest of us to enjoy. Everyone stayed in the kitchen with Lucy and gathered around the island as I poured coffee and tea for us.

"I love the way this family seems to enjoy food twenty-four hours a day," Ellen joked. "I haven't had this much food in a long, long time."

"Yes, and the Rosenthals have a way of showing it, too," Loretta said, patting her stomach.

"Like here!" Lynn chimed in, patting her rear end.

We laughed. After a big enough mess was made, Sarah took Lucy out of the highchair. It was time for her nap.

"Can we take a little walk?" Marc asked. "We can walk off a few of these calories. It's not too cold for you, is it?"

"No. That's a great idea," I said as I went to get my coat.

"Have fun, you two," Carl said as we neared the door.

Marc put his arm around my neck to keep me warm.

"This is such a beautiful neighborhood," I commented as we walked.

Marc nodded. "It's just nice to get away from all the chatter for a while."

"I think Carl and Lynn are doing well now, don't you?" I asked Marc. "Did you ever wish for a life like theirs?"

"Honestly?" Marc stopped walking.

I stopped walking and faced him.

Marc said, "Honestly, I don't think it was ever Lynn's dream, but it was Carl's. He seems to always want to give the impression of being very well-off and successful."

I nodded in agreement. "Lynn used to be envious of me in my little apartment on The Hill," I recalled. "She loved my porch and my being so involved in the neighborhood."

"Do you wish you were back there sometimes, or have you found the same feeling in Augusta?"

We began to walk again as I said, "I can be myself in Augusta, and I also like being part of a more artistic community. The Plein Air Festival is so impressive. Artists come from all over the United States. There's a gorgeous scene to paint in any direction you look. Lynn came out for it last year, and I think Ellen would love it as well."

"I really like Ellen," Marc said as we crossed the street. "Things seem to be going well with her visit."

I nodded and smiled, feeling a profound sense of relief that his observation seemed to hold true so far.

Chapter 89

"I think Ellen and Laurie are bonding. I hope to get a girl trip organized and travel to Paducah to see where Ellen lives. Perhaps that can happen after the New Year."

As we got closer to the house, my phone rang.

"Merry Christmas!" a familiar voice greeted.

It was Butler. "Oh, and the same to you!" I responded as I walked slower.

"How was Christmas morning with your family?"

"It was kind of wild, as we celebrated a one-year-old's birthday as well," I explained.

"It sounds like fun. Are you going back to Augusta tomorrow?"

"I'm not sure," I said slowly. I felt Marc looking at me. "It depends on when everyone here leaves."

"I understand. I want to visit with you about something. Can I give you a call in a couple of days when you get back?"

"Sure. That would be fine."

"Enjoy your family."

"I will. Take care," I replied. I hung up with a deep sense

of relief.

"Is everything okay? You looked a bit frazzled."

"Oh, it's just someone who wants to set up an appointment," I explained.

We went inside, and Carl immediately got Marc's attention by showing him a football game on TV. I went into my room to gather my thoughts and freshen up for dinner. A knock came at the door.

"Aunt Lily, can we talk for a minute?" Sarah said as she entered.

"Sure, come in."

"Aren't you interested in what's been happening with Lucy's father?"

"Sure I am. I hope it's good."

"It's very good! He's asked his wife for a divorce."

"Oh?"

"Well, I guess I really have Lucy to thank for that. He loves her so much and wants to be with her more."

"He wants to be with you as well, right?"

"Yes, of course! I want us to be a family." She corrected herself by saying, "We want to be a family."

Sarah had looked a bit uncomfortable with my last question. "Does he want to marry you?"

"In time, but first things first, I want him out of their house. I even suggested that he move in with me, but he didn't think that was a good idea right now."

"I hope things work out, but I caution you that he should do it because he loves you, not because of Lucy."

"Of course! Lucy calls him Dada. It's so cute."

"So, your mom and dad still don't know about him?"

"They may, but they never question me anymore, which

I appreciate."

"If you want to come back to Augusta for a while to think things through again, the guest house is still available."

"I would love that, but with this job right now, I can't afford to."

In the background, I heard Lucy crying to get out of her crib. "Somebody's looking for you. You'd better go. I'm glad you brought me up to date, and I hope things continue to work out."

Thanks, Aunt Lily," Sarah said, giving me a hug.

I closed the door, thinking how simple my life was compared to hers. My mind then went to Butler. I knew his excuse to talk to me about something was just a way to see me again. I didn't want to lose him as a friend, but I had to get the message across that I wasn't interested in dating him.

I dressed in black slacks and a red sweater. I accented it with a Christmas scarf I'd brought with me. I looked festive, yet casual. When I came into the living room, I was pleasantly surprised to see that Alex had arrived. "Merry Christmas, Alex!" I said, giving him a hug. "Did Santa come to see you this morning?"

"Yes, he actually did, even considering that I haven't been a very good boy," he joked.

"Welcome, Alex," Carl greeted him. "I just made some eggnog. Are you game?"

"I'll take some. If I remember correctly, you use a generous amount of good whiskey in that."

Everyone laughed.

"Ah, you remembered," Carl chuckled.

"Lily, what would you like?" Marc asked, going behind the bar.

"I'll have the same cab I saw you pouring for Lynn," I answered.

"Everyone, please remember that we will be serving champagne for dinner," Lynn informed the group.

"I brought some Wisconsin cheese and crackers," Loretta offered as she walked by with a platter heaped with different varieties of each.

Chapter 90

I sat down next to Marc and told him how much Carrie Mae and Betty had enjoyed the cookies from Main Street.

"I thought you said you were having cherry pie."

"It disappeared, so we had to settle for just cookies."

"Someone ate it?" He looked at me quizzically.

"You're not going to want to hear the answer, so I'm sorry you brought it up."

"You brought it up, not me."

His remark surprised me.

"How did it disappear?" he asked.

"We found it in Doc's office."

He gave me an odd look. "Is this a concern of yours, or are you going to blame it on your spiritual friends?"

"I'm not concerned. Let's just drop the subject." I was taken aback by the sudden negative turn of our conversation.

"So, Alex, what was it like to take the famous writer Lily Rosenthal to the party?" Marc asked sarcastically.

Alex chuckled and answered kindly, "She stole the show, as you might imagine. Did she tell you she left the party with a bonus? She's certainly caught the attention of the management there."

Marc looked at me evenly and said slowly, "She did tell me that she received a bonus."

"I'm sure Alex's check is in the mail," I joked.

"Marc, can you give me a hand with these logs for the fire?" Carl asked from across the room.

"Don't get me in trouble with Marc," I whispered to Alex while Marc assisted Carl. "He doesn't need to know anything about Richard's behavior."

"Whatever you say," Alex responded, seemingly amused by my discomfort.

"Oh, Alex, good to see you!" Sarah exclaimed as she entered the room.

"You too, Sarah," Alex returned, giving her a hug. "Where is Lucy?"

"She's still napping, thank goodness!" Sarah said with relief. "She woke up briefly and fell back asleep. Hopefully she'll be in a good mood for dinner."

Sarah quickly took over the conversation. For someone who had someone else in mind for her own future, she sure did flirt and turn on the charm when Alex was around. I'd witnessed that behavior before. I left the two talking and went into the kitchen to see what I could do to help.

"The turkey smells divine!" I said to Lynn.

"It won't be long," she responded as she gave it another basting. "If you and Ellen can fill the water glasses and light the candles, that would be good."

Ellen jumped at the chance to help, and I grabbed the crystal pitcher to pour water.

"Do you always have a big Christmas dinner like this?"

Ellen asked.

"For as long as I can remember," I said with a nod. "I've always loved everything about it—except the sweet potatoes."

"I've never liked them either!" Ellen agreed. "After Dad died, we didn't make any fuss at all about Christmas dinner. Many things were different after that."

"I understand." I nodded. "That's what's good about having siblings. We've all continued the traditions. Loretta, being the oldest, made sure of it. We girls made a pact that we'd never be apart on Christmas. We try to get together for our birthdays when we can. Laurie and I always shared the same parties and cake because our birthdays are both in June."

"That's special," Ellen said wistfully. "So you never had disagreements or were jealous of each other?"

I smiled. "I can't say it's been perfect, but I don't recall anything serious. When one of us is happy, we're all happy, and when one of us is hurt, we all hurt."

"That's beautiful!" Ellen said, looking away.

"I'm sorry, Ellen. I wasn't being very sensitive," I said softly.

"No, don't be sorry," she said, looking at me again. "You've been very fortunate."

"Hey! How about some Christmas music, Carl?" Lynn requested from the kitchen. "I think you need to turn off the TV. Dinner is almost ready."

"Consider it done, sweetheart." Carl saluted in jest.

Chapter 91

When Lucy woke up shortly before dinner, we mentioned what good timing that was. At least she let us know that she was hungry. Sarah had changed Lucy's outfit. She was now wearing a darling green velvet dress with a red bow in her hair. Everyone went crazy over her, including Ellen.

Lynn had arranged an elaborate and elegant table setting. It was nice to experience this kind of dining occasionally. The fire was roaring, and Christmas music was playing in the background. I was pleased to see that Lynn had set place cards by each plate. I was placed between Marc and Ellen. On the other side of Ellen was Alex, which was an excellent idea. I was sure Sarah would have liked to have been placed there, but she needed to be next to Lucy in her highchair.

After the rest of us were seated, Carl entered the dining room holding the biggest roasted turkey that I had ever seen! It was on our family's silver platter, which had held many previous turkeys. Everyone applauded as he set the platter right in front of his place setting so he could carve it. The smell was heavenly, and mouths were watering.

"I've asked Loretta if she would say grace today," Lynn announced. "She's been the matriarch of the Rosenthals since Mother passed and has quite a gift of spiritual understanding."

"Oh!" Loretta responded. "Bill actually does it better than me, but I'll give it a go and keep it brief. Please join hands."

Ellen was observing every detail and seemed somewhat uneasy as she took my hand and Alex's.

"Thank you, Lord, for bringing our family together to celebrate your birthday on this blessed Christmas," Loretta began. "We especially welcome Ellen to our table this year, and we all give thanks for our many blessings. In your name we all say, amen."

"Amen," everyone said in unison.

Ellen squeezed my hand, and I leaned over to give her a slight embrace. She was touched and at a loss for words. "That was lovely, Loretta. Thank you," she said quietly.

"Pass your plates and say whether white or dark meat is your preference," Carl instructed.

As Alex engaged in conversation, I looked over at Marc, who fit in perfectly with our family. As we exchanged looks, the earlier uncomfortableness between us disappeared. Gazing around the table, I saw nothing but happiness. Lucy's appetite kept her busy, so Sarah could enjoy the meal as well.

Marc was the first to toast the host and hostess for the dinner. As always, his comments were quite polished. We all clinked our glasses and continued eating. Minutes later, Alex held up his glass of champagne to make a toast. "I thank you all for including me in this special dinner," he began. "I guess I really have to thank my partner in crime, Lily, for without her, this invitation may not have occurred."

"Hear, hear!" everyone agreed.

Marc added, "Here's to Lily!"

We were about to have dessert when Ellen tapped her glass. Everyone was silent except Lucy, who was busy playing with her food. "I'd like to make a toast to the Rosenthal family," Ellen began. "I'd like to thank Carl and Lynn especially for inviting me to this special occasion and providing such a great meal. I thank you with all my heart. This has been the best Christmas ever. Merry Christmas to you all!"

We clinked our glasses again and said Merry Christmas to one another.

"That was so sweet," I said to Ellen.

Carl and Lynn jumped up to take our plates as they prepared to bring in dessert.

"I will never forget this moment," Ellen said softly.

Chapter 92

While the dishes were being cleared, I overheard various conversations. There were memories of Christmases past and wishes for the New Year.

"What were Meg's plans for today?" I asked Marc.

"I talked to her last night, and she was going to a friend's house in Brooklyn," he explained.

"Is there any sign of a significant other in her life?"

"None that she is willing to share with me," he said, shaking his head.

"I hope I can spend more time with her the next time she visits."

"That would be great."

I couldn't believe the extravagant presentation of desserts Lynn had just carried into the dining room! Her tray held an assortment of different pies, and behind her came Carl with a tray of cookies and various cakes. Even though I was completely stuffed, I felt compelled to have a traditional piece of pumpkin pie with whipped cream. Marc chose a piece of cheesecake with chocolate chips inside. There was much groaning in delight around the table. After dessert, I lingered at the table with leftover champagne and hot coffee.

"If you all would like to join me around the fire, I happen to know that Loretta and Bill could lead us in a Christmas carol or two," Carl suggested, teasing both of them.

Bill and Loretta immediately shook their heads and declined, laughing.

"I could ask you all to sing 'Jingle Bells,' because Lucy goes crazy and claps every time she hears it," Sarah suggested as she freed Lucy from her highchair. As we left the table, we brought our dishes to the kitchen, despite Carl urging us to leave them on the table. Some chose to sit by the fire, but it was then that I noticed Ellen looking as if she was preparing to leave.

Ellen went around and thanked each person and extended an invitation for them to come to Paducah. When she got to Laurie, she took both of Laurie's hands in hers and then gave her a hug. It appeared that the two had bonded. Ellen and Alex both left at the same time.

"Marc, its nine, so I'm ready to leave if you are," I suggested. "I'll get my things. I have everything ready to go."

"Sounds great. I'll say my goodbyes in the meantime," he replied.

It was now time for me to say goodbye to my family. I couldn't squeeze Lynn hard enough for creating such a perfect Christmas for all of us. Loretta, Bill, Laurie, Sarah, and Lucy were all lined up to say goodbye. As always, there were some tears. We always worried about when we would see each other again. Carl jokingly passed out tissues to elevate the mood. Marc stood by solemnly. I hugged little Lucy, hoping I would see her again very soon. Oh, what I wouldn't do to have that little sweetie around more often! Marc also said goodbye to her, and to my surprise, she gave him a hug, pressing her chubby cheek next to his.

I left with Marc and didn't look back as I went to my car. He helped put my things in the car and then went to his vehicle. The plan was to meet back at his place in St. Charles.

On the drive, I replayed the last three days in my mind. Christmas was nearly over. Only hours remained, and those few hours would be spent with Marc.

I arrived at his place first. When he drove into the large garage, I motioned for him to help me with my things. When he saw the large wrapped gift, he was puzzled. He lifted it up and was further surprised by the weight and awkwardness of the piece.

"Will this fit under your Christmas tree?" I asked, smiling.

Chapter 93

Once we got the gift inside, Marc placed it on the living room carpet. There was no sign of a Christmas tree. After we took off our coats, Marc asked what I would like to drink.

"I would like amaretto on the rocks, like you made for me once before."

"Let me turn on this fire so you can get warm and comfortable."

I sat down on the comfy leather couch that I loved and noticed that there was a very large box wrapped up nearby. It was definitely someone's Christmas gift. Maybe it was mine! When Marc came back into the room, he noticed my curiosity. He sat down my drink, lifted the big box, and gave it to me.

"Well, it's not a kitchen appliance or you wouldn't be able to lift it that easily," I guessed. "You open your gift first."

"Well, I don't need an ironing board, so I guess I can rule that out," Marc joked.

When the last piece of wrapping paper fell off, he was clearly puzzled. "Didn't you want a board with holes in it?" I joked. "It stands alone, see?"

"Okay, I give," he relented.

"It's a wine bottle holder," I explained.

"Well, that's pretty cool! Let me get a bottle and try it."

He took one of the wine bottles from his stash and placed it in one of the holes. "Very, very clever! I like this very much!" He leaned over and gave me a kiss.

"I'm glad you like it. I purchased it from a gallery in Augusta. Vic meets some very clever artists from around the country."

"Honestly, it's a piece of art even without the wine bottles."

"I agree. You are very hard to buy for, you know."

"It's your turn."

"Big is best! That's what we would always say when we were kids. Did you wrap this?"

He nodded. "I know it's not perfect, but it was a challenge! It's what's inside that counts, right?"

I began the tedious job of unwrapping, only to get to a smaller and then even smaller box. The boxes and wrapping paper were piling up on the floor as we giggled. "Okay, I know there must be a method to your madness!"

"Keep going!" Marc said as he continued to clear the trash.

I got down to a box of about six inches square, and there was a smaller box inside that rattled. The final box was black velvet. My heart sank as I thought that it might be a ring. I took a deep breath before I opened the small box. I was speechless when I saw a gorgeous pearl ring surrounded by beautiful diamonds.

"Don't worry, Lily Girl. I'm not getting down on my knee

to ask you anything. This ring had your name on it. I know you love pearls. I also know you would have killed me if this ring meant anything else."

"Marc, this is the most beautiful ring I have ever seen!" I said as I put it on.

"Well, I see it has competition from someone else who loves you, but this one is from someone who is *in love with you*," he said quietly, looking into my eyes.

"Marc, you are so special. I will cherish this ring forever. Thank you!"

"I can't ask for anything more than that. I do hope you wear and enjoy it more than the bracelet I gave you."

I ignored that comment. "I'm so sorry that my gift wasn't more personal."

"You know I like good art. That was a very creative gesture."

"This has really been an amazing Christmas," I said, taking a sip of my drink. "I wish I could stop the clock and feel this moment forever."

Marc grinned and kissed my forehead. "It's up to us make that happen," he whispered softly.

"I can't believe all the trouble you went to wrapping all of this!"

"It wouldn't have been as much fun if I just handed you a tiny box."

I laughed, agreeing with him.

It was then my turn to hand Mark a small wrapped package.

"What's this?" he asked, surprised.

"Just a little something for my baseball man," I teased. "Open it."

ANN HAZELWOOD

Marc carefully unwrapped the present and opened the box lid. Reaching in, he gasped in surprise when he saw the beautiful snow globe I had purchased for him in the gift shop of the National Baseball Hall of Fame and Museum. "Lily..." his voice trailed off.

Our eyes met, and I knew that it was the perfect gift.

As we continued our conversation throughout the evening, I kept looking at my ring. In a sense, it was a ring of commitment from Marc. It was comforting that the two of us were on the same page when it came to marriage.

Chapter 94

The next morning, I had a sick feeling knowing that my family was heading home. I, too, needed to head home to Augusta. I could tell that Marc was ready to get back to work after two days with the Rosenthal sisters.

"What would you like to do today?" Marc asked as he poured me a cup of coffee.

"Am I dreaming? Am I on vacation?"

"You could be."

"Nice of you to say, but neither one of us can afford that luxury. I feel guilty enough missing some days of Christmas sales."

"There will always be sales, but not always a family like yours to spend time with."

"You are so right."

"I see you still have your ring on."

"Yes. I love it so much."

"I'm glad. Now see if you approve of the blueberry muffins I just took out of the oven."

"They smell wonderful!" Just then, my cell phone rang. It

ANN HAZELWOOD

was Loretta.

"I hope I didn't interrupt your morning," she stated. "I just wanted to tell you that we're about to board the plane. We had a wonderful time!"

"Oh, I'm so glad you came. Marc and I are just having coffee and talking about what a wonderful Christmas it was."

"In my opinion, Ellen fit in very well."

"Has Laurie said much about it?"

"No, which is a good sign. By the way, your check to Sarah was very generous. Your sweet little quilt and knitted scarf and hat would have been sufficient."

"That's what aunties are for."

"Well, we have to get on the plane now. I love you, baby sister!"

"I love you, too. Let's all touch base in the New Year."

I hung up with a frown and looked at Marc. I wanted to tear up again.

"It's okay if you want to cry one more time." He kissed me on the cheek.

We chatted at his kitchen table for another hour before I needed to get on my way.

"Will Alex have his usual New Year's Eve party this year?" Marc asked when I put on my coat.

"I hope so. Do you have a date yet?"

He smiled. "I was hoping this gal I know in Augusta would ask me out, but she hasn't said anything."

"I'll check it out, and I'm glad you're free!"

After hugs and kisses, I drove away from St. Charles. As I drove along, I had fine memories to think about, a generous bonus to spend, and a gorgeous ring on my finger. What more could I want? The air was terribly cold and windy, but there was no chance of snow. The traffic was light, and as I drove into wine country, I looked forward to arriving at Lily Girl's Quilts and Antiques. When I got to Augusta, I decided to stop at Carrie Mae's shop first. Her sign indicated that she was open. She would want to know that I had returned.

"Welcome back, Lily," Carrie Mae said as she sat by her woodstove. "How was your Christmas?"

"It was great!" I said, taking her hands. "It will take me a long time to fill you in."

"Is that ring on your finger what I think it is?"

"It's not, but I think I'm going steady with the baseball man. He's quite generous."

She chuckled.

"How is Betty?"

"She's doing better than me. My arthritis has been killing me. My body's giving out, Lily."

"Now, don't talk like that. You stand all day on these concrete floors, which is taking a toll on you. Why don't you hire Korine to come in and work? She knows this place backwards and forwards from helping you all these years. That way, if you didn't feel like coming downstairs, you wouldn't have to. Don't tell me you can't afford it."

She looked surprised at my suggestion. "You act like you know what you're talking about," she retorted, smiling impishly.

"I'm serious. I know how much this place means to you. No one would suggest that you give it up. What does your daughter have to say?"

"Nothing. Really nothing. She has no interest in this place."

"Carrie Mae, you know these things have a way of working out!"

She shook her head.

Chapter 95

"Have you been busy?" I asked Carrie Mae.

"Not really. I suppose it will pick up after the holidays."

"Is there anything I can do for you while I'm here? By the way, everyone loved the ring you gave me. That was so generous."

"Honey, you have become like a daughter to me. I'll think about your idea regarding using Korine."

"Good. If you're okay, then I think I'll head home."

"Thanks for checking on me, hon."

As I got in my car, I thought of Bertie and how she would say similar things to me. I hadn't checked on Bertie quite enough. One day Harry and I found her dead. We had taken her competence for granted. There was probably a fine line about staying independent as one ages. We want someone to care enough to know how we're doing, but we want to have a final say about our activities and freedoms. Betty had enough of her own problems that kept her from watching Carrie Mae too carefully. She was fortunate to have Ted helping her almost every day.

When I walked into my house, it felt very cold. I took the first load of my things upstairs and turned on the fireplace to take the chill out. My poor Christmas tree looked very dry and forlorn. Ted would have to remove it soon. I turned the tree lights on for the very last time. As I began to unpack, I put Ellen's quilt aside to hang somewhere in my bedroom. As the house warmed up, I was glad to be home once again.

My landline rang. It was Karen.

"Welcome back!" she greeted me. "Carrie Mae said you were gone for the holidays."

"Yes, I had family in from Wisconsin, so we gathered at my sister's house in St. Louis."

"I'm calling to tell you that Buzz and I are having a New Year's Eve party. We wanted to include you and your significant other."

"How nice of you. Every year, I have an invitation to my friend Alex's party, but he hasn't mentioned it, so perhaps we can make it. I'll let you know."

"Wonderful! I'm hoping that we have a large turnout."

"Knowing your reputation for entertaining, I'm sure you will." I smiled when I hung up. I realized I was an established person in the community. Now I began to wonder about Buzz and Karen's friend Anthony. Would he be there?

I went downstairs to make myself a cup of hot tea, and something felt different. When I got to the kitchen, I opened the bottom cabinet to get a new bottle of dish detergent. The open space was hard to ignore. All of Doc's things were gone! Even the large plastic container was missing. In a panic, I started opening cabinet doors to make sure I wasn't mistaken. I even looked on the back porch. Had his things gone to his office? Was I losing my mind?

I quickly put on my coat and ran to open Doc's office. The only thing I saw was Santa's chair and the rug I had placed it on. The sprays of cedar on the ceiling were falling and needed to be removed, just like my Christmas tree. I closed the door, feeling sad and bewildered. Where else could I look? I didn't want to tell the Dinner Detectives until I had searched everywhere. There was only one place left to look, and that was the basement. I would likely conduct that search alone.

I sat down to think it all through. It was obvious that Doc was not happy about me collecting his things. Funny how Rosie never made me feel that way. She was my friend and companion here in this house.

My phone rang. It was Alex. "Alex!"

"Yeah, baby, what's up? Are you back in Augusta?"

"I am. I'm having tea in front of my Christmas tree as if Christmas never happened."

"Whatever. I'm just calling to thank you for including me in your Christmas dinner."

"It was special, wasn't it?"

Chapter 96

"Should I be so bold as to ask if you are having a New Year's Eve party this year?" I asked Alex.

"I haven't said anything because I've gotten an invitation to go elsewhere. I really want to go to it. Are you upset?"

"Of course not! We've had some great parties at your place. What was so special about this invitation?"

"Mindy's parents are coming in from Minnesota. Did I tell you that her dad owns a couple of small publishing houses? Well, they are having a big bash at the Ritz Carlton, and nothing can get my attention more than that."

"My heavens, I guess not. You hadn't told me that little detail about Mindy. Now you're meeting her parents. Have you been holding out on me?"

He laughed. "You know me better than that. It's a big deal for her, and it could be a big deal for me as well."

"Yeah, like marrying into a publishing family! How sweet is that? I get it."

"Lily, I guess you are forcing me to say that I don't love Mindy. She's been a bit more fun lately, but I'm not attached to her in any way."

"That is only your opinion, Mr. Alex! She's going to lure you in with this ammunition, so be careful!"

"So will you and Marc find something else to do?"

"Well, just today I got an invitation from a couple out here in Augusta, so we'll see if Marc will be willing to come."

"Then it all worked out. Hey, don't you have a busy day planned for spending that big bonus check?"

"Okay, Alex, our conversation is done."

I was more than a little disappointed that Alex was not having his party. I was concerned about Alex being sucked into a relationship that had a career bonus to it. Alex loved to name-drop and was easily impressed by successful people.

Now I just needed to contact Marc about Karen and Buzz's party invitation. Someone was knocking on my front door, so I went down to answer it. I saw that it was Betty.

"Welcome home!" she said, holding something in a bag.

"I'm glad to be back. Come on in. Did you have a good Christmas?"

"Sure did. How about you?"

"It's always good to see my siblings. What smells so good in that bag?"

"Well, it's your late Christmas gift. I kept one of my homemade coffeecakes for you, as well as some of my banana bread that everyone seems to like."

"Oh, this is perfect. I didn't bring home a bite of anything from our family gathering. Thank you so much! Would you like a cup of coffee or tea?"

"Oh, I don't want to keep you. I thought your shop would be open."

"I suppose it should be, but I've been unpacking and

tending to other matters."

"Like what?" Betty asked, concerned.

"All of Doc's things have disappeared from under my kitchen sink. I've looked everywhere."

Betty's face looked grim. "What do you make of that?"

"I don't know. I even looked in his office and didn't find anything."

"What if they went to the basement?"

"I don't think I want to find out."

"Well, take Ted with you. I'll pass!"

"He won't appreciate that offer either. That reminds me. Will you tell him to come and take my tree away?"

"Will do. Good luck with the hunt!"

"Thanks for the goodies, Betty. You are such a sweetheart."

Chapter 97

The next day, I decided to get back to work. It was cloudy with a threat of snow. I went ahead and put out Rosie's rocker and draped a yellow-and-white Snail's Trail quilt over the back. What I wouldn't give to have yellow tulips to display with it.

"Good morning, Ms. Lily," I heard from afar.

"My goodness! You're back!"

Snowshoes gave a chuckle.

"I've missed you!" I gave him a little hug, which he awkwardly accepted.

"I guess it's good to be back," he said, shaking his head. "I sure got tired of sitting around. I really miss the Mrs., but she isn't coming back."

"I know it's been hard, but I'll bet she'd want you to get back to work. Before you know it, you'll be back in your garden, too."

"Yeah, I get up early from habit, so I decided that I may as well get back to work."

"You are making many folks happy. How was your

Christmas?"

"I made it through. I'm glad you're still here, too. Thanks for coming to the funeral."

I smiled and waved to him as he went on his way. I hoped that I had been an encouragement to him.

Ted pulled up in his new truck and said he had cleared his day to help me with the tree and whatever else I needed. "I brought this drop cloth to put under your tree to carry it out to the sinkhole, so we won't have needles everywhere."

"Good idea. Doc's office needs the cedar cleaned out of there, too, so I'll let you get to work."

As I was doing some dusting in the shop, I got a call from Marc. "I'm on my way to Kansas City to get a deposition. I'll be back tomorrow."

"Great, I'm glad that you let me know."

"Did you get unpacked?"

"I did, and now I have Ted over here taking down all the mess from Christmas. I'm glad you called, because Alex informed me that he's not having a party this year. It just so happens that a nice couple I know out here in Augusta have asked us to come to their house party. They would love to meet you. Would you consider that?"

"Sure! Whatever you would like to do."

"Great! I'll fill you in on the details later. I've still got that beautiful ring on my finger, by the way."

"I hope so, darling. Talk to you soon. Love you!"

"Love you too!" Now that the party plans were settled, I'd call Karen later.

In walked two women who looked like antique buyers looking for a bargain.

"How are you two ladies today?" I asked cheerfully.

"We are having a wonderful time," one said as she began looking. "Do you have any day-after-Christmas sales?"

"You know, I just got back into town, but it's a nice thought. How about twenty percent off whatever you purchase?"

"Great!" the other woman said. "We love quilts, and Mary here collects antique sewing tools. Do you have any?"

"Sure," I answered. "The quilts are all in this next room. I have some sewing tools in this display case on the counter. I'm happy to get any out for you to look at."

I followed the first lady into the quilt room and offered to unfold any quilts that she might want to see. When I went back into the front room, I saw her friend coming out from behind the counter.

"Oh, I can show you anything in there," I offered.

"That's okay. I looked, but didn't see anything I didn't already have," she replied. "Do you have any vintage pillowcases? I make doll dresses out of them."

"Yes." I nodded. "They are in the quilt room as well."

We made our way there.

"Oh, these are lovely!" she responded when I handed her several pairs.

"Well, I'll pass on the quilts," the first woman reported. "I'm ready to go if you are," she said to her companion.

"I like these sets of pillowcases, so I'll take all of these," her friend said, handing them back to me.

"Okay, I'll wrap them up," I said as we all walked into the other room. "Thanks so much. I hope you find some good sales today."

Chapter 98

As they were leaving, a customer immediately entered the shop and looked around for a short while. After he departed, I noticed that the back lid to my display case was open. I went over to close it, and my heart sank. Three antique needle holders and a pair of German needlework scissors were missing. What had I been thinking? I should have suspected something when I saw that customer behind the counter! My next thought was to alert Carrie Mae. I gave her a call and described the two women.

"Yes, they were here a good while ago, but I can't say that I noticed if they took anything. One bought a child's cup."

"Well, a sale is a distraction for them, so check your sewing tools."

"I will, but I have to go right now."

I was beginning to think I shouldn't have opened today. Ted came in to get his payment, and I asked him the dreaded question. "Ted, I have a gigantic favor to ask you."

"Sure, ask away!"

"You know I have a basement that I've only been in once

since I've lived here."

"Really?"

"Yeah, it's kind of creepy. Carrie Mae, your grandmother, and I went down there one day. We found a lot of Doc's things that he'd left behind."

"Oh, I think Grandma mentioned that."

"Well, I need to go back down there to look for something. It wouldn't take me long, but would you go with me?"

He chuckled. "Sure. You surprise me. I always think of you as such a brave, gutsy person."

I shook my head emphatically.

"Let's do it now, if you're ready," he offered.

"Okay. Let me put on my coat and get a couple of flashlights."

Quietly, I led the way. As we opened the door, the smell reminded me of my first visit.

"No electricity down here?" Ted inquired as he felt around the wall at the bottom of the steps.

"Not that I've found. That's why we each have a flashlight."

"Yeah, it's creepy, alright. What are we looking for?"

"Never mind. I see the things I wanted to know about," I said as I saw everything on Doc's workbench.

"Okay, so let's get out of here!" Ted immediately turned around to go back up the stairs.

I was glad Ted hadn't asked a lot of questions. He did exactly as I had requested and then wanted to move on. After he left, I thought that I was glad that the Dinner Detectives didn't need to get involved. Doc had reclaimed his things, and I now understood to leave him alone. After Ted left, I called Carrie Mae to give her a report. I knew Ted would tell Betty. Carrie Mae got a real chuckle out of the situation.

"You did the right thing by leaving it all down there," She said.

"I think so, too. After all, he was here before any of us."

"By the way, I got a nice New Year's Eve party invitation from Buzz and Karen. I can't believe they would want an old lady there."

"Great! If you want to go, Marc and I can pick you up."

"Oh, lands, no, but thank you. So you're going?"

"Yes, it appears so. Alex isn't having his usual party this year."

"Well, I haven't stayed up until midnight for many years, so I hope you all have fun."

"I hope my new outfit will arrive in time. I just couldn't show up in black again."

"What? You shopped? What color?"

"A bright aqua. Rather Tuscan-looking."

Chapter 99

My aqua blouse arrived not a moment too soon. Marc deserved to see me in something besides black. Underneath the flowing sheerness of the bellowing sleeves and overlay was a chemise that fit me perfectly. There was nothing like something new to perk me up.

As I drank my coffee, I watched light snow falling on the ground. It was not going to be a good day to open the shop, so I decided to spend most of my day calling everyone and wishing them a Happy New Year. I wasn't even dressed when my cell phone rang, showing that Sarah was calling.

"Happy New Year," I said.

"Oh, Aunt Lily, I just have to talk to you," Sarah blurted out.

"What's wrong? Is it about Lucy's dad?"

"Yes, of course. He said he'd asked his wife for a divorce, but now she's told him that she's pregnant. He's not going to leave her."

"What? That doesn't make any sense."

"No, it doesn't, but I didn't want to see the truth. I've told him not to bother Lucy and me again. We will make it on our own. I'm just so hurt."

"Of course you are. I'm so sorry. I know how much you wanted to make a family for Lucy. Are you going to be okay?"

"I have to be. I just have to be smarter."

"Things will work out for the best. You and Lucy deserve to have somebody who truly loves the two of you."

"Are you going out with Marc tonight?"

"Yes. We're going to a house party here in Augusta. Do you remember meeting Karen, who had the shop that sold barn quilts?"

"Yes, she was so sweet. I wish I was out there with you."

"Maybe you can visit soon."

"I hope so."

After we hung up, I was sad and happy for Sarah at the same time. I'd known all along that Lucy's father wasn't going to leave his wife. I wondered if he would still try to be part of Lucy's life.

I was shocked when I opened my group email and saw a message from Ellen. It was very upbeat, wishing all of us a Happy New Year. She then invited us to come to see her in April, when QuiltWeek was taking place at the convention center in Paducah. She described how grand it was and how we could all stay at her place.

I responded immediately with a New Year's greeting and told her I was putting QuiltWeek on my calendar. As I was typing, Loretta messaged and said she was excited about the idea. She said going to Paducah to the show had always been on her bucket list. So far, there hadn't been a response from Laurie. That may have been because Laurie generally checked her emails at night. Loretta added that she and Bill were going to a neighbor's house for New Year's, and Ellen commented that she and her friends were going out for an early dinner before the town got crazy. When I logged off, I called Alex to tease him about the big night ahead of him.

"You're going to ruin it for me if you don't stop. You know why I'm going."

"Yes, I do. It never hurts to get to know other publishers."

He laughed. "What are your plans for tomorrow?"

"The weather is getting to be a concern, so probably nothing."

"I guess there won't be a New Year's hug for you, Lily Girl! Have you made any resolutions?"

"Nope, I never keep them. How about you?"

"I'm afraid to say mine out loud. So, here's to you, sweetheart. Have fun tonight."

"You, too!"

It was bittersweet knowing I wouldn't see Alex that night after all these years of spending this holiday together. I took a short nap and then decided to call Holly.

"I'm so glad you called," she answered.

"I wanted to wish you a Happy New Year. Do you have plans tonight?"

"Mary Beth and I are going to dinner and a movie."

"Wonderful!"

"I need your advice, Lily," Holly said. "Maurice's only friend Clete, who came to see him in his last days, thinks I should have a memorial service for him here in town. I told him no one would come because Maurice had made so many enemies. What do you think?"

"I can't advise you on it. Only you know what that may be like and how it would make you feel. Right now, enjoy your evening. You have a whole new year ahead of you."

"I hope so. I have so many people coming to pick up things at the house, which is really making me feel good. In the process, I have to decide whether to move or stay in this house."

"You'll figure it out. Happy New Year, my friend!"

"The same to you, Lily!"

Chapter 100

Getting gussied up for a party was a lot of trouble, but was also exciting. If Marc arrived early enough, we could have a drink by the fire. I kept assessing the snow accumulation, but most of it was not sticking. Checking my watch, I saw that Marc was running late. The roads and traffic were not going to be kind to him tonight. I poured myself a glass of wine and finally heard Marc pull up in front of the house. I opened the door, and he stood there staring at me.

Stepping inside, he said, "Is this the same Lily that I know? My, you look amazing. I hope I'm not underdressed."

"You always look amazing. Come in. Do you want to have a drink before we go?"

"I apologize for running late. The traffic was terrible. Perhaps we should just go straight to the party." He followed me to the top of the stairs and helped me with my coat. "Happy New Year," he whispered in my ear as he straightened my collar.

The ride to Karen's house was brief. When we drove up to her house, a valet service was provided. That could only mean that this party was going to be big.

"Welcome!" Buzz said as we approached the door.

I quickly introduced him to Marc, and Marc was gracious as always.

"We've heard a lot about you, Marc," Buzz teased. "I, too, am a Cardinals fan and get to go to games every now and then."

"Great!" Marc responded. "I'll remember that when I have tickets available. Perhaps we can make it a foursome."

"There are several bars set up throughout the house and a buffet on each floor," Buzz informed us as he ushered us into the festivities. A young woman took our coats, and we ventured into the crowd. As we approached the first bar, I introduced Marc to Vic and Ruth Ann, who were standing there. I told Marc that it was Vic's gallery where I had purchased the wine rack. Gracie then joined us and introduced herself. She mentioned to Marc that she and I were the single girls in town. He got a kick out of that. As we left that group, I saw that Anthony had arrived. He wasn't with anyone. To my dismay, Buzz and Anthony came over to us right away.

"Marc, I want you to meet Anthony Giuliani," he began. "Lily met Anthony when we hosted a dinner party here. Anthony is a wine sommelier. He can tell you anything you need to know about wine. His family are winemakers from Italy."

"Is that right?" Marc responded. "I've never met a sommelier. Just the other day, my law partners and I were talking about having a sommelier at one of our dinner meetings. Would that interest you?"

I tried not to look at Anthony as he answered.

"Absolutely!" Anthony responded enthusiastically. "Here's my card. I think Lily enjoyed the experience, did you not?"

I cleared my throat. "Yes, it was very informative. The menu Karen and Buzz prepared was perfect for the occasion."

Marc sincerely seemed to want to continue the conversation, so I excused myself to talk to Judy, who was standing nearby with Randal and Marge from the coffee shop.

"You all clean up well," I joked.

They laughed.

"You look gorgeous!" Judy exclaimed. "I don't think I've ever seen you wear much color."

"I see you brought your significant other," Randal noted. "He does look like the handsome lawyer you described."

I blushed. "Thanks," I replied. "He's quite taken with the wine sommelier right now."

In the next room, where there was a trio of musicians, people were dancing. I turned the corner and noticed wonderful artwork displayed along the hallway. I'd no idea that Buzz and Karen had such good taste in art.

"None of these pieces of art are as beautiful as you tonight, Lily," Anthony said from behind me.

I didn't respond.

"Don't worry, your gentleman friend saw someone he knew and is engaged in conversation."

"You keep showing up everywhere," I said quietly.

"Like a bad penny or like a burst of flowers?"

I giggled.

"How have you been? Was Christmas good with all of your family?" he inquired.

I nodded. "Yes, it was very good. How about you?"

"Surprisingly pleasant," he stated.

"Oh, Anthony!" Karen cried as she came near us. "I want you to meet someone who has just opened a winery in Ste. Genevieve. You may already know him."

"Sure," Anthony agreed.

"Your collection of art is wonderful," I said to Karen.

"Thank you. You should go downstairs, where we have paintings of barns that feature our barn quilts. There is quite a collection down there."

"Oh, I will!"

Chapter 101

I met up with Marc, and we picked up a few appetizers since we hadn't had dinner. As we chatted and munched on the delicious food, I was able to introduce Marc to Susan and Heidi from my quilt group. I could tell that everyone was impressed with Marc. Not much later, he said we should take advantage of the music and dance.

"I've never danced with you, Marc," I said, suddenly feeling shy.

"Shall we give it a try?"

I nodded and hoped for the best. Of course, like everything else about him, Marc's movements were as smooth as glass. Out of the corner of my eye, I could see Anthony watching me as he stood by the bar with a glass of wine. I didn't feel too self-conscious until the music turned to an upbeat selection. Marc knew exactly what to do, and I followed. Had this guy gone to dance school or what?

"Go, Lily, go!" Marc teased as he waved his arms.

It was rather comical. Knowing Anthony's eyes were on me made me feel awkward at first, but then I got into it. Marc surprised me with an old-fashioned dip at the end of the song. After that dance, we went to get drinks, and I saw Anthony headed our way. I could hardly swallow. Fortunately, Karen was also approaching us. She immediately commented about what good dancers we were.

"Marc, since I'm a lonely, single guest at this party, would you allow me to ask your date for this dance?" Anthony asked.

"I think that could work, if Karen will allow me to dance with her," Marc responded.

Anthony put his arm around my waist and led me onto the dance floor. My heart was beating ten miles a minute as he guided us to a place out of Marc's sight.

"Relax, Lily," Anthony said as he pulled me closer. His salt-and-pepper beard felt soft against my cheek. I had often wondered what it would feel like to be this close to him. He was so close that he must have felt my heart pounding.

"You are light on your feet, as I have imagined," he whispered in my ear. "I wondered if I would ever be able to hold you in my arms, and here you are. Your hair smells like roses, as I remembered from when I first met you."

"You know I can walk away from this at any time," I whispered back.

"You wouldn't dare, because you are loving this as much as I am."

"You have a tremendous ego," I whispered.

"And your body language tells me everything I need to know about you," he replied. "Why are you breathing so heavily?"

"Because you're smothering me," I said, leaning back just a bit.

"Then tell me to back away," he challenged, as his lips

got closer to mine. "I want to kiss you right here in front of everyone."

"Don't you dare," I said, feeling suddenly panicky.

"Okay, Anthony," Buzz said, interrupting us. "My wife is preoccupied, so I'm cutting in on this beautiful lady, if you don't mind."

"I mind very much, but I can't say that I blame you," Anthony said, letting me go with a twirl. "You are the host tonight."

Buzz swung away from Anthony and into the dancing crowd. "You can begin thanking me now for saving you," Buzz teased with a grin. "I wasn't sure if you really wanted me to intervene, but I thought it best before Marc saw the two of you."

"I'm a bit embarrassed, but Anthony is very charming and persuasive. I was trying to be polite."

Buzz chuckled. "I know what Anthony's intentions are," he then said more seriously, "You have a very nice man with you tonight."

I nodded in agreement. "I do, don't I? By the way, Karen said you didn't dance. You are quite good!"

He smiled. "I have to tell her that or she'll drag me out on the dance floor every chance she gets," he confessed. "We used to dance a lot, years ago."

"There aren't many places where you can dance anymore," I complained.

"That's what Karen says. That's why she insisted that we have some music at this party."

The song ended, and my eyes met Marc's. I was glad he had seen me with Buzz instead of Anthony.

Chapter 102

Marc and I continued socializing until it got close to midnight. Every now and then, Anthony and I would trade glances. I was just as interested in what he was doing as he was in my activities. So far, he hadn't danced with anyone else.

Gracie came up to us to say goodbye. She wanted to get home before midnight and was concerned about the snow. "I couldn't help but notice, Lily, that guy Anthony seemed to be coming on to you," she whispered when Marc wasn't paying attention.

"Another time," I whispered back. "Drive safely and have a Happy New Year."

"Okay, maybe a lunch," Gracie suggested. "After all, you know more about me than I do about you." She grinned. "It's been nice to meet you, Marc."

"Nice to meet you, Gracie," Marc responded. "Are you okay to go home alone?"

"Sure. Happy New Year!" she said, making her exit.

After she left, I wondered who else might have seen

Anthony and me dancing.

"It's almost midnight, Lily," Marc observed. "Do you want to stay here or find a more private place to bring in the New Year?"

I laughed. "Remember last year when we were in Alex's kitchen and you kissed me, and I backed into a plate of deviled eggs?"

He began laughing as well. "Yes, and we left with some of it on our clothes, if you remember."

Marc and I decided to join the others as they gathered on the dance floor for the final song of the year. I loved seeing Marc so relaxed and enjoying the party. As we danced toward some double doors leading onto the patio now covered with snow, Marc looked at me in wonder.

"Are you thinking what I'm thinking?" Marc said suggestively. "Let's see if this is locked."

I casually tried the doorknob, and to my surprise, it opened. Marc opened the door and gently led me out into the falling snow. The countdown to midnight had started, so the timing was perfect. It was magical as we heard the crowd cheering "Happy New Year" and singing "Auld Lang Syne." With flakes landing on our faces, Marc kissed me gently on the lips. "This is better than egg salad, don't you think?" he joked as he licked snowflakes off my lips. "I love you, snow angel."

"Ah, I love you too, snowman."

Others could see us outside and tapped on the windows to get our attention.

"Guess we'd better go in," Marc suggested. "Are you ready?"

"Ready!" I responded as I dusted snowflakes off my

shoulders.

"Hey, you two!" Buzz commented when he saw us. "Did it get too hot in here for you?"

We laughed.

"It's beautiful out there!" I said, shivering a bit.

Buzz shook his head in disbelief. "Happy New Year," he said, giving me a kiss on the cheek.

"Thanks for inviting us to a great party," Marc said graciously. "We'll be heading out now."

"Tell Karen that it was a great evening," I added.

We had just gotten our coats when Anthony approached us.

"Marc, I'll give you a call this week so we can set that date," Anthony said as a follow-up to their earlier conversation.

"That would be great, Anthony," Marc replied, shaking his hand. "I'm glad I met you. Have a Happy New Year."

"The same to you," Anthony responded as he directed his gaze at me.

I was glad to leave. The valet quickly brought Marc's car, and we were off. The drive home was slow, and a gentle snow continued to fall.

"Remember that night when we walked in the snow and ended up on your front lawn?" Marc recalled with laughter.

"Oh, I do! I hope you don't have any notion of doing that this evening. I think we've had our share of snow. My fancy blouse is still damp from being out on the patio!"

Arriving at my home, we made a quick run to the front door. Happy New Year, Lily Girl's Quilts and Antiques!

Chapter 103

It was such a luxury for Marc and me to not have to worry about work the next day. The snow had stopped during the night, but I knew Ted would be coming by at any time to start cleaning things up. Marc and I sat leisurely by the fire with our coffee as we munched on the banana bread Betty had given me.

"What are you writing about these days?" Marc asked.

"I've been lazy lately. I had gotten ahead on my columns, but now I need to turn something in this next week or so."

"When you decide to write your column, do the ideas just flow automatically, or do you have to wait for an idea to surface?"

"That's a good question. It's a little of both. My experience in making Ellen that wish quilt has given me some thoughts I might share. It was so fun to make, and the rewards were wonderful."

"I'm sure, and what a relief it was for Ellen to know you all thought that much of her."

"Yes, and it made me realize that a gift like that could be

a great option for many occasions. When Loretta married Bill, Bill's mother made a Double Wedding Ring quilt for them and had all the guests sign it, so it turned out to be more than just a quilt."

"I see. That's so interesting! It sounds like you could write about those uses and call your column 'More than Just a Quilt.'"

"It would make a good title, and there are plenty of stories to back it up. Thank you, Marc."

"Well, I need to be on my way. Traffic should be clear, and I have plenty to do. This was a great New Year's experience, my love!" He kissed me quickly on the lips.

"I agree that it was a pleasant change from Alex's party, but I won't tell him that."

Marc chuckled.

"I can't believe he didn't call me at midnight to wish me Happy New Year."

"I think Mindy from Minnesota had something to do with that," Marc quipped.

After he left, I still had a smile on my face. Last night could have gone horribly wrong, but it hadn't, thank goodness. Buzz's intervention had saved the day.

After I'd dressed for the day, my phone rang. I was sure it would be Alex, but I was surprised to see that it was Karen. "Have you recovered from your party?" I asked her.

"I have. Thanks to my speedy cleaning lady, you can't tell that a soul was here."

"We really enjoyed it."

"I wanted to ask you something before you left last night, but you got away from me."

"What's up?"

"I wanted to tell you that I have a family friend named Bonita Cadez."

"Was she there last night?"

"No, she wasn't. She's from Honduras and has worked for my father's company for many years. She is quite an asset to my father because she has a keen sense of business. She also has a heart for her friends and family, who remain in Honduras and are quite poor. She's heard of quilting and sewing groups in America who are working to help women and children in her home country. When I shared with her that you collect and sell quilts, she expressed interest in coming to see your collection. She knows little about quilting. She is hoping to educate herself on sewing and quilting and come up with a business plan to help her family and friends support themselves and hopefully work themselves out of poverty."

"Well, that's quite noble of her."

"She'll be out here visiting in a couple of days. I told her about you, and she would love to meet you. Can I bring her over?"

"Sure. It may be best to do so when my shop is closed so we can have a conversation without interruptions. How about some evening around cocktail time?"

"Perfect! I hope you don't think I'm being too pushy, but when I also told her a little bit about Doc's office, she was quite fascinated."

"I've come to a bump in the road with him recently," I said, rolling my eyes. "Let's just hope he behaves himself while the two of you are here."

"I hope he does, too! Okay then. I'll call you."

That had been an interesting conversation. Thank

goodness Karen hadn't mentioned anything about Anthony. Maybe Buzz hadn't shared anything with her.

While I had some free time, I started on the column that Marc had suggested. An incoming call interrupted my thoughts. By golly, it was Alex! "It's about time you called," I scolded him. "At midnight, I waited and waited for your call, and it never came."

There was silence. I guessed Alex didn't think my rant was funny.

"I had a good reason."

"Is the reason called Mindy from Minnesota?"

"Now you're just being mean. Just listen. Mindy and I had dinner before we went to her dad's party. As you recall, the weather was bad. At least, it was here. We were halfway there, near The Cheshire, when a car came out of nowhere and hit me broadside."

"Oh, no!"

"It gets worse! I then got hit by an elderly woman in her Cadillac."

"Is everyone okay? Are you okay?"

"Mostly, yes, but that old lady was mighty upset. I think she did get checked out at the hospital."

"I never imagined such a thing had happened to you! So where were you at the stroke of midnight?"

"You really want to know? I was standing in the middle of a busy road directing traffic until the police got there to take over. It was not a happy beginning to the new year, my friend!"

Chapter 104

"You can just imagine the great mood Mindy was in by then," Alex continued. "We didn't get to the party until one, so Happy New Year to us."

"Alex, I am so sorry. Did Mindy get over the disappointment?"

"Time will tell, but at this point, things are very cold, you might say."

"I see. Wow. You can hardly be held responsible for something that wasn't your fault!"

"No big deal. How was the fancy party in Augusta?"

"It was great. I want you to know that I, too, was standing in the snow when midnight came, but that's another story."

"I'll bet it is. Well, back to me. I'm now driving a rental car. By the way, why didn't you call me at midnight?"

"Well, since I happened to be in Marc's arms, I'm sure he would have loved that! I did think of you, however. I even told Marc that I was disappointed when I didn't hear from you, and that it was a first for us not to communicate at the stroke of midnight."

"Well, the lesson learned here is that next year, I'm having a party again."

"I'm glad to hear it. By the way, I forgot to tell you that Butler called me again to wish me Happy New Year and said that he needs to see me about something. What should I do?"

"I think Lily Girl is quite capable of playing both sides. I think he hopes you still feel sorry for him over his loss of James."

"Yes, I do think he's lonely. I really do want to continue to be his friend."

"Does Mr. Marc know about these suitors who are trying to date you?"

"Not really." I thought of Anthony. Alex didn't even know about him.

"I think Marc is sometimes jealous of what you and I have," Alex remarked.

"I don't. He likes to tease me about it, but Marc isn't a jealous kind of guy."

"So he knows you can't live without me?"

I giggled. "Pretty much!"

"Atta girl! Hey, are you coming back into town soon?"

"I want to. I really feel like I need to see Holly now that she's footloose and fancy free."

"Man, I'll bet she's a new woman!"

"We'll see. Sometimes you just replace your solved problems with new ones."

"Okay, keep me posted. I'm happy to join the two of you, if you like."

"Okay."

"Have you spent your big bonus yet?"

"No. The first thing I have to purchase is a new water

heater. Would you mind picking one out for me?"

"Sorry, that's not my field of expertise."

"For today, I'm going to call my friend Lisa. I've purchased quilts from her before. She just moved and told me she has another pile for me to look at."

"Now that's much more exciting."

I hung up feeling better about connecting with Alex, despite his bad luck. While I had Lisa on my mind, I decided to give her a call.

"Happy New Year!" I greeted her when she picked up the phone.

"The same to you!"

"I was just telling a friend of mine that I needed to call you to set up a time to see your quilts."

"Well, come out anytime. Are you closed today?"

"Yes, and I need the day to catch up and get started on my inventory."

"How about coming by after you close tomorrow? We'll have a cocktail before you start looking through the quilts. I'll make some nibbles for our dinner."

"You sound like a single woman now! I would love that."

"Why don't you come around five thirty? Here's my address."

I wrote the information down, and we said goodbye. Perhaps it was a little presumptuous to spend money on quilts when I had no idea how much a hot water heater would cost. I guessed the first thing I had to do was to get that check in the bank. Details, details!

Chapter 105

Augusta Shores was an upscale neighborhood of new houses that all had a fantastic view of wine country. Lisa's directions were simple enough, considering the winding roads. I parked in the driveway of a huge and impressive house. I couldn't imagine living in that big place alone.

"Come on in, Lily," Lisa said after I rang the doorbell.

"Lisa, your home is amazing!"

She looked down as if embarrassed. "I'll give you a quick tour, and then we'll have a drink. It's too bad the weather is cold. The outdoor patio and view are two of the reasons I liked this house."

"Ah, I see you also have a pool!"

"Yes, at first I was concerned about it, but I think it will be great for entertaining, which I like to do every now and then."

As we wandered from room to room, I noticed that some of them weren't even furnished.

"This is my quilt room. It's not organized yet, but I have someone helping me with that. I put this pile aside for you to consider."

"Very nice. Do you know the provenance for any of these?"

"I do for some. Do you want to just go ahead and look at them now?"

"Yes. I can already see one that has my name on it."

She smiled a knowing smile. "The red-and-white Courthouse Steps?"

I nodded. "You know me well, Lisa. I love the variation on that one. It has a contemporary look but still uses the traditional pattern."

"I agree," Lisa said as she held it up.

"Price?"

"Let's see what all you're interested in, and then we can discuss prices."

"I like this Log Cabin. I can't stock too many of those. I think it may be everyone's favorite pattern."

"I agree. This one is called Sunshine and Shadow. I think Barn Raising is the favorite of the variations, but this is pretty striking."

"It's a bit worn, but I like that it has a lot of reds and blues in the prints. I think this blue-and-white Drunkard's Path is striking, but I'm worried about the blue fading. I'd better pass on that one. The rest of these are too scrappy. I have trouble selling quilts like those."

"Well, that's all I have right now," Lisa said as she folded up the blue-and-white quilt.

"Do you wash the quilts when you bring them home, Lisa?"

"Most of the time I just air them out. I'm very sensitive to fragrances, and I don't like bringing those odors into the house. Let's have a drink while I think of a price."

"Sounds good."

We chatted for the next thirty minutes. Lisa was very interesting and was obviously happy with her new single life.

"If you don't mind me asking, do you date very much?" I questioned.

She smiled. "Some. Everyone my age has a lot of baggage by now. I'm certainly not looking, but I do enjoy male companionship every now and then. Why? Do you have someone in mind for me?" She laughed, clearly not particularly expecting a response from me.

I thought of Butler and Anthony. They would love Lisa.

I watched Lisa go behind her bar, which was better stocked than most public bars. She poured herself a glass of scotch and then poured me a glass of red wine. On the coffee table was an assortment of cheeses and crackers. We began to help ourselves to the food.

"How is Carrie Mae?" Lisa asked out of the blue.

"Slowing down. She seems more and more fatigued every time I see her."

"She is such a gem. I've known her for a very long time."

Chapter 106

I left later that night than I had planned. I was always fearful of the winding roads after dark. Lisa's asking price for the two quilts was more than reasonable, but I wished I had found a couple more. Every little bit would help my shrinking inventory. I really wanted to keep the red-and-white quilt for myself, but decided to bump up the price to make up for the cost of my purchases. At home, I was exhausted and fell into bed quickly. I was almost asleep when the phone rang. I answered quickly, thinking something must be wrong. It was Butler.

"Lily, did I wake you?" he asked apologetically.

"Sort of," I said with a yawn.

"For some reason, I think of you as a night owl."

"I used to be, but not any longer. It's pretty quiet out here compared to living on the The Hill."

"I'm sure. I was wondering if you're free for dinner this weekend."

"Oh, Butler, I don't know what to say. I so appreciate our friendship, but I'm in a relationship that I don't want to lose.

When you said you wanted to start seeing me, it made me nervous."

"I see. I guess I didn't realize how serious you and this gentleman are. Are you talking marriage?"

"I think I told you before that marriage isn't something that we're interested in."

"I really do want to talk to you about something, however. I'm serious, and it's business related. Would you still agree to hear me out?"

"Sure. I'm sorry. I didn't mean to react so coldly. Why don't you come out next week and we'll discuss it here at my place?"

"Whatever you say. I'll check my calendar and get back to you."

"Great." I hated the way our conversation had to end, but Butler was not getting my message. I wondered if he would even come here to talk to me about the business thing he'd mentioned.

I tried to go back to sleep, but my mind went to Marc and how much I really cared for him and didn't want to lose him. If anyone tested my loyalty, it was Anthony! He was so different from anyone I'd ever met. It had truly been a test when he'd almost kissed me at Karen's party. What would have happened had I let him? I don't think Marc or anyone at the party would have approved, but it was such a temptation!

By now, I was wide awake, so I decided to get my laptop and check some emails. I positioned myself under the covers and got myself comfortable enough to stay warm. There were emails from my siblings that I had missed.

Loretta was glad to be back home, but disappointed that she'd had to cover some extra shifts at the hospital to make up for her time away. She said Sarah had been very moody lately, but she didn't know why. She once again thanked us all for being so generous to Sarah and Lucy at Christmas.

Laurie said all the shops in her area had remained closed for the holidays. She was doing more to promote her oils online and had taken up a new craft of making jewelry to sell in her shop. She made no mention of Ellen.

Lynn thanked everyone again for making the trip and commented about how quiet her house was now that everyone had gone. She also mentioned going to Paducah for the quilt show in early spring. She thought we would have a blast.

I decided to respond by backing up Lynn's comments about going to see Ellen in Paducah. I reminded my sisters about the quilt museum, which was known worldwide, and told them that I'd always wanted to see it. I then described where I'd hung Ellen's quilt in my bedroom. I briefly told them about Alex having an accident on New Year's Eve and that Mindy from Minnesota had not been too happy, then I closed by saying that Marc and I had enjoyed a wonderful time celebrating New Year's Eve in Augusta. I closed my laptop knowing that responses wouldn't come until the next day. Having a close connection to my family through the internet made me feel safe and content—content enough to go back to sleep.

Chapter 107

I woke up on Sunday morning and decided to go back to the church where I had attended Pauline's funeral. I had been impressed with the pastor, and I didn't like putting off choosing a church any longer.

When I arrived, the service had started, so I sat in the back row. It didn't take long to recognize some people, such as Edna and her daughter Marilyn. When Marilyn saw me, she waved and smiled. As soon as the service ended, I quickly made my way out to avoid getting engaged in conversation with anyone. I stopped at the coffee shop to get lunch afterward. It was very crowded with tourists. I didn't recognize anyone until Judy appeared from the kitchen.

"I didn't know you worked on Sundays," I said when she saw me.

"Typically, I don't, but I'm filling in for someone, and we had a lot of baking to do this morning. The group that's here now is part of a tour."

"It smells wonderful in here."

She nodded. "Are you going to quilting tomorrow? Don't

forget, tomorrow we find out who our secret sister is."

"Oh, I forgot. I wonder what Susan has planned for us this year?"

"Well, I'd better get back to the kitchen," Judy said as she eyed the crowd.

"Would you add an order of your soup special for me to drop off at Carrie Mae's?"

"Is she sick?"

"No, but I don't think she takes the time to eat very well," I explained.

"Okay. Well, I'll also add a piece of our apple pie that just came out of the oven."

"That would be awesome. Thank you."

I was pleased to see Carrie Mae's shop sign indicated that she was open when I arrived with my delivery.

"Well, what's this?" she asked, surprised.

"Have you had lunch?"

She looked puzzled. "It's too early for me."

"When you're ready, I brought you something from the coffee shop, and Judy added a nice piece of pie."

She smiled. "Aren't you something! Thank you. While you're here, look who's working in the other room."

I looked inside the next room and saw Korine cleaning a shelf of old silver and copper items.

"Hello, Lily," Korine called out.

"Hello to you! Carrie Mae has you working on a Sunday?" I asked jokingly.

"She says to come any day I can, so I've been coming in most days, thanks to you, Lily."

"I'm so glad I succeeded," I said, walking closer to her. I whispered, "Please keep an eye on Carrie Mae. If she doesn't come downstairs at any point, please check on her. I've been a little worried about her."

"Oh, I will, but she's the one who keeps an eye on me most of the time."

We shared a laugh. When I returned to where Carrie Mae was sitting, she was enjoying her lunch.

"This pie is delicious!" she said between bites. "It's almost as good as your pies, Lily."

"I'd better get back to open the shop. I'm so glad you asked Korine to help you."

"Thanks for everything. You are a dear," Carrie Mae said as she blew me a kiss.

When I got back to my shop, a couple was just parking their car. I went inside and quickly turned my sign to indicate that the shop was open.

"Lily?" the woman questioned.

"Yes? How can I help you?"

"I just want to tell you how much I enjoy your column. I told my husband that when we came to town for a wedding this weekend, we just had to stop and meet you. I'm so glad your shop is open."

"I'm glad you came," I responded. "Please come in and look around."

"Would you autograph this magazine for me?"

"I would be honored," I said, taking it from her.

Her husband seemed unimpressed as he looked around the shop.

"I want to see all of your quilts while I'm here," the woman said, glancing around the room.

"I'll be happy to show you to the quilt room here," I directed.

"Oh, don't you need to put out Rosie's rocker?" she suggested.

I laughed. "I do! You go ahead and start looking at the quilts."

When I returned to check on the customer, she had the red-and-white Courthouse Steps quilt that I had just acquired from Lisa in her hands. "I love red-and-white quilts like you do, and this one is very striking."

"I think so, too."

"Honey, I'm going to take this quilt so I can tell Mary Alice I got it from Lily Girl!" she bragged. The husband shrugged his shoulders and walked to the counter to pull out his charge card. When the couple happily went out the door, I felt triumphant. It was times like these that gave me hope in the retail world. The added amount I had put on that quilt hadn't seemed to be a problem for either of the customers.

Chapter 108

I felt I hadn't been to quilt class in a long time. Everyone was present and seemed to be talking all at once. Judy had brought fresh cinnamon rolls from the coffee shop, so we all took a little extra time to socialize.

"Welcome back, everyone!" Susan said to get our attention. "Happy New Year to you all! Now, as you know, today we are supposed to find out who our secret sisters are, unless you have already found out somehow. If you brought a gift for them today, you will go first and can give it to them." Susan immediately walked over to me and handed me a small gift. I smiled. After that occurred, Susan instructed everyone to go their sister and give them a hug. I looked at Susan and proceeded to do so.

"I knew it was you!" Susan admitted. "Thank you so much for everything!"

I opened my gift from her, which was a beautiful writing pen with my name on it. I told her, "Thanks, this is special, just like all the other gifts."

Susan got our attention once again and announced that

she had an idea for us for the new year. "I know you all love this wine country community," she began. "I know I've told myself so often that I would love my own quilt representing this area. This next quilt will be for us!"

Everyone cheered.

"You have had a little experience now with many different techniques, so you choose what you would like, just as we did with our Christmas quilts. This time, however, there will not be any kits. The only thing I ask is that you make two of everything. We will use the extra blocks to put together a raffle quilt to make money for the library. They have been very gracious to let us use their facilities. Many locals and visitors will enjoy seeing something like that hanging on the wall. What do you think about that?"

Everyone seemed to be excited about her proposal.

"That's a great idea, Susan," I was the first to say. "What size should the blocks be?"

"I think we need to stick to the twelve-inch blocks that we're accustomed to making," she advised. "Remember to leave a quarter-inch around the edges."

Susan had increased everyone's interest. I knew I would love my own wine country quilt. My skill level was limited, but I wouldn't worry about that just yet.

"Gracie will continue to give us a discount at the quilt shop, so I encourage you to shop there for your supplies," Susan suggested. "I also wanted to announce that Amy has found a location for her knitting shop in Washington, Missouri. It's close enough for us to drive there, and she's right downtown. She wanted to make sure I told you and that I thanked you again for the purchases that you made when she came to our group."

"Oh, that's great news," Judy exclaimed. "Some of us should go together and visit Amy."

"Great idea, Judy," I agreed. "If she's open on Mondays, that would be the best day for me to go."

We left our class with excitement for what was ahead. When I got back to the shop, I started rearranging things now that the holidays were over. My phone rang. It was Karen.

"Lily, have you given any more thought about when I could bring Bonita over to your place?"

"No, I haven't. Later in the week, I guess. I have so much to do, and I still haven't finished my inventory. Last year, I had Korine to help me, but I'm pleased to say that Carrie Mae has basically employed her full-time now."

"I'd heard that. She's giving her a lot of freedom in the shop, which Korine loves. She's moving some things around that haven't been moved in years. By the way, we appreciated the thank you note regarding our New Year's Eve party. No one does that anymore."

"I believe in the written word, my friend," I reminded her. "We had a wonderful time."

"It looked like Buzz and Marc hit it off well. How did Marc react to Anthony?"

"Pretty well. Anthony is coming to Marc's law firm to do one of his sommelier appearances."

"Now that's interesting," Karen responded.

"Now, Karen, don't go there!"

We burst into laughter.

Chapter 109

The next morning, I stayed in bed to take a few minutes to plan my day. The phone interrupted my thoughts. It was Holly. It was most unusual for her to call me early in the morning. "Holly? Is everything okay?"

"Oh, sure. Did I wake you?"

"No, but what's up?"

"You won't believe this!"

"I wouldn't be surprised by anything from you, Holly."

"Clete. Remember Clete?"

"Yes, the visitor at the hospital."

"Well, he called last night and asked to take me to dinner. Should I consider that a date?"

I chuckled, a little surprised by her latest news. "I guess you'll have to decide that. Maybe he just wants to be helpful, and perhaps he feels a bit sorry for you."

"I know. I thought of that, too, but he said a few things that made me think he may be interested in me."

"I can certainly understand that. You're attractive, smart, and very funny."

"You're just saying that because you're my friend."

"That's my point! I know you better than anyone. Hey, enjoy a night out. You deserve it."

"Thanks, I think I will. Something weird also happened recently that I wanted to share with you. I got a sympathy card from a woman I'd never heard of before. The card was quite elaborate, and there was a letter inside."

"And?"

"She started out by saying how disappointed she was that there wasn't a memorial service for my husband because she had wanted to be there."

"Okay."

Well, she went on and on about what a marvelous person the monster was. She said he was the most generous and kindhearted man she'd ever known. Who in the world would ever say that about him?"

"Do you think she was serious?"

"I guess. She didn't give any contact information. She must have met him online, because he never left the house much."

"Maybe Clete will have some information about that."

"Good thought. It will be interesting to see if I continue to hear from her."

"I have got to get going. I'm doing inventory, but when I get this done, I'll come by and we'll go to lunch."

"That would be great. I would be happy to cook for you."

"Yes, I would love that. Have fun with Clete, okay?" It was so nice to have a positive conversation with Holly for a change. Perhaps Clete could boost her self-esteem.

I finally got in the shower and got dressed for the day. I dreaded inventory in some ways, but the part of touching and examining my quilts was quite enjoyable. It gave me a chance to refold them and recheck their prices.

When I put Rosie's rocker on the porch, I displayed the Log Cabin quilt that I had purchased from Lisa. Hopefully, that would sell as quickly as the Courthouse Steps quilt. The sun was out, but it was bitterly cold. Rosie always said that after Christmas, sales could be good since people had received gifts of money for Christmas. I could only hope that she had been right.

I saw Snowshoes approaching my shop. The poor guy was moving slower than ever and even had a slight limp. "How are you feeling, Snowshoes?"

"Not bad. Nothing a full day of work won't cure."

"Now that's the attitude! I need to remember that today."

After I tidied up the shop, I got back to the laptop to complete my latest column. I still had no customers. The dead of winter was so hard on shops out here. What could I do to change that?

Finally, an elderly gentleman came in looking for antique walking sticks. I had several from Rosie's inventory. He chose one that he was pleased with and asked for ten percent off. I was thankful for the sale and agreed. He placed the cash on the counter and left.

Chapter 110

Around noon, when I was munching on a banana, Butler called. "How's business?" he asked immediately.

"I have a feeling you know the answer, because it's January."

He chuckled. "I know I was supposed to get back to you after I checked my calendar, but time got away from me. If you don't mind, I would like to come out to your shop today."

"I suppose so. What time?"

"How about after you close the store around four? We can talk over a glass of wine."

"Fine. See you then." Hanging up the phone, I sighed. I truly hoped this was a business-related visit.

The slow-moving day allowed me to straighten up as I did inventory. Two sales had taken place by the end of the day, which brought my total to $159.68. Last year, there had been days when I had no sales at all because of wintry weather.

Just before four, I went upstairs to freshen up for Butler's arrival. It wasn't long before he knocked at the door. He looked chipper and quite handsome in his camel overcoat, a plaid scarf draped around his neck.

"Come on upstairs. I have the fireplace on. They say it will get down to ten degrees tonight."

"So I hear! I brought a bottle of merlot that I think you'll like."

"You didn't have to do that. I live in wine country, remember?"

He smiled, took his coat off, and got comfortable while I opened the bottle of wine and poured a glass for each of us.

"You've made this apartment quite cozy."

"Thanks. I love all the windows on this porch, so I spend a lot of time out here, even in the winter. Butler, what's on your mind?"

"As I may have indicated to you before, I now deal in fine art rather than quilts."

"Yes, I'm aware that you have made that change."

"Well, I still have a nice inventory of very good quilts. I would like to turn them over to you."

My eyes widened in surprise. "Me?"

"Yes. You decide what you can get for them, and I'll be happy with twenty percent of the sales."

"Seriously? That's hardly fair."

"It is for me. When I gave you that Christmas quilt, it felt very good. You have such a passion for quilts, rather than just seeing it as a business. You take excellent care of them and give them a good home. When I sell a quilt, it's a cold process from one dealer to another. No matter how special they may be, they all get treated in the same way. I looked at my quilts the other day and felt rather sorry for them. Maybe I'm getting to be a softy in my old age."

I gave him a look of concern.

"There was no one to caress or admire them. Then I thought of you."

"How sweet, Butler. I'm not sure I'm the answer."

"Yes, you are. I've given this a lot of thought."

"How many quilts are we talking about?"

"Maybe twenty or so."

"Oh!"

"They're good ones, trust me. None of them have a value under a thousand dollars."

"I'm just not sure my little shop will do them justice."

"I think they'll feel like they've died and gone to quilt heaven when they come here."

I smiled. "You are so caring and trusting, Butler. What if I can't move them? Most of my quilts are priced under a thousand dollars."

"All the more reason that you need them. You'll never establish a reputation as a complete quilt shop if you don't have something for everyone. I'll leave the pricing up to you, but keep in mind that all of these have certified appraisals and are quite unique."

"I don't know what to say."

"Say you'll be happy to take them, and then tell me what you think of this merlot."

I shook my head in disbelief. "I like it, but as I've told Carrie Mae, I've never met a merlot I didn't like."

He laughed.

"It's good to see you laugh, Butler. I don't see that side of you very often. It becomes you."

He flashed me a big smile. "Thank you, sweetheart, and I'm glad you like the wine. Now back to business. When can I bring them out?"

"Anytime, I suppose. Do you approve of my quilt room?"

"I have seen it, and I do like that it doesn't have daylight coming in from any windows. However, I don't want to see any of them displayed on the back of your rocker on the front porch!"

I threw back my head and laughed. "I promise!"

Chapter III

"I wish we could have gone to dinner," Butler said as he gave me an even gaze.

"It's just not necessary. If you're hungry, I'll be happy to fix you something like a frozen pizza."

"I'm fine, but I will take a refill of wine. Tell me more about this gentleman you're involved with. Is he a jealous sort who would be offended if we had dinner?"

I shook my head. "He's wonderful, and certainly isn't the jealous type. I just feel it would be inappropriate."

"Well, tell him that if he doesn't treat you right, he has competition."

I smiled. "I've never asked, but are you seeing anyone? I've always felt that it was none of my business."

"I think I have a problem with trust. It takes me a long time to trust anyone. I can say that I trust you, Lily."

"I'll take that as a very nice compliment," I replied. I decided that it may be best to change the subject. "When do you think you'll have the paperwork ready for the quilts?"

"Will next week work for you? You may need time to

rearrange some things."

"Sure. You probably feel I should do a little more advertising, and I'm not sure I can afford to do that in the way you're accustomed to."

"You do what you can afford. I'll alert my former buyers about you, which will help. You do have a good security system, I assume?"

"I do, but let me share a little something with you."

"What's that?"

"I have a couple of spirits that seem to hang out here."

He nodded as if it didn't surprise him. "Is one of them the doctor who used to live here?"

"Yes. He's the one that is the most unpredictable. The other one is Rosie. I purchased her inventory, remember?"

"Yes, I remember Rosie. What a sweetheart she was. She doesn't give you any problems, does she?"

"No. In fact, she rather protects me."

"I can understand that. Why did you feel you needed to tell me about that?"

"Because it's rather unpredictable as to what these spirits get up to."

He laughed. "Just tell Rosie to protect these quilts with all she's got. I trust her. Do you feel the doctor is unhappy with you being here?"

"I can't tell."

"Well, I think I need to be on my way. If you have any questions regarding the quilts, just let me know. I'll bring them out next week."

"I'm excited. I really can't believe this!"

"It's a good deal for both of us."

I walked Butler to the door. When I opened the door,

he put his hands on my shoulders and leaned in to kiss me softly on the cheek. "Good evening, Lily."

I smiled, then closed the door and thought about how the evening had gone. For Butler to think that much of me was unbelievable. It was obvious that money wasn't a concern to him. Perhaps getting rid of the quilts was one way for him to erase the bad memory of James's suicide.

I went back upstairs and finished the rest of the wine in my glass. Now serious planning would have to begin as to where these quilts would go. Carrie Mae would flip when I told her about Butler's plan!

Later, I finally got into bed. My mind began to wander. What would it be like to be in a romantic relationship with Butler? I'd never felt attracted to him, but I couldn't ask for a better man. What had his wife been like? Was there anyone I knew that I could introduce Butler to? I tossed and turned. How could I erase these thoughts from my mind and get some sleep?

Chapter 112

The next day, I was determined to get the paperwork done for my inventory. It was a cold, cloudy day, and I once again wished winter would come to an end. When the shop phone rang, I was surprised to see that it was Karen. "Good morning!" she said.

"Good morning to you!"

"I wondered if it would be okay to bring Bonita over tomorrow."

"Sure."

"How about around five?"

"Sounds good. I'll serve the wine."

Karen chuckled. "I'll bring something to munch on. See you then!"

Before a customer came in, I decided to call Carrie Mae and tell her about Butler's offer regarding his quilts.

"Good morning," Korine answered.

"Well, good morning, Korine. Is your boss downstairs?"

"Yes, she's sitting right here drinking a cup of tea. She is quite the slave driver. She's got me polishing more of her silver today."

"Oh, yuck! You're welcome to tackle some over here if you like."

"Good morning, Lily," Carrie Mae said, taking the phone.

"I called to tell you about my visitor last night."

"Oh? Who would that have been?"

"Butler. He told me over Christmas that he wanted to talk to me about something."

"Is everything okay with him?"

I assured her that he was fine. I began explaining what was on his mind as she listened without interrupting. Then I waited for a response when I told her I had accepted his offer.

"I guess I'm not surprised. He has really moved on in his business and personal life. I don't think he wants to work anymore, and frankly, he doesn't have to. It's a wonderful opportunity for you. You may need to think of a way to effectively market quilts of that price range."

"I've thought about that. It is quite a responsibility."

"Well, he thinks an awful lot of you, sweetie."

"I know. I'm not sure why."

"That was obvious when he gave you the Christmas quilt. I can't wait to see these other quilts!"

"He should deliver them next week."

"I think the Dinner Detectives should be the first to see them, don't you?"

I agreed to her request and hung up when a woman came in pushing a stroller. I held the door open so she could maneuver it inside.

"Thanks!" she said as the baby started to fuss. "Whew! I decided to walk down here from Walnut Street. I don't look forward to going back up that hill."

"Would you like to sit for a bit?"

"No, I just want to shop. I hardly ever get time to do that anymore."

By now, the baby had really started to cry, and the woman appeared a bit frustrated. She picked up a baby girl from the stroller and put her on her shoulder.

"What a sweet baby girl. Maybe she's just hungry."

"No, I fed her before I left," the woman claimed as she rocked the baby back and forth.

"Would you like me to hold her while you look around?"

"That would be great!" she said, placing the baby in my arms.

I gently held the baby like I had just been handed a handful of glass that was about to shatter. To my surprise, as I held her closer, she stopped crying.

"See, she likes you," the mother claimed as she began looking around the shop.

I didn't know whether I should follow the mother around or sit in a chair with the delicate child. Just then, Judy stopped by on her way to work.

"Well, Lily, you've certainly added something new since I've been here," she teased.

"Very funny, Judy," I replied. "The baby's mom is doing a little shopping. I did get this little one to stop crying, by the way."

"You must have the knack," Judy suggested. "Look, she's even smiling at you."

Chapter 113

"Can you help me?" the mother called from the quilt room. "I don't see a price on this quilt."

I started to make my way to help her and Judy offered to take the baby. I gladly obliged. "She likes to keep moving," I said.

"Oh, you're the expert mother now," Judy teased.

When I got to the quilt room, I knew the woman had looked hastily at many quilts, as they were now in piles.

"Is this the quilt you were referring to?" I asked, pointing to the one on top of the pile.

"Yes, I love those colors."

"All of the price tags are on one of the corners, unless someone has pulled them off," I explained. "This one is four hundred dollars."

"Really?" the woman questioned. "How can that be? It's an old quilt, isn't it? Did you see the worn edges?"

"I have all antique quilts, and there are numerous factors that go into pricing a quilt," I explained as I refolded it. "There are no two alike, and actually, this one is really in pretty good condition."

"Boy, I don't get it," the woman said, shaking her head. "Are you telling me that none of these are new quilts?"

"None are new," I confirmed. "This is an antique shop with antique quilts."

"Well, my mom has plenty of those," she replied. "I want to fix up my bedroom in the colors of this very quilt."

"I see," I said as I began to straighten her mess. "Maybe you should learn to make a quilt like you want. I'm now a quilter, and if I can do it, anyone can."

She looked at me like I had suggested that she become an astronaut. By now, the baby was crying, so Judy brought her into the quilt room.

"I don't think she likes me," Judy commented as she swayed back and forth.

"Here, I'll take her," the mother said abruptly. "I think I'm done here." At that, she took the baby, marched into the room where the stroller was, and tucked the baby inside.

"I hope you make it up the hill okay," I said as I held the door open. "Thanks for stopping by. You have an adorable baby."

After she was outside and making her way back up the hill, Judy and I looked at each other.

"Well, if that isn't something!" Judy said.

"There are some days when I don't think I have anything anyone wants," I said, annoyed. "What was she thinking?"

"You don't have to have something for everyone. After you were nice enough to hold the baby and then listen to her insults, you shouldn't feel bad. I hope she huffs and puffs all the way up the hill."

I smiled wearily. "I have to admit that the baby was

adorable. I think she liked me."

"It brought back memories for me, but do you ever wish you had a child? Maybe that's too personal to ask."

"It's okay. I'm not sure. Watching Sarah raise Lucy has been such a joy, but that's her baby. My life didn't go in that direction, and maybe there's a reason for that. I never met the right person to make me even consider marriage, much less motherhood."

"You don't have to be married to be a parent these days," Judy pointed out. "Look at Sarah." Then she added, "You could always adopt."

"Oh, Judy. I have enough problems," I said, dismissing the topic. "By the way, what brought you in today?"

"Oh!" she giggled. "I was wondering if you wanted to go with me to the new knitting shop in Washington."

"I do, but not just yet. I have a friend bringing in lots of quilts for me to sell, so I'm going to have to do a lot of rearranging. From the looks of things in my quilt room, I think that last customer began the task for me."

"Do you need some help?"

"I'll let you know. Thanks!"

"When we go to Washington, there's a great coffee shop where we can have lunch. We can go on a Monday when we don't have to work."

"I would like that. I want to start exploring more of that area. I think Amy will be very successful there."

Judy agreed to wait for a week or so before visiting the new shop and eventually went on her way to work. I went to the quilt room and started assessing what I could do differently to prepare for all the additional quilts.

The end of the very unprofitable day ended with a phone

call from Marc. He told me about his trip to Kansas City and then talked about how excited he was about a recent trade for the Cardinals. He was a peach, and my day felt more complete.

Chapter 114

Carrie Mae called quite early and offered me one of her glass cases for some of Butler's quilts. It had a lock, and she thought it would display them nicely. When I asked about the price, she said to consider it a loan. She said it had a price tag on it, and if I sold it, she would split the profits with me. How was I so lucky to have friends like Carrie Mae and Butler looking after me? I was glad Carrie Mae shared my excitement about receiving the quilts, but then she always seemed to approve of everything Butler did. She closed the conversation by telling me that Ted and a friend would deliver the case next week.

It seemed that the morning would be filled with phone calls. As soon as I hung up with Carrie Mae, Holly called to report on her date with Clete.

"Lily, it was so weird to be seen with another man out in the open. I couldn't help but feel a little guilty!"

"Did you have a good time?"

"Very much so! I had no idea Clete knew as much as he did about our marriage. He knew the control issues had to be difficult for me."

"That was probably helpful to hear. Will you be seeing him again?"

"Yes. There is a play at the Rep that we both want to see. Do you remember when Maurice and I used to have season tickets there but never used them?" Holly paused before saying happily, "It's just nice to be with someone who is kind and who I share similar interests with."

"I'm so happy for you."

After we hung up, I realized how quickly Holly was moving on. She was now focused on Clete and getting her husband's things out of the house!

As I continued to think and plan for the extra quilts, I remembered that I needed to choose a quilt block for Susan's wine country quilt project. There were so many choices. When I used to come out to Defiance and have lunch at Wine Country Gardens, I would stare out at the incredible view of the hills and valleys that seemed to transport me into another world. If I could make a block to depict one of those scenes, it would remind me of the early days before I moved out here. Another scene in my mind was from Montelle Winery. The view extended for miles and miles, and you could see the church steeple in Augusta in the background. I had taken Alex to lunch there one day so he could see it for himself.

Making a scene like I wanted would certainly present a challenge. My fabric stash would also be limited. Maybe I should do a redwork block to get all the places I wanted in the scene. Perhaps when I paid a visit to Gracie's shop, I'd get some ideas.

The afternoon brought rain and more dark skies.

There were storm warnings as well. I brought in Rosie's rocker, knowing something could happen at any moment. I wondered if the weather would postpone my visit from Karen and Bonita.

I turned my sign to say "Closed" and decided to check my emails. There was nothing from any of my siblings, which was unusual. I hoped that my having included Ellen in our email hadn't kept the others from replying. I decided to wait to tell them about Butler's offer. Concentrating on my guests for the evening, I decided to make a small veggie tray to go with the wine, despite Karen's offer to bring something.

I opened my last bottle of Vintage Rose merlot. I hesitated as I thought of Anthony's generosity. It really was my favorite wine, but now I would have to purchase it from Ashley Rose if I wanted more. I turned on the fireplace on the porch upstairs and suddenly jumped when a loud clap of thunder struck close by. I hated loud noises.

Right on time, I heard a knock at the door. I quickly ran downstairs to get my visitors out of the rain. "Hurry! Get in here!" I said as the wind and rain entered the shop when I opened the door. "The weather is dreadful. I wondered if you would cancel."

"This really reminds me of the spring weather we get," Karen said. "I hope it isn't cold enough outside to make it freeze on the roads." She continued, "Lily, I'd like you to meet Bonita. Bonita, this is Lily."

"I've heard so much about you, Lily," Bonita said with a Spanish accent. She was a short, stocky woman who wore her hair pulled straight back into a bun.

"I'm glad to meet you, too. I have a nice fire going upstairs so you can warm up."

"Oh, that sounds good," Karen said. "Here is a little something to share. I made a few appetizers for us."

"Thanks! I have hot coffee or red wine ready for you, along with some veggies."

Up the stairs we went.

Chapter 115

"I brought some of the homemade cheese sticks that you liked at our party," Karen announced as we got settled.

"Yes, I do remember these," I said, pleased that she'd remembered. "Thanks so much! I should learn how to make them." I poured each of them a glass of wine. "Bonita, how are you enjoying your visit to Augusta?"

"I am enjoying it very much. Karen and Buzz are wonderful hosts. There are so many lovely small businesses here. It gives the area so much personality."

"I'm glad you're enjoying your time here. I've always liked the variety of businesses here, too. Whether it is quilts, food, wine, or art, there's something for everyone here," I replied.

"Lily, I do like this wine," Bonita said. "What is it called?"

"Vintage Rose. It's one of my favorites," I answered, happy that she liked my selection for the evening. Just then, a loud clap of thunder gave us a bit of a jump.

"Here it comes!" Karen said, referring to the weather prediction. "My, you can really hear the rain up here."

"It reminds me of a tin roof, it gets so loud," I said. "I rather like it, and it's great for sleeping."

"When we got out of the car, my attention was drawn to the little building out front, Lily. It is charming," Bonita said.

"Yes, I can see why your attention would be drawn to that area," I acknowledged. "We really know very little about the doctor who had an office there long ago, but I did get a pretty good description of his activities recently from a woman who came here as a child with her mother."

"That's interesting," Bonita said as she rose from her chair and walked toward the porch windows. At that moment, a large flash of lightning looked like it came through the glass. Bonita jumped back. We looked at one another as if one of us could have gotten hit by the lightning, relieved to see that we were all just fine. Bonita started to say something when suddenly the electricity went out.

"Great. That's just what we need," I said, getting up to find some candles.

"Thank goodness for this gas fireplace," Karen pointed out.

"Stay put, ladies," I cautioned. "I have candles close by. This has happened to me before." I left them to get the candles stored in my bedside table drawer. I brought them into the room and lit several. The gas fireplace and the candles illuminated the room enough for us to see one another.

"I wonder if the power is out all over town," Karen

said, sounding concerned.

I responded, "Well, we knew the storm was coming, and you don't want to leave in the middle of it, so tell me about your concern for your friends and family in Honduras, Bonita."

"Thank you, Lily," Bonita said, settling back in her chair as the rain continued to pour. "Honduras is the second-poorest country in Central America. Rural communities suffer the most. The people mostly depend on agricultural production for their livelihood and to feed their families, but natural disasters and severe weather can occur at any time, wiping out their resources and ruining crops. When that happens, families are at risk of not having enough to eat. Among the poor, housing consists of basic shelters built from whatever they can find, and those structures also sustain damage when big storms come through the area."

"I had no idea, Bonita. I can't say that I know very much about Honduras at all," I replied.

"Since I started working for Karen's father, I have been able to live differently. However, it haunts me to know how harsh life is in those rural villages. Lily, I hope to learn some things from you that will help me reach out to women there and help them secure a better life for themselves."

I looked at Bonita. She was intelligent, articulate, and had a good job. She could easily create a life in America and live comfortably, content that she had escaped such extreme poverty. Yet here she was on this rain-soaked night, seeking information so she could help others. I swallowed hard, feeling for the families she had just described. What could Bonita learn from me? I heard myself say, "Bonita, I would like to know more. Tell me how I can help."

Chapter 116

"There are many single mothers in Honduras, and it is particularly difficult for them to make a living," Bonita explained.

"Bonita tells me that some mothers have risked their lives trying to get out of the country in hopes of getting a job so they can send money home to their families. So many of them are abused along the way before they finally make their way back to the homes that they originally fled," Karen added. "It is very difficult for them to relocate safely."

"How awful," I commented.

"There are those who hope that times are changing," Bonita continued. "Some are trying to develop new sources of income through the textile industry."

"Textiles?" I asked.

"Yes, textiles and items made by artisans. My interest is primarily in the areas of sewing, quilting, and fiber arts."

"I see," I said. "How could that help a single mother?"

"Sewing is a life skill. If women there learn how to sew, then they can repair school uniforms, or make clothing to sell. From there, they can learn other skills—like quilting. When given small loans, some women have purchased sewing machines and started small sewing shops. It gives them an opportunity to be an entrepreneur—to own something and build a business capable of providing for their families. Some have even been able to hire other women to work for them as their business expands."

Karen said, "The problem is that they don't have sewing machines, fabric, or instruction. However, when given an opportunity, they realize that they can change their economic future. They become excited about all that it could mean for their family."

Bonita leaned forward, looking intently at me in the dimness. "They need solid business plans. If they have plans that work, then they stand a better chance at having their businesses survive. That is something I can help them with, since I have a business background."

"A business plan is essential," I agreed. "It also takes a lot of effort and introspection to put one together."

"Tell me your story, Lily. How did you start this business?" Bonita asked. "I am always interested in how people turn their passion into their livelihood."

I told her about working for the publishing company and how I'd felt discontent there. I talked about my quilt collection and how I would drive out to wine country and purchase quilts from Carrie Mae. Then I told Bonita about my sweet friend Rosie. It had been after her unexpected death that I acquired the inventory from her shop. Carrie Mae had helped me get settled in Augusta by allowing me to purchase a house that she owned. Without her support, things would have been much more difficult as I attempted to open my shop. Bonita and Karen listened attentively. I also described how Alex had helped me get connected with *Spirit* magazine and how that income had supplemented my finances to help me make it through the first year. "I wouldn't have made it without the support of Carrie Mae and Alex. They have cheered me on from the very beginning."

"Lily has worked hard to establish her business and become involved in the community here," Karen offered with a smile.

"Yes, I have made some good friends during my brief time as a resident of Augusta. I'm even part of a little group called the Dinner Detectives," I said with a laugh.

"Dinner Detectives?" Karen asked. "Who are they?"

"Carrie Mae and Betty Bade," I stated with a grin. "They are good friends. They knew I was too scared to go into the basement of this house by myself, so they went down there with me to investigate the items left there from years ago. They've been a tremendous help with research, too, because I'm curious about the history of this house."

"Dinner Detectives! Well, if that doesn't take the cake!" Karen said with a chuckle. "You all are something!"

"We have a lot of laughs together, and there is generally food involved, which makes everything better," I replied.

Another loud clap of thunder made us jump once again.

"I wonder if we should take shelter," I said, feeling ill at ease.

"I'm going to call Buzz and see if we have power," Karen declared. "We could be here all night! Perhaps we should come back at another time—when we can see the quilts in the light. It's turning into a pretty eerie evening."

Bonita smiled. "The conversation tonight has been very

interesting. I so enjoyed hearing about how you came to be a shop owner, Lily."

As if on cue, the room lit up and the power was restored, giving us a profound sense of relief. The storm still rumbled in the distance, perhaps flirting with a repeat performance.

Chapter 117

"Let's go home," Karen said, getting up from her seat.

"Lily, I would like to return some other time, if you would agree," Bonita suggested. "I honestly would like to see your quilt collection and learn more about the process of making and selling quilts."

"I'm sorry that the lack of power kept us from taking a look at the quilts," I said. "You're welcome to come back any time."

She smiled. "Thank you so much. I loved the wine, and I appreciate your openness and hospitality. You have such an attractive little place here. I do hope to come back soon. It is important to me that I help my people by connecting them with sewing or quilting opportunities so they can begin their own businesses. I think you are someone who could give me the type of information I need, since you are making a living selling quilts and have experienced success in running a business in a small town. Perhaps you could even sell some of the goods made by these women if we could get them shipped from Honduras at a low cost."

"Bonita, please know that I am certainly interested in having a discussion about how I can help these women," I said.

By the time we got downstairs, it had started to pour again, and lightning could be seen striking in the distance. We said our goodbyes, and I closed the door and turned on the alarm system before going upstairs. As I cleaned up our wine glasses and snacks, I began thinking about the things we had talked about. My heart went out to the women that I had learned about from Bonita. I had never had to struggle to acquire food. While I had never lived in a mansion, my housing needs had always been met, and I lived comfortably. I had no idea what it meant to wake up each day and wonder where my basic necessities would come from. It was disturbing. What would be my role in helping these women?

Rain pounded on the roof, and I wondered when the storm would end. I brought the candles to the bedroom in case the power went out again. Crawling into bed and even hiding under the covers, I weathered each bolt of lightning and clap of thunder. I tossed and turned as I continued to consider all the things Bonita, Karen, and I had discussed while they were here.

After a while of sleeplessness, I checked the clock on my bedside table. I was surprised to see that it was five in the morning. Perhaps I had dozed off a time or two. I got up to look out the window. The rain was still pouring, and the thunder seemed constant. I could see that the front lawn was soaked, and I watched as a large amount of water ran down the hill. I decided to forget going back to sleep and got dressed in jeans and a sweater to get warm. I went downstairs to make a pot of coffee. I wondered what the basement must look like with all the rain. I knew I wasn't about to find out!

Finally, the rain began to lighten, and I breathed a sigh of relief. I had just poured my first cup of coffee when suddenly, a bolt of lightning seemed to come right into the kitchen! I jumped as if I had been struck. What had just happened? Something was very wrong. Should I take cover under the stairs? Should I go back to bed where I felt safe? Scared beyond belief, I headed toward the stairs. I glanced out the front window and saw hell appear before my very eyes. Enormous flames were coming from the back of Doc's office.

"No!" I shrieked.